Curiosity Can Kill

Bob Doerr

Jim West mystery/thriller™

TotalRecall Publications, Inc.
1103 Middlecreek
Friendswood, Texas 77546
281-992-3131   281-482-5390 Fax
www.mousegate.com

Copyright © 2024 by: Bob Doerr
All rights reserved
ISBN: 978-1-64883-340-3
UPC: 6-43977-43403-6

Library of Congress Control Number: 2024942710

FIRST EDITION
1   2   3   4   5   6   7   8   9   10

This book is dedicated to my buddy Fitz.

Thanks for keeping me inspired.

Save a tee time for me up there.

Award Winning Author: Bob Doerr

Award winning author Bob Doerr grew up in a military family, graduated from the Air Force Academy, and had a career of his own in the Air Force. Bob specialized in criminal investigations and counterintelligence gaining significant insight to the worlds of crime, espionage, and terrorism. His work brought him into close coordination with the security agencies of many countries and filled his mind with the fascinating plots and characters found in his books today. His education credits include a Masters in International Relations from Creighton University. A full-time author with twenty one published books, Bob was selected by the Military Writers Society of America as its Author of the Year for 2013. The Eric Hoffer Awards awarded *No One Else to Kill* its 2013 first runner up to the grand prize for commercial fiction. Two of his other books were finalists for the Eric Hoffer Award in earlier contests. *Loose Ends Kill* won the 2011 Silver medal for Fiction/mystery by the Military Writers Society of America. *Another Colorado Kill* received the same Silver medal in 2012 and the Silver medal for general fiction at the Branson Stars and Flags national book contest in 2012. In addition to *Curiosity Can Kill*, Bob has written nine prior novels in the Jim West series. Bob lives in Garden Ridge, Texas, with Leigh, his wife of 51 years, and Cinco, their ornery cat.

About The Book

An old friend of Jim West is murdered in Big Bend National Park, Texas. The authorities have no witnesses and no leads. West is contacted by his friend's wife, now his widow, who asks him to meet her in Alpine, Texas. She's been asked to go there and identify the body, and she wants Jim there to support her. Although he'd rather not, Jim travels to Alpine and does what he can to help her. A joint investigative team has been established to run the investigation, and as the murder occurred on federal property, the FBI has the lead. A second seemingly unrelated murder occurs at the same location. At the same time, Jim is thrilled to discover that his long-distance romance has gotten closer when FBI Special Agent Rose Luna joins the team. When his friend's widow disappears and is later found dead, things begin to get personal. The son of the second victim arrives in Alpine. He's a retired police officer from San Antonio and starts aggressively interviewing his dad's acquaintances. The team asks Jim to stay with him to keep him from hurting anyone. A role Jim doesn't like, and one that soon puts the two into the crosshairs of the killer's sites.

Curiosity Can Kill is the 10th Jim West mystery/thriller.

Chapter 1

The Gila monster crawled closer to the campfire's flames and to Pat's feet. The wind picked up, and a lone tumbleweed raced by, traveling wherever the wind might take it. The Gila monster snuggled in close to one of the larger rocks that surrounded the small fire. Like Pat, it did not belong here in the Big Bend.

A light covering of dust blew in through the driver's side window of Pat's old pickup truck parked nearby. In the distance, heat lightning flashed in the sky with its false promise of rain. This part of the Big Bend hadn't seen rain in twenty-seven days.

Pat's new prospecting gear, tossed about in the bed of the pickup, had brought with it a dreamer's optimism that this would be the year. Pat had moved to Marfa, Texas, two years earlier, abandoning his family and his job with a boast that he would return one day with his fortune.

He was too broke and too ashamed after one year to return. This should've been a better year. It could've been.

The Gila monster had escaped from a run-down, now-closed, exotic animal attraction a year earlier. Movement in the sand a few yards away caught its eye, and it started moving toward what could be dinner.

Pat wouldn't be moving. His lifeless eyes continued to stare at the fire long after the Gila monster had crawled away.

Chapter 2

The call came in at six in the morning. Neither Chubbs nor I were awake, and neither of us appreciated the interruption to our sleep.

"Hey, Jim, Jim West?" the caller said, after I mumbled a hello, or what was meant to be a hello.

"That's me."

"I'm sorry, but we have some bad news. The General wanted me to call you," the voice said.

"Hold on," I said and went into the bathroom to splash some cold water onto my face. "What general, and who are you?"

"I'm sorry. General Davrik and I'm Lieutenant Green," the voice said.

The information did nothing for me for a few seconds. Then it did. "Steve Davrik?"

"Yes," Lt. Green replied.

I remembered hearing that my old acquaintance Steve Davrik had been selected to be the new commander for the Air Force Office of Special Investigations.

"What's up?" Not the most intelligent response I could've made, but my brain hadn't caught up with my mouth.

"General Davrik said you and Patrick MacCumber worked together and were close."

"Yes, we had two assignments together."

"He said you two worked a couple big cases."

I didn't know where this conversation was going, but my mind had cleared, and I knew something wasn't right.

"Something come up with one of the cases? Those were long

ago."

"No, we thought you should know he was murdered last week."

The news shocked me. "What? What happened?"

"No one is sure at this point."

"He's no longer in the air force. I thought he retired shortly after I did," I said.

"That's right. One theory is that something in one of his old cases may have caught up with him. There's a joint effort looking into his murder. We've recommended they talk to you."

"I'm not sure how much help I can be. I haven't seen or talked to him in years."

"We're trying to hit all angles. You understand."

I did. "Can you give me any details?"

"We'll let the team do that. They should be getting in touch with you in the next few days. The general did say not to worry, you're not a subject or anything."

I almost laughed at his comment, but he was a lieutenant and probably young and inexperienced. He meant well.

"Is Pat's wife, Janice, alright?"

"As far as I know. She wasn't with him when he was killed."

I had a lot more questions, but I figured I would have more luck with the internet. Even in today's world, murders usually get some publicity.

"Thanks for the call," I said. I felt like reminding him that New Mexico was on mountain time. However, he likely showed up to work and had a list of things to do. Calling me happened to be one of them.

The call did bother me. Those two military assignments spanned a seven-year period. We didn't work all investigations together, but we saw each other most days at work. I hadn't stayed in touch with Pat even though he was a good friend. My ex used to do all the letter writing and phone calling. After my divorce, I didn't pick up the habit. A character flaw I never had the energy to correct. I tried to go back to sleep; however, my mind wanted to know what exactly happened to Pat.

Chubbs, my faithful Heinz 57 mutt, didn't want me to go back to sleep either. Since we were both awake, he wanted me to get out of bed to feed him or let him outside, preferably both. He started making those little whining sounds he knew I couldn't sleep through.

"Alright, I'm getting up. You're not suffering," I said to him. I let him out to the backyard, while I went back to the bathroom.

After I fed Chubbs and made a cup of coffee for myself, I started my internet search. It didn't take long, but the information caused more questions than answers. Patrick MacCumber had been shot and killed while camping in Big Bend National Park. The article said the authorities had no witnesses, no motive, no weapon, and listed the time of death as either July 10th or 11th. The article inferred that his body was not discovered right away. It also pointed out that prospecting in the park was illegal.

The Patrick MacCumber I knew never expressed any interest in prospecting. In fact, if my memory was correct, he never liked camping either. I continued my internet search. While I found a half dozen more references to the murder, none provided any additional information.

I gave up on my search for information. When the investigative team reached out, I would learn more.

A business card on my kitchen table caught my eye. Today,

my big plan was to buy a new car. The name on the card read "Trixie Lee, new car specialist." I had wanted a new Mustang for months. I also knew Trixie's good looks and big smile might be the bigger motivating factor in my wanting to buy the car now.

"Come on, Chubbs, want to go for a walk?"

He didn't respond, and I didn't see him in the kitcher with me. When he was young, he used to enjoy the morning walks more than I did. Now, it was a fifty-fifty chance that he would have any interest at all. It didn't take me long to find him.

"Want to go for a walk, boy?"

Curled up on my bed, he gave me a look that said, "No way."

Somewhere, early in our relationship, he had stopped thinking of me as his master. Sleeping on my bed was a major rule violation which he broke shortly after moving in. Now it was a reminder I wasted money on his obedience class, and that I wasn't in charge.

The news about Pat dominated my thoughts, so I decided to go out for breakfast rather than try to decide which brand of cereal would be best this morning. Why would someone kil Pat? I couldn't think of any of our old cases that might have resulted in a revenge killing. Pat had been killed while he was alone, out somewhere in south Texas. To me, it had all the markings of a random act of violence, maybe a robbery by some psycho who enjoyed killing.

The drive to IHOP took less than five minutes. In my morning restaurant rotation, I had already been to Teddy's Tacos, Dale's Donuts, and The Coffee Shoppe in the last week or so. IHOP would complete the list, and I could start over.

"Good morning, Jim," El said when she brought water and coffee to my table.

"Morning."

El had never explained how she got the nickname. She had acknowledged that it was abbreviated from her real name, leaving the actual name to our imagination. My guess was Elspeth.

"I think I'm going to trade in my Mustang today."

"That girl's got you hypnotized, too?"

"What girl?" I asked, trying to hide my grin.

"You know who. She's set a six-month sales record for them, you know. Maybe a sales record for our little city of Clovis, New Mexico. Some of the guys and even that other woman there are upset."

"Come on, El. Why do you think I always ask to be in your section? It's the same thing."

"I wish. I just remind you of your mother. Besides, half our waitstaff can't even spell pancake."

"That's harsh."

"Unfortunately, it's true. These young kids come and go too quickly for me to learn and remember their names."

"Well, I am happy you're here."

"Blueberry pancakes?"

"Yes, please, the full stack."

"Well, if you do buy a car from her, make sure she gives you a good deal. She's like a car saleswoman honeypot. You know, like in those spy stories. Except I hear she's more of a tease than the real thing."

El walked away. In a feisty mood, I thought. Yet, I knew she was correct. Trixie Lee had been the talk of the town since she showed up on the salesroom floor of our local Ford dealer. To be honest, I knew she was the reason I had suddenly become ready to trade in my car.

Before my pancakes arrived, my phone rang again. The chance of me getting two real phone calls in one morning were slim. I almost didn't answer, thinking it was another spam call, but then I thought it might have something to do with Pat's murder.

"Jim, Jim is that you," a woman said in response to my hello.

"Yes." I thought I recognized the voice.

"It's Janice. Have you heard?"

"Janice, I'm so sorry. I heard about Pat a few minutes ago."

"I asked them to get in touch with you. I didn't know who else to tell them. They asked me if his death could be related to some old case. I told them I didn't know. You were the only other agent I could think to tell them to ask. I hope you don't mind."

"No, not at all. I'm so sorry, Janice," repeating myself.

"He changed, Jim. After retiring, he kind of slowly fell apart. I hadn't seen him in over a year. Hadn't seen much of him in the past three years."

"Why? If you don't mind my asking."

"No, not at all. He started getting addicted to all these crazy websites. At first it was UFO stuff, then it was government conspiracies, and most recently, hidden gold mines or buried treasure."

"Seems harmless," I said.

"Well, it wasn't. He became obsessed. It got him killed."

"Can I do anything for you?" I asked, believing it was the right thing to say, and fairly certain there would be nothing I could do to help.

"Actually, yes. You live right there on the Texas border. They want me to go there to identify the body and fill out some paperwork as his next of kin. I would like you to meet me there and help me through the process."

"I'm not sure what help I can be."

"Please, Jim. I can't do it alone."

"When are you going?"

"Today, I'm flying into San Antonio and driving a rental car from there. I'll help you with your expenses. I didn't want to go, so I put it off a couple days. They're insisting now, and I know they want to talk to you anyway. Please, Jim, don't make me beg."

I felt my stomach knot up. I didn't want to go and didn't like being put in these type situations.

"Please, Jim," she repeated, realizing I was debating her request. "I'll be staying at the Cattle Rustler Inn in Alpine. Any chance you can get there tonight?"

"I'll try," I finally said.

Chapter 3

I left Chubbs under the supervision of the gaggle of teenagers who live next door. He would have a better time than I anticipated having. Despite Janice's comment that I lived on the Texas border, the drive would still take me six or seven hours. Texas is a huge state.

I packed for several days. If I was going to the Big Bend, I might as well spend a few days sightseeing. I even brought my barely worn cowboy boots. They might come in useful as most of the land down there was desert.

Once out on the highway, I let my mind drift back a decade or so to when Pat and I worked together. I thought we made a pretty good team. We were young officers and thought we had the world by its tail. His wife and my wife never really hit it off, but that didn't bother us. We went to work, travelled the world, and did our thing. We were never neighbors. While I saw Janice at the occasional office social functions, away from work, the four of us didn't hang out much.

Janice was one of those people whom I classified as pushy. She was too vocal, always trying to get people to do things her way. Getting me to meet her in Alpine reinforced my opinion. I didn't believe she needed me, and she likely knew she didn't need me.

Most of my drive took me straight south through extreme southeastern New Mexico. It made me think of Rose Luna. Being optimistic, I considered we were still in a long-distance relationship. She was the first woman with whom I have had a serious relationship since my divorce. There had been others that had the potential, but life always got in the way. With Rose, fate had given us more time together before pulling the rug out from under us.

When I met her, she was a deputy sheriff in El Paso County, Texas. She didn't care for her boss and had a dream of becoming an FBI agent. As our relationship was getting serious, the FBI hired her, and she moved to the east coast. Between the training and now being a rookie agent, she had little time for me other than the occasional text or phone call. I kept telling myself it was for the best.

I had to use the car's cruise control. The road, NM 218, had a speed limit that I had a habit of ignoring. I hadn't been on this road in months, but the few times I had taken it south, I never saw a police car. You can drive for miles without seeing another vehicle and then suddenly come up behind a slow-moving tractor. Despite the scarcity of vehicle traffic, I'd seen a lot of wildlife, dead and alive, on the road. On highways like this, I had to work on keeping my mind focused. Driving too fast, even in the middle of nowhere, can be deadly.

About halfway into my trip, I crossed into Texas. The speed limit went up, and the road appeared to get better. The volume of traffic didn't change.

I kept driving south, following the signs to Alpine. I had the sensation that despite the movement of time and the speed I was driving, I wasn't getting any closer. This last stretch of driving covered a hundred miles and seemed to go on forever. At least the terrain changed with several hills and rocky mesas improving the scenery.

I drove through the small town of Marfa before taking Highway 90 due east to Alpine.

Chapter 4

As I approached the city of Alpine, my phone rang again, startling me.

"Hello." I had stopped identifying myself years ago with the advent of the flood of spam calls.

"Mr. West?"

"Yes."

"I'm Caleb Wilkins. I'm a Texas Ranger assigned to a team investigating the murder of Patrick MacCumber. I've been asked to call you. We understand you used to be close to him. Has anyone briefed you on what happened?"

"Only that he was killed, and someone would be calling me," I said, thinking Caleb's bedside manner, like that of the lieutenant who called me earlier, could use some improvement. What if I hadn't heard?

"Well, that would be me," he said.

"What happened?"

"That's what we're trying to piece together. Do you have idea who may have wanted to harm Mr. MacCumber?"

"No, not at all?"

"Did he say anything to you that might indicate he felt threatened?"

"I hadn't had any contact with Pat in at least five years."

"Your previous organization gave us your name. Do you know why they would do that if you haven't had any contact with him?"

"I have a good guess that his wife passed my name onto them, or somebody else did in an effort to be helpful. I worked a lot with him in the old days."

"You haven't stayed in touch?" he asked.

"No. After I retired, we went separate ways. Can you tell me what happened?"

"Someone shot him, Mr. West. We'll be in touch if we need to speak to you again. Thank you for your time." He ended the call.

"Well, that was a waste," I said out loud to myself.

I wondered why the Texas Rangers were involved in the investigation. While I never expected the investigative team to share much, the scant information he provided, and the way he cut short the conversation piqued my curiosity. For the first time since my conversation with Janice, I looked forward to seeing her and, maybe, getting some answers.

Thanks to modern technology, I had no difficulty finding the Cattle Rustler's Inn. The fact that the hotel sat in the middle of Alpine on Highway 90 helped. I wondered if people still rustled cattle. The hotel looked old.

Inside, I approached the long polished, wooden reception counter.

"Welcome to the Cattle Rustler's Hotel," the man behind the counter said. Despite his remark, he didn't seem pleased to see me. A short man with black hair and an old scar on his chin, he kept twirling a pencil in his left hand.

"I think you have a reservation for me. I'm Jim West. The reservation would've been made by Janice MacCumber. She may already be here." I wondered why he said hotel rather than inn.

"Nope and nope."

"Are you sure?"

He stared at me but didn't respond.

"Okay, how about this, do you have a room I could check into for a couple of nights?"

Rather than respond, he walked over to a nearby computer and picked at a couple keys. He looked back at me. "I can put you on the second floor."

"That's good," I said.

He gave me a form to fill out and then sent me on my way with the key but without another word. Strange, I thought.

I unpacked the car and threw everything onto the small couch in the hotel room. Janice's journey would put her in sometime later in the day, so I stretched out on the bed and fell asleep.

The sun had gone down when a knock on the door woke me up. I opened it and stared at a man in a deputy sheriff's uniform.

"Mr. West?" he asked in a deep voice.

"Yessir."

"Glad to meet you," he stuck out his hand, and I shook it. "I'm Tony, Deputy Tony Anaya. Can I come in for a minute?" Unlike the receptionist, Tony never stopped smiling.

"Sure," I said and let him in.

He walked over to the only chair in the room and sat down. His black hair had patches of grey. He was about my height, six feet, maybe an inch shorter with a stocky build.

"We didn't know you were coming down here until Mrs. MacCumber called us a little while ago."

"She insisted. I'll leave as soon as I can."

"No, no, that's okay. It's just we would've reserved you a room and met you upon your arrival."

"That's okay," I said. "Is Janice here now?"

"No, when she discovered how long of a drive it was from San Antonio, she decided to spend the night there and drive here tomorrow. I understand you knew the victim."

"Yes, but I haven't had any contact with him in years."

"Terrible thing." Tony shook his head and looked around the room. "Listen, I'm not supposed to ask you anything. Someone from the team will likely do that tomorrow, but as they're all out-of-towners, I thought I could at least welcome you to our little city. Have you eaten dinner?"

"No."

"Then why don't you come with me. The least you can do is let the county buy you dinner. Besides, I bet you have a lot of questions."

"Sounds good. Can I meet you in the lobby in about five minutes?"

"Sure, but don't get dressed up."

I grinned. "No sweat, I didn't bring any good clothes."

He laughed and left. A few minutes later, I joined him in the lobby, and we walked a block to a restaurant named Beef and Beans. I followed his lead and we both ordered beef fajitas, charro beans, and Sol beer. He drank his beer in large gulps.

"Why is there a joint team running the investigation? Wasn't he killed in your county?" I asked.

"MacCumber was murdered in the park, Big Bend National Park. A lot of agencies have an interest. They don't need or want us, except to help out with the administrative things. That's okay. They'll spin their wheels here for a week or two, and all go home. Can't see how they'll solve it."

"I had a Texas Ranger call me and ask a few questions."

"The rangers are helping out, but it's really the FBI and National Park Service investigators in charge. Mostly the FBI, I guess."

"No leads, then?"

"None. He was shot twice in the back of the head. Once would've been enough. Nothing left at the scene that would give us anything. Nothing appeared to be taken. Maybe money, but he still had thirty-two dollars in his wallet. He could've had a lot more. Animals messed up the scene. We don't know where he'd been since he was last seen at a small convenience store in Lay-By. A clerk saw him there a few days before we believe he was killed."

"It does sound like you would need a giant break to solve it."

"You got that right," Tony said. "At least they're making a good show at trying to solve it. They kind of have to. The killing took place in the park, so people back in D.C. are interested. If it happened only a few feet outside the park, we'd be on our own."

"I wouldn't think you'd get too many like this. At least, I hope you don't."

"Not murders. However, it's not that uncommon to find someone who simply got lost out there and died. Not locals, they know better. Some illegals and a few tourists who make a foolhardy attempt to hike out there without a map or a guide. A shame really."

"I thought I might take advantage of being down here to see part of the park. There must be some well-marked trails."

"Oh, there are. I recommend you stay on them and not wander off," Tony said.

"I will. There're a lot more mountains down here than I imagined."

"Not very tall mountains, but rugged." Tony nodded and took another large bite of meat he had wrapped in a flour tortilla. "We have our Twin Peaks."

"Are we close to the park?"

"Not far, it's a large park, but it only covers a portion of the Big Bend. There's also a state park near it."

"Is the team located here in Alpine? I thought I saw something that said he was found near Marfa."

"Not really near to anywhere. The first reports went through Marfa. He had a place over there, but he was found in our county. Better hotels here, too, because we have the college."

I wondered if his definition of better hotels included the Cattle Rustler's.

"Thanks for filling me in on the background."

"Haven't told you anything the whole city doesn't know."

"His wife said he was prospecting. Do you get a lot of people coming here to do some prospecting?"

"It's not unusual to get several each year. There are stories of bandits burying stolen gold or stolen money chests, but most of that stuff is fiction. I think people here spread half that stuff to drive the tourist trade."

"Can't blame them. I understand Pat drove his pickup truck to the spot where he was found. Why did it take so long for someone to notice him?"

"We have a number of old roads, not all of them paved, that meander around. Most will take you to someone's ranch or to some long-abandoned house or even town. He was found next to a dirt road that serves no purpose anymore."

I shook my head. What in the world had caused Pat to throw his family away and go on some wild goose chase?

Chapter 5

The next morning, my phone rang and woke me at eight.

"Mr. West, this is Ranger Caleb Wilkins again. I understand you're in town."

"Yes, I am."

"Can I get you to come to the sheriff's office to answer a few questions?"

"Of course. When do you want me there?"

"Now, if possible."

"It will take me a few minutes to get dressed and cleaned up."

"I'll wait. Do you need directions?"

"I think my phone can get me there. The sheriff's office, right?"

"Yes, Brewster County, right here in Alpine."

It didn't take me long to get dressed and drive the short distance to the station. Outside, the warm breeze did nothing to lessen the heat I felt from the morning sun. Inside, multiple fans did their best to supplement the air conditioning.

Ranger Wilkins waited for me in the lobby. He personified the stereotype I had in my mind of a Texas Ranger, tall and lanky with short brown hair. His tan uniform appeared to have been recently pressed. His skin had the appearance of a permanent suntan. He even spoke in a voice that sounded a little deeper than it should. His smile when he saw me seemed natural, but his eyes could have been those of a falcon, watching for any sudden movements.

"Come on back. We have been given a workspace with a few private rooms," he said after we shook hands.

We walked down a short hallway and through a larger room that appeared to be a conference room. One man in civilian clothes sat at a computer near a wall.

"Grab a cup of coffee." He stopped in front of a coffee pot.

I filled a paper cup. "Thanks."

Ranger Wilkins led me into a small office and closed the door.

"That's our work space out there," he said, motioning to the room we had walked through. "It gets busy in there when everyone is here. Right now, we have a rep from the medical examiner's office, two FBI agents, and I believe one more is due in today or tomorrow, a rep from the state police, a park ranger, and me. Two local deputies are helping us, too. We do our interviewing in one of these two side rooms."

"Any suspects yet?"

"I understand you have some law enforcement background, so you know I couldn't tell you if we did."

I smiled at his roundabout way of telling me no.

"How can I be of any help?" I asked.

"Not sure you can, but since you're here, let me ask you some more questions. You told me on the phone you haven't had any contact with Mr. MacCumber for several years. Do you know why your former agency would have given us your name?"

"Only a guess."

"Good enough for me."

"I'm thinking they really had nobody when asked by your team, but when they talked to Janice, his wife, widow, she mentioned that someone should talk to me since we knew each other so well while we were on active duty." I knew I had already told him this on the phone.

"Janice or Patrick?

"What do you mean?" I asked.

"Which one did you know so well?"

"Him, not her, I was never a big fan of her."

"So, they passed on your name, because they really had no idea how they could help?"

"I'm sure they wanted to help, but with Pat being retired for so long, and being out of contact for years, they didn't have anything to offer to the investigation."

"Makes sense. They've provided us a list of cases that resulted in prison time or individuals being booted out of the air force. We know people can always carry a grudge, and some are irrational in their desire for revenge, but we didn't see anything that stood out."

"I can't think of any either. I never received any hate mail, threats, or whatever and never heard that he did either. His wife, Janice, might know of some, but she didn't mention any when she called me and asked me to meet her down here."

"So, that is why you came here."

"Yes. No offense, but I'd rather be back home. I was supposed to be buying a new car yesterday."

"What kind?"

"Mustang."

"Good choice," he said, nodding and smiling. "Did he have any other friends that might have come down here with him?"

"I have no idea. Didn't he have any friends here?"

"Not really, as far as we know, he was definitely a loner. He rented a trailer over in Marfa. We've been through that. Nada. Apparently, he spent a lot of days and nights out prospecting. A waste of time, but I guess slightly better odds than playing the lottery."

"Could you tell if the killer was someone he knew, someone who might have been with him out there?" I didn't expect an answer.

He stared at me for a second. "We know the obvious. Someone shot him, but we have no clue how long he or she may have been there."

"Is the crime scene still sealed off?"

"I think so, but I know we're done examining it. You thinking about driving out there?"

"Just a thought. His wife will be here today, and she may want someone to take her there. If she went, I'd want to tag along. If I had directions, I could take her myself."

"We'll see."

I left the building and drove back to the hotel. I didn't know any more than I knew earlier, and figured unless the investigative team got a break, I'd be heading back to Clovis in a few days without any idea why someone killed my old friend.

Chapter 6

Raymond Stahl looked down from the rocky ledge near the area cordoned off with police tape. He squinted, trying to minimize the burn in his eyes caused by the morning sun. He knew the map that his friend Patrick MacCumber usually kept with him had not been discovered by the deputies. That meant it had fallen out and blew away, or it was still out here somewhere and overlooked during the search of the area.

At least, that's what Raymond hoped. The obvious other option was that the murderer took it when he killed Pat. Raymond thought he knew who had killed his friend, but he was afraid to tell the police. If he did, he believed he would never see his next birthday.

Raymond climbed down from the ridge and walked over to the crime scene. Despite the police tape, the terrain in the crime scene looked the same as the ground around it. He imagined the tape was simply left up so the police could come back and find the spot.

"Whatch-ya doing here?"

Raymond spun around. He recognized the voice.

"Well?" the man spit. He chewed on a tooth pick

"I wanted to see where Pat died. How about you?" It took all of Raymond's willpower to ask the question and not start whimpering.

"He died right over there?" The man pointed to the center of the crime scene.

"Yeah, I figured that."

"What do you know about this map of his?"

Raymond swallowed. "It was a fool's map. I told him a dozen times. He bought it off the internet for God's sake. Probably made in China."

"Other than the time at Nessy's, did you see it again?"

Raymond ran the calculations through his mind. What answer might keep him alive? He didn't see a weapon, but he could have anything tucked behind him in in his jeans. His presence further convinced Raymond that the man in front of him killed Pat.

"Yes, he showed it to me, but I didn't study it or anything. Like I said, I told him he wasted his money."

"Have you told anyone about the map?"

"No, I never thought about it again. Why the questions? Where were you? I looked around from up there before I came down and never saw you."

"Pat told me he believed the map was genuine."

"And you believed him?" Despite the stress, Raymond almost started laughing.

"I never liked you," the man said and drew a large pistol from the back of his jeans. He fired two shots into Raymond's chest. He watched Raymond fall, then he walked up close and fired two more rounds into the already dead man's head.

Chapter 7

I watched Janice walk out of the elevator and look around. She had called me a few minutes earlier, letting me know she was here and had checked-in. She wanted me to take her somewhere for lunch, so we could talk.

Only one other man sat in a chair in the lobby, so it didn't do my ego any good for her to look twice at both of us trying to decide which one was me. I stood up.

"I thought that was you," she said. She came up to me and we hugged. I don't think either of us put any emotion in the hug. "Have you been sick?"

I remembered why she wasn't my favorite person. "Just tired from the long drive, and a little sad."

"I'm still madder than sad. Where can we do lunch?"

The only place I could think of was where I had dinner and it was nearby. "There's a good little place we can easily walk to."

"Lead the way."

She appeared to be a little overdressed for Alpine. She wore what looked like expensive blue slacks and a long sleeve black blouse. Her hair style hadn't changed, a little too wavy and long. Not that I don't like wavy or long hair, but on her it didn't seem right. Her hair had always had an unnatural look.

"Something in my hair?"

"No, sorry, my mind was elsewhere. Have you talked to any of the investigators yet?"

"No, I will let them know I'm here after I eat. Have you seen Pat?"

"No, I thought I would go with you."

"Of course," she said. "Has anyone given you any idea why he was murdered or who did it?"

"No, they may tell you more."

"I hope so. This wasn't an easy trip."

"Let's order," I said, wondering for the umpteenth time why Pat had married her.

My phone buzzed in my pocket right after I had taken a big bite of my chopped brisket sandwich. I did my best to say hello.

"Jim, is that you?" Ranger Wilkins asked.

"Yes," I said with less difficulty.

"After we talked did you go out to the crime scene?"

"No, you never gave me any instructions how to get there."

"Have you seen Mrs. MacCumber?"

"She's having lunch with me right now."

"She was supposed to call us when she got in. The hotel said she had checked in."

"Do you want to talk to her now?"

Janice shook her head, "Tell him I'll call after I have eaten."

"I heard her. Can you bring her by after your lunch?"

"I'll try. Same place?"

"Yes."

"They want you to bring me there after lunch?" Janice asked. She either had good ears or the conversation was obvious. She didn't commit to going or not.

"Might as well get it over with," I said. She didn't answer. I finished my sandwich and wondered why Ranger Wilkins wanted to know if I had visited the crime scene.

After lunch, Janice agreed to my taking her to talk to the investigative team. Ranger Wilkins escorted her back to the interview room and left me sitting in a chair by the coffee pot in the large bullpen. Two men, whom I assumed were FBI agents sat across from each other not far from me. One had finished a phone call as I sat down.

"Can you believe it? They're sending us a rookie agent. We've got our hands full and could use another body, but a rookie? She'll only get in the way."

"From D.C.?"

"I think that's what they said. Maybe New York."

"We got rookies here in Texas."

"Working the illegals, oh, excuse me, the migrant issue. They won't want us focused solely on this much longer. I often wonder who's running the show."

I had to smile. I remembered too many situations when I grumbled about the support higher headquarters sent me back in the day.

Deputy Tony Anaya walked into the room. He glanced at me and nodded but didn't say anything. He went over to the FBI agents, who were apparently waiting for him. They stood up and all three left together.

Shortly after they left, a woman in a deputy's uniform walked into the room. She glanced over at me, then she took a seat in the center of the room and started fiddling with her phone. Babysitting me, I imagined.

Janice and Ranger Wilkins came out and headed towards me. He looked over at the deputy and nodded. She stood up.

"This is Deputy Lanier. She will be escorting you to see your husband. I'm going to have to run. Can I count on you two not to leave before I can get back in touch with you tomorrow?"

"Of course," I said.

Janice didn't commit.

"Ma'am, I'm very sorry," Deputy Lanier said.

"Thank you. Please, let's get this over with."

Deputy Lanier looked at me. If she wanted an explanation, I didn't have one for her. She led us to a back room in an adjacent building. The air conditioning in the room was jacked up too high and the floral scent too strong for me. They had already wheeled out a metal table with a body covered in a clean white sheet on it. A thin man with a pasty face and wearing a dark suit stood next to it. We approached the table.

"Are you ready?" the deputy asked Janice.

"Yes."

I wasn't sure I was, but nobody asked me. I had to look twice to recognize him. Janice turned away almost immediately.

"Yes, that's him, my husband."

"Are you sure, ma'am? Would you take another look."

I thought Janice might bite the deputy's head off, but she looked back for a long second before turning away again. "That's him. I want to go now."

"Please follow me. There's a form I need you to sign. It's a formality."

We followed the deputy, and Janice surprised me by grabbing ahold of my arm as we walked. She wiped a lone tear away with her other hand. The one form needing a signature turned out to be three.

The sun brought us both to a halt when we stepped outside.

"I need a drink," Janice said as we both put on our sunglasses. "Any place open?"

"I imagine we can find something. It's afternoon, early afternoon, but still."

"How about there?" Janice pointed across the street to a sign that read Spirits and Sandwiches. It hung above what looked to be a restaurant or bar.

"Let's go check it out," I said. We crossed the street and walked fifty or so yards. I paused at the door, but Janice walked right in.

"It's a deli. I'm not hungry, but I need a drink," she said

I followed her. The place seemed out of place, but that might have been its attraction. It looked like an upscale deli you might find in a big city. You could order at the counter or sit at one of the small tables for service. A long bar with stools ran across the front of the deli. Janice plopped down at the only empty table.

"Ranchers, farmers and bankers," she said looking around.

A young woman in a short black skirt and a white blouse followed us and asked, "Can I get you all a drink?"

"Can you do an old fashioned?" Janice asked.

"Yes, we can."

"Bring me a tall one."

The server turned to me.

"A beer, a Sol."

"Coming right up," she said.

"A Sol? I never heard of it," Janice said.

"It's a Mexican beer."

"Oh yeah, I remember you moved to Mexico."

I felt like correcting her. New Mexico wasn't Mexico, but it wasn't worth the effort.

"You know, Jim, I didn't know him anymore. The Pat lying there seemed a stranger to me or maybe a cousin I hadn't seen in years. Why did they need me to come down here? You could have done it as easily as me."

"I believe they need next of kin." I tried to keep my voice from sounding sarcastic.

"He asked me twice if Pat had ever mentioned a guy by the name of Ray Stahl. Maybe he said Raymond Stahl. He thought they might be friends. I don't know how many times I had to tell him I didn't know anything about his life here or who his friends might be. He did tell me that Pat lived alone. I was wondering if he might have had some woman living with him."

"Was there?" I asked.

"No, apparently not. He wasn't much of a catch, you know."

I thought of so many things to say but remained silent.

Our drinks arrived. Mine came in a bottle along with a frozen mug. At least the day wouldn't be a total loss.

"The ranger wouldn't tell me if this Stahl guy might be a suspect. Think you can find out? I would like to think they have caught the guy. Plus, did you know in situations like this, the insurance companies slow ball paying out the claims."

I guess I wasn't surprised that she had already contacted the insurance companies. Maybe most people would have by now, but in my mind, identifying the body would be the first step.

"Insurance companies are notoriously slow in paying out claims," I said.

"I don't like insurance companies. He said someone will be driving me over to Marfa later today, so I could have access to his apartment. They have already gone through it. I don't imagine there will be much there."

"Would you like me to go with you?"

"Of course, I don't want to do any of this alone. Where's Marfa anyway? Why aren't they doing the investigating there if that's where he lived?"

"They will be investigating there. However, he was killed in this county, and Alpine is closer to the crime scene."

"I thought he was killed in the national park," she said.

"He was, and that's why the federal investigators are involved. The county folks are supporting them as that spot in the park is in this county."

"I don't think people say folks anymore."

When we left the deli, we went straight back to the hotel. Janice said she wanted to relax until they came to take us to Marfa.

Chapter 8

"Are you one of the FBI guys?" the waitress said as she put the frozen mug and my second Sol beer of the day in front of me. I had returned to the deli to think. It felt more like an escape. If I had to hang around Janice too much in the next day or two, I'd be drinking a lot more.

"FBI? No, why do you ask?"

"There's an FBI office here. It's brand new, but I don't think they keep someone here full time. I know there are some of them here for the investigation. It's big news here in town. More so, now that a second body has been found."

"A second body?"

"Yes, it's only rumor now, but this is a small town. My sister's friend has a boyfriend, well, he's not really a boyfriend, you know, with the fire department. They sent an EMS team out to the same spot that first guy was shot. They found a second man. I don't think they could've missed him the first time."

"Your sister's friend knows why these people keep getting shot?" I asked.

"No. I don't think anyone knows. By the way, is that woman you were with earlier your wife?"

"No, thank heavens."

She giggled and used her hand to brush her blond hair off her ear. I guessed she was in her mid-twenties and cute. "I'm Konnie, with a k. What's your name?"

"Jim. Have you always lived here?"

"No, I'm from Lubbock. I came here for the college, got engaged to another student who is from here, and I stayed. Long story but after waiting five years, he could never agree to a wedding date."

"But you stayed here."

"My sister is a student in the college now. Besides my parents moved to Costa Rica. I guess a lot of Americans do that."

"I've heard that, too."

"I overheard that woman talking to you. That's why I thought you might be the FBI. Is she the dead man's widow?"

"You do have your sources, don't you?"

She smiled. "This isn't a big city, and I'm friends with a lot of people. There's nothing wrong with that."

"No, I know. I didn't mean anything negative. I was just impressed."

"Besides, if I want to hear the gossip, I need to have some to share, too," she winked and walked over to the only other table that was still occupied.

My phone interrupted my thoughts.

"Jim, that woman deputy is ready to drive us over to Marfa. I'm in the lobby waiting for her now. Where are you?"

"Out walking around. I'll be there in a few minutes." I sat there long enough to drink most of my beer. As I got up to leave, Konnie hurried over to me. I gave her a ten-dollar bill and didn't ask for change.

"Come back, Jim. I work here most afternoons until six."

I said I would. By the time I got to the hotel, Deputy Lanier was already there. Janice gave me a look that showed her displeasure at my being late.

The drive didn't take long. I sat upfront with the deputy. She wouldn't talk about the investigation, so we chatted about the park, the two cities, and the weather. She claimed the climate was nice in this part of Texas, except for the summer which she explained ran from March to November. During the occasional long stretch of straight road, the heat shimmering off the distant pavement created a mirage with the road breaking away and floating above the ground.

"Why would anyone live down here," Janice said more as a statement than a question.

"It's not bad. You get used to it, and in a lot of places, it's really quite beautiful. If you have the time, I could give you a list of places to visit. You'd be surprised."

"Thank you, Deputy, but I think not. Should you be driving this fast?"

Deputy Lanier slowed down a few miles-per-hour. I could see her jaw tighten.

"I do plan on staying here and seeing the sights. Any recommendations you could give me would be appreciated. Visiting here has actually been on my bucket list for a long time," I said. It might have been a minor white lie, but it brought out a small smile on Lanier's face that made it worthwhile.

We pulled to a stop at a rundown lodge. Behind it sat a dozen old trailers in various stages of disrepair.

"What is this?" Janice asked.

"It's where your husband lived."

"His address said an apartment."

"Yes, it gives a tenant a little cover."

"False pride, I would say," Janice did say. "OMG, how far down had you fallen, Pat."

"Would you like to come in with me? I need to speak to the manager and get the key."

"No, and Jim you don't go either. You need to stay with me. I don't believe it's safe here. We'll wait here for you."

"I won't be long," Lanier said. She gave me a look as she was getting out of the car that I read as "If I shoot her, will you keep it a secret." At least, that's what I would have been thinking if I was her.

Police crime scene tape surrounded the last trailer to my right behind the lodge building. I assumed Pat lived there. I started to point it out to Janice, but the deputy came out of the lodge.

She drove the car around the opposite side of the building to a different trailer. This one also had crime scene tape around it. I counted eleven trailers, and two had recently been visited by the police.

"This is it. We've processed it. That one over there was a drug lab." She pointed to the trailer I thought was Pat's. "We found out when they started shooting each other in there."

"Idiots," Janice said.

"Inside, please identify anything you want to be sent to you. Feel free to go through everything."

"Deputy, you mean I can't take something back home with me when I go?"

"Yes ma'am. We'll make sure you get whatever you want, but the FBI doesn't want anything to leave the scene yet. I'll wait out here for you. Take your time."

I thought I heard Janice whisper idiots under her breath again. Deputy Lanier either chose to ignore it or didn't hear her.

"Jim, please go in and make sure it's safe," Janice said.

"I'm sure it's safe," I said, but I accepted the key from Lanier and entered the trailer. After a second, I called for Janice to come in.

"I thought it would be messier than this," I said. After seeing how run down the trailer looked from the outside, the contrast with the inside surprised me.

Janice stood inside the doorway and looked around. "I'm glad he stayed the same organized person that he was. Still made his bed."

Sunlight streamed in from the windows where the blinds had been left opened. Some sand on the floor and a light covering of dust marred an otherwise tidy room. Clothes neatly hung from hangers in the closet and folded in the drawers. Clean dishes sat on a small shelf over the sink.

Janice scoured the room for fifteen minutes. "There's nothing here. Think the police took things?"

"I'm sure they did. They'll have an inventory."

"I didn't see my letters or emails."

"They may have taken all the documents and his computer. They would have wanted to go through them looking for clues."

Janice nodded. "Did you notice if he was wearing his wedding ring?"

"We didn't see his hands, Janice. I think they would have removed it."

"I want it back. Can you get it from them?"

"They won't give it to me, but I'll go with you and see what they have and what they'll return now." I doubted he still wore his wedding ring.

"He rarely wrote to me. I tried to write to him more often. We would text now and then, but what's in a ten-word text? He never called."

I didn't expect the tears that started falling from her. She reached for a paper towel before I could offer her my handkerchief.

When we arrived back at the sheriff's office, the investigative team had not returned. Janice asked about the wedding ring but Deputy Lanier claimed to have no knowledge of it or anything else to do with the investigation. She would contact us when the team returned.

"Think they have a suspect? Is that why they're all gone?" Janice asked, as another deputy drove us back to the hotel.

"I have no idea. Maybe we'll find out later this afternoon."

"They should tell you things. They know you used to be a special agent. You're representing the air force –"

"Whoa, don't say that. I'm not representing anyone. I have no official role. I'm only here to help you. When you go home, I'm done."

"I'm going to call the general. Do you have his phone number?"

"No, Janice, I don't. He won't tell you any different."

"We'll see. I expect to be kept informed."

We parked in front of the hotel. Janice got out and walked away without saying a word.

Chapter 9

A man holding his cowboy hat down against the wind walked by on the sidewalk in front of the hotel. I heard sand being blown against the side of my car. Like my mood, the weather had started to change. Clouds formed in the west and appeared to be heading this way. I imagined everyone in town had their fingers crossed for rain.

Once in my room, I considered calling someone working the investigation and telling them I was leaving in the morning. I didn't bring enough Tylenol to continue babysitting Janice. I only held off calling because I thought someone from the team would call me in response to Janice's complaints. They would want me to calm her down. I would rather kiss a fire ant mound. I had fulfilled my obligation to her and didn't feel guilty about leaving.

An unexpected knock on my hotel room door changed everything. I opened it, and as much as Janice depressed me, the woman in front of me skyrocketed my mood. She smiled at me but didn't speak. She put her arms out and we hugged.

"So, you're the rookie," I said.

Former deputy sheriff and now FBI Special Agent Rose Luna pushed me away. "Rookie?"

"Not my word," I said. "It's great, it's fantastic to see you again." I stared into her face. Her pretty brown eyes and jet-black hair brought back memories that seemed like they happened yesterday.

"I couldn't believe it when I heard you were here."

I touched the side of her face, and we kissed. A good kiss with a hint of passion, and all my thoughts about leaving disappeared.

"May I come all the way in?"

"Of course," I said. "How have you been?"

She sat on the one chair in the room. "Busy, but loving it. It's like I'm in a whole different world. Not only the job, living in Washington D.C. is so strange for me. I always thought El Paso would be the largest city I'd ever see."

"How'd you get picked to come down here?" I asked.

She looked at me like she was trying to figure something out. "That's a long story. How about we get into all that later." She stood up and started unbuttoning her blouse.

If there had been any woman, since my divorce, who had me seriously thinking about taking the plunge again, Rose was her. We even went on a cruise together. Somehow, despite our differences, we fit together very well. That she didn't blame me for almost getting us both killed, twice, made her a special kind of gal in my mind.

"You know, your comment about me being a rookie does tick me off a little," she said later. We both lay in bed looking at each other.

"I missed you," I said.

"Don't change the subject. I have more law enforcement experience than most the agents I work with. Yet most of them like to refer to me as the rookie."

"It's part of the initiation process. Ignore it."

"I know," she said. "I better get dressed. Having sex with our number one suspect is frowned upon."

"Number one suspect?"

"Well. Maybe not yet, but I think I can convince them," she grinned.

"I'm glad you're here, but how did that happen?"

"Simple minds and faulty logic."

"So, typical front office management?"

"Yes. Someone in Texas requested help, and someone in FBI headquarters figured that being from the El Paso area, I would be an expert on the Big Bend area. Being a rookie, as you say, I was also expendable."

"They were wrong on both accounts," I said.

"You got that right," she said and kissed me. She got out of bed, grabbed her clothes, and walked to the bathroom.

"You look absolutely fantastic."

She didn't respond, but I could see a smile form on her face. I wasn't in a hurry to get out of bed, so I sat up against the headboard and waited for her.

"This is strangely déjà vu. Don't you think?" Rose said when she came out of the bathroom.

"You mean being out in the middle of nowhere trying to find a missing treasure while people are being killed around us?"

She nodded.

"Maybe," I said.

"Except in this case there is no buried treasure, right?"

"I don't think there is either, but I can't see any motive. What can you tell me?"

"I can tell you that we have no idea why your old friend was murdered. To compound things, someone murdered a second person at the same spot early this morning."

"Can't be a coincidence."

"No, and we don't have anything that would link this second guy with Pat. We're scrambling to find out. This second murdered guy was a Raymond Stahl. Do you recognize the name?"

I shook my head. "Never heard of him."

"Didn't think you would. He was shot, too, but we believe with a different weapon."

My phone vibrated on the bed stand. "It's Janice, I better answer it or she'll come knocking on the door."

"The widow?" Rose asked, and I nodded.

"Hey Janice…. No, but I'm working on that now…. Ok, I'll get back to you shortly." I ended the call.

"What does she need?"

"She wants Pat's wedding ring. She figures it was either on his finger or in the trailer somewhere, and that your team has it."

"They may. I can find out today, and if we do, I can't see why it can't be returned to her right away. I take it there's nothing going on between you two?"

"Mutual dislike, maybe. I can see why Pat may have needed his space, but I have no idea what motivated him to come down here. I can't believe he was really prospecting."

"It appears that he was," Rose said.

"I know. I knew him for years and never heard him ever mention the topic. Of course, Janice said he became fascinated with the UFO conspiracies, too."

"A passion for solving mysteries maybe?"

"Possibly. Does your team know about our past?"

"No, but it shouldn't matter. You're not a suspect, at least not yet," she teased.

"Good, and I have no intention to get involved with the investigation. I was going to leave tomorrow, but now, if you don't mind, I'd like to stay for a while."

"I'd like that. I'm sorry I messed up our relationship, Jim."

"What? You did the right thing."

"I don't know. Joining the FBI was a life-long dream, but it took me away from you. You're the only person that has meant this much to me in a long time."

"You did the right thing. I'm a mess and certainly not worth throwing away your future."

The alarm on her phone went off.

"I need to get back for a team meeting."

"You better go. Won't look good if the rookie is late."

She smacked me in the arm, and we both laughed. We kissed, and she left. I sat back down on the bed and tried to get my arms around the menagerie of emotions bouncing around inside me. I was happy that the FBI recruited her, but I also had wished she would've turned it down. Selfish of me, but I couldn't help it.

My wife had divorced me for too many years of my taking her for granted. It hurt me, hell, it broke me, but deep down I couldn't blame her. There is something in some professions that suck all the attention, all the purpose, out of an individual who is seriously devoted to doing a good job. I had let that happen to me. Married to the job, I think that's the term for it. I never wanted to be. I had simply let it happen. I solved it by retiring shortly after my divorce.

Chapter 10

"Who was that woman who was in your room?" Janice asked. Her tone made it sound more like she demanded an answer.

"An FBI agent. She's going to get your ring back for you." I could have answered her in two words but decided to play nice.

She had called me and asked me to meet her in the lobby. "They want me to come back over for a few more questions. I have a few questions of my own."

"Want me to go with you."

"Yes, I may need a witness."

I didn't know why she thought she might need a witness. She certainly wasn't considered a suspect. More than likely, she would want me to corroborate her story if she decided to sue them. Good luck to that, I thought.

"If the FBI agent is looking for my ring, why didn't she come to me instead of you? That doesn't sound right? I don't like being cut out of my own husband's murder investigation."

"She didn't know you were looking for a ring. We're old friends. When she heard I was here she stopped by to say hello. While she was here, I asked her about the ring."

I drove us to the sheriff's office. I could tell Janice wanted to say something more, but she remained silent for the two minutes it took us to get there. She got out of the car and went into the building without waiting for me. So much for needing a witness, I thought.

By the time I entered the team's large room, I saw Janice being led off to a smaller side office by the Texas Ranger and another man I had not met. This second man was in a uniform I didn't recognize. She didn't look around for me, so I didn't follow them. I sat down on a chair that had been placed alone against a wall, out of the way, for people who were here waiting.

After about ten minutes, Janice came out of the room followed by the Texas Ranger. Neither looked very happy. She walked straight to the door passing me and looking at me long enough to say, "Drive me back to the hotel."

Rose, the two other FBI agents, and a woman I didn't recognize came out of another office and into the larger bullpen. They were discussing something, and Rose didn't look over at me. I followed Janice out the door.

"Janice, slow down," I said once I stepped outside. "I'm here as a friend to help you. I'm not here as your employee to order around."

She looked back at me. Her hard expression mellowed a bit. "I'm sorry, but you know I'm under a lot of stress."

"I understand, and I do want to help. Just don't make it hard on me to do so."

"They said they didn't know anything about my letters or my ring. They weren't even real policemen."

"Of course, they were –"

"No," Janice said interrupting me. "One was some park ranger and the other a Texas Ranger. They should be out rescuing baby bears or something."

I fought the urge to laugh at her. "Believe me, they are both trained and qualified to be involved in this investigation. They are supporting the FBI, but they are capable of conducting interviews, searches, etc. on their own."

"Well, all they did was ask me more questions. They didn't

tell me anything. They asked me about some other person who was murdered. How would I know?"

"I'm sure they are trying to determine if there is a link between that person's murder and Pat's."

"God, what's next, a bunch of masked men riding through on their horses?"

"I'll follow up with Agent Luna later today to see if she's located your ring. You might want to call Deputy Lanier, too. She gave you her card, and it wouldn't hurt to have two people looking for it."

"We should have asked about it at the morgue. They have it, I'm sure," she said.

"That's a good guess."

"You know you should never have anyone buried with their rings on. The people at the funeral homes steal them before the casket is sealed."

"Well, we can make sure Pat isn't buried with his."

"They did say they would take me out to the spot where they found him. I want to see it. I don't know why, but I do."

I wanted to see it, too. Morbid curiosity maybe, but I knew it might help give us both closure.

"When did they say they would take you out there?"

"You have to go with me," she said.

"I will."

"Today. They said they would have that Deputy Lanier drive me out there."

While we were still in the lobby of the hotel talking, I saw a county sheriff's vehicle pull up to the front of the hotel.

"That may be her now," I said.

She hadn't come alone. FBI Special Agent Rose Luna entered

the hotel lobby with her. She smiled at me but let the deputy do the talking.

"Ready to go?" Lanier asked. "It's about an hour drive, so we can wait if you need to go to your rooms first. You will need good hiking shoes, too."

Once we started the drive out of town, Lanier said, "Agent Luna is going with us. She recently arrived and hasn't been out to the scene either."

Janice didn't acknowledge the comment. She sat in the front passenger seat, while Rose and I were in the back.

"Any luck with the wedding ring?" I asked Rose.

"Yes, I want to know what happened to my wedding ring?" Janice asked in a voice louder than necessary.

"When we get back, I'll track it down. Agent Luna mentioned you were looking for it. I'm sure it's with the rest of his personal items," Deputy Lanier said.

"What else was there?" Janice asked.

"I'll get you a list," Deputy Lanier said.

The conversation during the rest of the trip consisted of small talk about the topography and wildlife in the Big Bend. For whatever reason, Janice did not join into the discussions, choosing to remain silent.

"Here we are," Deputy Lanier announced and pulled the car to a stop.

I looked out the window and saw no signs of a crime scene or anything else.

Chapter 11

"It's hot out here," Rose said as we stepped out of the car.

The thin layer of pavement seemed soft under my feet.

"We have about a hundred-yard hike to get there. We could get closer by using the old dirt trails, but that would take another half hour of bumpy travel. After this small rise, the terrain is fairly flat. It shouldn't take us more than five minutes. I have water bottles in the cooler in the trunk."

"Are we in the park?" I asked. We hadn't gone through a control point.

"Actually no. We're on private land. The park starts a handful of yards before the crime scene," Deputy Lanier said.

Once we all had a bottle of water, the deputy led us toward our destination. Rose walked next to Lanier, and I could hear them talking. I stayed next to Janice. She made little effort to keep up with the pace set by our leaders. It took a good ten minutes, not five, to reach the crime scene. The hundred yards turned out to be twice that much, but surprisingly, no one complained.

The afternoon sun reflected off steep rocky cliffs about a half mile away to our left. Smaller, rocky hills dotted the landscape to my right. The ground where we walked consisted of hard-packed dirt, maybe clay, and rock. We appeared to be in a narrow valley.

The trail took us around a few large boulders and then started a gentle descent for the last thirty yards. I saw Deputy Tony Anaya leaning against a jeep. He stood up as the first two in our party got close.

Police tape cordoned off a wide circular area next to him

"Is this it?" Janice asked me. We were still a good twenty paces away.

"It appears so."

"I don't see anything."

"You'll see the exact spot where Pat died. Everything else that didn't belong out here would have been taken in as possible evidence."

"This sucks."

"Let's let them explain what they found. That will help you visualize how it was."

"Didn't they take pictures? They could've simply shown me those."

"You asked to be taken out here."

"You should've have told me they had pictures."

"Mrs. MacCumber, I'm Deputy Tony Anaya. I'm very sorry for your loss."

His greeting allowed me to take a few steps away from Janice. I needed the space. Anaya nodded his head at me but didn't say anything.

"What happened here?" As usual, the tone of her question made it sound more like a demand than a simple question.

"When we responded to the scene, we found your husband lying over there. His feet were close to the small campfire. You can see the ashes," Deputy Anaya used his fingers to point to spots on the ground some ten yards in front of us. "His pickup was parked at the far edge of the police tape. We found no evidence of anyone else being here."

"Of course, someone was," Janice said.

"Yes, we know that, but we didn't find any footprints or trash or anything to help us identify who was here."

I could see why they had so little luck in finding any evidence. The ground was hard, and the constant breeze would eliminate any surface impressions in a day or two. I already knew they hadn't found any shell casings.

Rose motioned me to join her off to the side. We stood with our backs to the crime scene.

"This is a rough place to die. They were lucky to have found him. In the dark, it would be easy to sneak up on someone out here," she said

"The campfire would have hurt his night vision. The bushes and uneven ground would conceal someone's approach, too. Of course, it may have been someone he knew and expected."

She nodded. "This second murder puts everything in a new light. An obvious understatement, but it does."

"Where did the second one happen?"

Rose looked over at Lanier. She seemed to have an interest in what we were talking about. Rose signaled for her to join us.

"Anne, where did the second murder happen?"

Anne paused for a second, looking at me like she wanted to ask "does he need to know?"

"It's okay, I'll explain later," Rose said.

"Just over there, about fifteen steps from here. There's no real landmark other than the white stone," Anne said.

"Different weapon used, but same location, what do you think, Jim?" Rose asked.

"Seems they have to be connected. There are thousands of square miles out here. For two murders to happen in the same spot, one right after the other, there has to be some connection. Did they know each other?"

"The victims? We're trying to find out," Rose said.

"Both of them lived alone. Neither had any close associates that we are aware of. Neither grew up around here or have any family here. MacCumber lived in Marfa, and Stahl lived outside Alpine. But, both liked to wonder around the Big Bend looking for things," Anne added.

"Hopefully something in their phones or computers will provide us more," Rose said.

"We should know that in a day or two. Stahl didn't use any password protection," Anne said.

"I don't want to get either of you into hot water for talking to me," I said.

"You won't. I've talked to the boss, and he said to clue you in. At this point, I believe they feel there's nothing to lose," Rose said.

"Not sure if I should thank you or not."

"I didn't tell him that mayhem usually follows you around."

"Now you have my attention, Agent Luna," Anne said.

"Please, it's Rose. We're teammates, and as far as I'm concerned, it's a level playing field. I spent many years in your shoes."

"Jim! Jim, I'm ready to go back now," Janice called over to me. They had drifted a little further around the police tape.

"Guess we're heading back," Anne said and started walking back to the car.

"I'll catch up," I said to Rose as she started to follow the two.

"I can wait," she said.

"I want to say hi to Deputy Anaya. Have you met him?

She hadn't, so the two of us walked over to him and said hello. We only stayed for a minute and had no trouble catching up before we all reached the car.

"Good thing you made it, Mrs. Macumber and I were going to leave you," Anne said, grinning.

"I told her we weren't waiting for you. I'm hot," Janice said. Unlike Anne, her tone had no humor in it at all. "You would've had to catch a ride with that other man."

On the drive back, Janice looked back at me, "Can I sell his pickup?"

"I would think so. You'll have to wait for it to be released to you, but as you're his surviving spouse I would think everything would go to you."

"I still have his will. I doubt if he had the energy or imagination to change it. At least, he never gave me any indication that he was going to."

"When I check on the ring, I'll also get a list of everything we have. I do know that we have the pickup," Anne said.

"Good, I'll be in my room all night," Janice said.

"No dinner?" I asked, immediately wondering why I asked or cared.

"I'll have something delivered."

At the hotel, Janice got out of the car and walked into the hotel without a comment to the rest of us.

"A hard one," Anne said.

"Is she always like this?" Rose asked.

"Yep. Never cared for her."

"Jim, I'll see you in the morning. We have a team dinner," Rose said.

Anne and Rose drove off. I wondered if Rose's remark was for Anne's benefit, or if I wouldn't really see her until morning. She was staying in the same hotel, so I hoped I might see her again that night.

Chapter 12

I didn't. Noise in the hallway outside my door woke me up at half past six in the morning. I contemplated going back to sleep, but my knowledge of a nearby coffee shop motivated me to get up. Not in any hurry, I took my time getting dressed and to the coffee shop where I worked my way through two cups of coffee and two cinnamon cake doughnuts.

The front window of the coffee shop gave me a clear view of the hotel. I was reading a regional magazine targeting tourists that had been left on one of the empty tables when I saw Deputy Anne Lanier drive up and park in front of the hotel. She went inside.

Early, I thought, wondering if Janice was even awake. Anne came out a few minutes later and looked up and down the street. She took out her phone and called someone. My phone, as it turned out.

"Good morning, deputy," I said.

"Jim, I'm glad you're up, is Janice with you?"

"No, you didn't find her in the hotel?"

"No...., did you see me?"

I could tell she was wondering how I knew where she was. "Look across the street. I'm in the coffee shop. Come join me."

She looked in my direction. I doubted if she could see me inside, but she smiled, put her phone in her pocket, and started walking. Once inside, she immediately went to the counter and ordered something, then she came over and sat down next to me.

"What a crazy twelve hours," she said. Before I could respond, she continued, "Another family member showed up wanting answers."

"I didn't think Pat had any other family."

"No, not him, Stahl," she said. "Claims to be his son."

"Is he?"

"Could be, but we didn't notify him. These people, like Stahl, like MacCumber, they move here alone from who knows where. They aren't social. They don't join things. Somebody here probably knows them enough to talk to us, but we don't yet know who they might be. If the people who know them don't come forward, it's a hard struggle to develop information on the victims."

"They don't frequent any bars –"

She cut me off, raising her hand, "Jim, please, we know how to do all that." She paused for a second. "Sorry, I'm venting. It's not supposed to be our case, but the feds keep looking at us like we should know all the answers. It's like they think we're letting them down."

"Rose?"

"No, she just got here. Forget I said any of that. I chased down all the information Janice wants, and now I can't find her. I was hoping you might know where she is."

I took out my phone and called her.

"I did try that already," Anne said.

"I know, but she might not have recognized your number. And, she's not very responsive. She'd call you back when she felt like it." I let the phone ring for another fifteen seconds. "No answer for me either."

"I'm thinking of having the hotel clerk let me into her room."

"It's a good idea. It's not like her to run off. Is her car still here?" I asked.

"I don't know. Do you know what kind of car she has?"

"Yes, let's go see. It should be in the lot."

She grabbed her coffee off the counter, and we walked across the street to the parking lot adjacent to the hotel. The Toyota Janice had rented still sat in the same spot it had been since the day before.

"Come with me to check her room. I don't want her to later claim I did an illegal search or something," Anne said.

The hotel clerk gave us a key to Janice's room without hesitation. We explained that we only wanted to make sure she was okay.

"Not here," Anne said. We stood a couple feet inside the room.

"The bed wasn't slept in last night."

"She wasn't with you?"

"Give me a break. I'd rather hang myself."

She grinned. "Let's go check with Rose. She's on the third floor, right?"

"I don't know."

"So, you don't have an alibi?" She walked out of the room and waited for me. Her grin had grown.

We ran into Rose in the hallway outside her room.

"No coffee for me? Or is that for me?" Rose said looking at the one in my hand.

"Sorry, we didn't know we'd be coming to see you," Anne said. "Have you seen or heard from Mrs. MacCumber this morning?"

"No, why? Has she left us already?"

"Hopefully, she's out having breakfast somewhere, but she's not answering her phone," I said.

"And, it doesn't look like she slept in her bed last night," Anne said.

"Her car?"

"Still parked where it's been since yesterday," I said.

"That's not good. Do you have a key to her room?"

"I do. Want to see it?" Anne asked.

"I'm not doubting that she's not there."

"It's no problem, Rose," Anne said.

We returned to Janice's room.

"Should we knock first?" I asked.

They both nodded, so I did. We didn't wait long for the response we didn't expect. Using the key, we once again entered the still empty room.

"Is the sink or shower wet?" Rose asked.

I went to check and found both dry. A hand towel had been used and left on the sink, but it too had dried. The other towels did not appear to have been touched.

"Everything is dry. I think it's safe to say she didn't spend last night in this room," I said.

"That is not good," Anne said. "Let's hope we contact her soon. This wouldn't be a big deal, you know, some woman not spending the night in her own hotel room. But this woman happens to be the wife of our first victim, and she's here on our request. If something's happened to her," Anne looked at Rose and shook her head.

"Let's don't overreact, yet. She could be next door," Rose said.

Deep down, I knew that wasn't the case. A terrible feeling overcame me. I didn't say anything, hoping I was wrong.

"What should we do?" Anne asked.

"Let's keep looking for her. I'll report this to the team, and

Anne can you talk to whoever was working the desk last night here at the hotel and see if they remember anything. Also, see if they have any CCTV. Jim, would you mind walking up and down the street to look for her in any of the restaurants. I know there's only a couple. Maybe her phone's battery died, and she's nearby."

"Sounds like a plan," I said. We left the room and all went our separate ways.

Chapter 13

An hour later, I sat in the middle of the investigative team's conference room. Chairs had been pulled into a circle-like pattern, and questions were being tossed around looking for answers. Everyone but Janice was there.

"Where is she?"

"Why would she leave her hotel?"

"Why would she become a target?"

"Who saw her last?"

"Have we distributed her picture to everyone?"

"Is it too early to up channel her disappearance?"

The questions weren't aimed at me, but when they ran out of things to ask, they had me tell them everything I could remember about Janice. I had the feeling a few thought I was holding something back. The younger of the two male FBI agents had sufficient suspicion to suggest I hand over my room keys to allow someone to have a quick look through my room.

I gave my room key to Anne, and after a nod from the team leader, she hurried out of the room. We were still continuing our fruitless discussion twenty minutes later when Anne returned.

"Not there and no sign of a struggle," Deputy Lanier said. She returned my key.

"Okay, let's get back to work. Let's have all road patrols have an eye out for her. Hell, maybe she'll show up. If not, I'll call it in at noon."

I waited in the room as everyone started to scatter.

"Has anyone else asked you about Pat's murder?" The older FBI agent asked me.

"No, no one at all."

"By the way, I'm Joe Rodriquez," he said and held out his hand.

I shook it. "I can't see how her disappearance can be related to her husband's death. I may have been away from all this too long, but I can't see a link." I motioned with my hand to the room.

"I can't either," he said. "Have you met Rhett Stahl?"

"No."

"He's the son of our second victim. He's a former San Antonio police officer. He's at your hotel. I'm only mentioning him as you may run into him. He's as confused as we all are. You two should meet each other at some point."

"Okay," I said, not really having much interest in meeting anyone else.

"You're welcome to poke your nose in this as much as you want. As you know, we have zilch. Agent Luna says you're pretty good at all this. Just keep us informed and don't be surprised if at some point we tell you to back away."

"Not a problem."

He nodded and walked away.

Rose stood in a corner of the room talking to the park ranger. They both looked serious, so I left the building without interrupting her. Janice's disappearance didn't make any sense to me. I started walking down the street without any destination in mind.

I stayed on the main road, glancing down the side streets as I went. While many on the team thought it plausible that Janice was simply out on her own, I couldn't imagine Janice doing much on her own. Not that she wasn't capable. It wasn't her style. She saw me as her personal assistant on this trip. If she wanted or needed anything she couldn't get in the hotel, she would've called me to take her wherever she needed to go. As unexplainable as it was, something bad had happened to her.

The call from Rose came as I reached the edge of town.

"They found her."

"Bad?"

"Yes, she's been killed. Where are you?"

Five minutes later, Deputy Tony Anaya and Rose pulled up next to me in a sheriff's sedan.

"Hop in," Tony said through the driver's side window.

I did, and he sped off. No sirens but he turned the flashers on.

"A rancher, checking out his new Cessna and flying some approaches to the local airport spotted the body out in a field. He called it in. It's her, but they want you to confirm it," Rose said.

"Ranger Wilkins and Deputy Lanier responded immediately. The sheriff should be out there now, too," Tony added.

This would belong to the county, I thought. It didn't happen in the park. Rose looked back at me from her front seat position. I couldn't tell if she was trying to read my mind or wanted to tell me something.

"What are you thinking?" I asked her.

"This makes no sense. No one knows her here. She's only been here a few days."

"I don't think she would have gone anywhere without dragging me along. I can't explain it either."

We drove in silence for several minutes before we came to a field. I could see a half dozen emergency vehicles with flashing lights about a hundred yards into the field. Tony turned off the road and followed the tire tracks of the cars already there.

"The city police and fire department arrived first. They sealed off the scene. I'm not sure if this is inside city limits. The airfield is," Tony pointed to the small airport in the distance.

As we climbed out of the car, a short heavy-set man in civilian clothes shouted at Tony and waved him over. Tony left us. Rose and I walked toward Deputy Lanier who was talking to a young city cop. I could see who I imagined was the medical examiner bent over the body. Another person stood nearby taking pictures.

"It's definitely her. Looks like someone hit her on the side of her head with the proverbial blunt instrument. A finger looks broken, too. She's fully clothed, so no signs of anything else done to her," Anne said to us.

I knew she meant she wasn't sexually assaulted, but getting killed might have been bad enough.

"Ronny has a good theory. Someone may have been trying to get some information out of her. He may not have meant to kill her, at least, not right away."

"I mean why else break her finger?" Ronny said. He looked to be in his early to mid-twenties.

"Good point," Rose said.

Ronny beamed. His city police uniform was spotless.

"Mr. West, can we have you come take a look," Tony asked.

"That's our sheriff next to him," Anne said.

Tony led me right up to the body, and the medical examiner positioned her so I had a good look at her face.

"That's her," I said. "She's wearing the same clothes she had on yesterday."

Tony escorted me back to Anne and Rose. "Thanks, Jim. It's a formality, we all knew it was her."

"No introduction to the sheriff?" Annie asked.

"He's a busy man, and when he heard Jim didn't vote in this

county, he said he would meet him later," Tony said. The two smiled at each other. "It's nothing personal, Jim."

"I know."

"How do you think he got her out here?"

"We didn't see any tire marks when we responded. Sergeant Robles and I found her. We came straight out from the end of the runway. That was how the location was described. After we found her, the EMS wagon and a couple county and city cars drove right out here. The way you came, and everyone else," Tony said.

"Messed up the scene," Rose said.

"Well, we had a good look at the ground around her and didn't see anything to mess up. There's enough buffalo grass and taller brush that made her hard to see until we were right on top of her, but there was no sign of another vehicle being here," Ronny said.

"Must have carried her," Tony said.

We all looked toward the road.

"He would've come the most direct way. It was most likely dark, but still it would've been risky," Rose said.

"More of a reason to think he may not have meant to kill her right away," Ronny said.

"The disposal of the body could've been a sudden decision. Where does this road lead?"

"It doesn't go anywhere, Rose. It circles this open field at the end of the runway. Both ends take you back into the city," Anne said.

"Why would he have come out here in the first place?" I asked.

Everyone shrugged.

Chapter 14

Ranger Caleb Wilkins, Rose, and I sat at a small table in a side room off the team's larger conference room.

"The way I see it," Caleb said, "we have one or two possibilities. Her murder is connected to the other two or it isn't. Neither make any real sense, but it doesn't need to. It happened. How could it be related?"

"It has to be related," Rose said in response to his question. "If it's not, then it really defies the odds."

"I agree. It's related. Doesn't have to make sense to us. The killer is either looking for something he thinks these people had or is trying to prevent something from being discovered that he thinks these people may be aware of," I said.

"Ideas?" Caleb asked.

"No, not really. I can't buy that this is over a buried treasure," I said.

"Our killer is probably not as logical as you. In fact, my guess is that he or she is nuts, so I wouldn't rule out the buried treasure angle. There doesn't have to be any. Our killer just has to believe it's out there," Rose said.

"Your other theory," Caleb said to me.

"Could be anything at all. Something that our killer wants to be kept secret. Maybe it's his real identity, information about a past crime, who knows. It may not be a physical thing. It could be knowledge of something he wants to keep secret," I said.

"So, you're saying that perhaps we have someone living here who may be, say, a fugitive from the law. He's living here under a different identity. Somehow, MacCumber finds out about it, so the killer shoots him. Then to be sure, he kills Stahl whom he thinks MacCumber may have told, and finally MacCumber's wife who he may have also shared his suspicions." Caleb thought about it a second and nodded his head.

"That's plausible. It may explain why the killer broke her finger before killing her. He wanted to find out what she knew," Rose said.

"But it doesn't get us any closer to identifying our killer," I said.

"How did he get her out of her room?" Rose asked.

"That's a tough one. I have a hard time thinking she'd go anywhere without asking me to go with her," I said.

"But he did, so what theories do you have?" Caleb asked.

I shook my head. "Maybe someone called her room and said they were with the team and had something for her or needed her signature."

"Would she have left the hotel, though?" Rose asked.

"All the person had to do was get her out of the hotel. If he could get her to the parking lot, that may be all he needed. Could there be two people involved?" Caleb asked.

"Anything's possible," Rose said.

"If the caller identified himself as a cop or a sympathetic reporter she might have gone alone to the lobby. They must have had a good ruse to get her outside," I said.

"Hopefully, forensics will give us something to work with," Caleb said.

Rose's phone buzzed, and she looked at it. "I've got to go," Rose said and stood up.

We stood up with her. She left the room.

"How close are you two?" Caleb asked.

I looked at him not sure what to say.

"Rumor mill, you know."

I did know and had expected it. Our history was never a secret. "We're close, but it won't affect her job. She won't let it." I smiled, and he smiled back. I thought I noticed a little understanding sympathy in his smile.

I left the building and walked around, going nowhere. The early afternoon sun finally drove me inside. I selected Spirits and Sandwiches as my place of refuge for two reasons. First, I needed a cold beer, and second, I wanted to talk to Konnie.

A dozen or so late lunchers occupied the tables, so I grabbed a seat at the bar. I didn't see Konnie at first, but then she came through the door to the kitchen carrying a tray with someone's order. An older man with an obvious limp ran the bar. I ordered a Sol and watched Konnie in the mirror behind the bar. I didn't think she saw me, but she walked directly up to me after she delivered the customer's lunch.

She didn't smile, but she grabbed my arm. Her eyes looked like she might start crying. "Are you okay?"

As I expected, the news had spread fast, and Konnie had already surmised who the victim was. I let her hand linger on my arm.

"I'm okay, just trying to get my head around all this. What have you heard?"

"It was your lady friend? The one who was here with you."

"Yes, someone murdered her and left her in the field at the end of the airport runway. Probably killed her sometime last night."

Konnie's hand went from my arm to her mouth. The bartender placed the beer in front of me. He stayed close, listening.

"I'm sorry. I mean she was only a friend, I know, but still," Konnie said.

"It doesn't make any sense. She didn't know anyone here. What have you heard?"

"Everyone has been talking about it. Nothing like this has ever happened here. Nobody knows anything. That's what's scary. Usually someone has a theory or two. It's all over social media. No one has a clue."

"Konnie," the bartender said and nodded at a couple sitting at a table. Konnie hurried off. The bartender looked at me for a second and then walked over to his stool in the corner.

I looked back at Konnie. She looked the same as she had when I was here before. The outfit must be her uniform for the job. The short black skirt and white blouse, along with her short blond hair gave her an anime look. At least with my limited knowledge of the Asian anime culture, that's how she looked to me. I liked the look on her.

I sipped on my beer. These weren't my murders to solve, but I took Janice's killing very personal. She may not have been my favorite person, but I had agreed to meet her here, to help her. Someone had snatched her right out of the hotel we were both in and killed her.

"Sorry about that," Konnie said, interrupting my thoughts.

"You stay busy."

"Does the FBI have any suspects?"

"No, not yet, but they will," I said.

"What are you going to do?"

"I'm going to help them catch the bastard."

Her eyes widened.

"If you or your friends hear or see anything, tell the police. If they don't want to go to the police, call me." I wrote down my phone number and gave it to her. She took it and then hurried off to greet another new arrival.

She came back a few minutes later. "I wish I could do something to help. It's all kind of scary."

"I don't think anyone else is in danger at the moment. These killings seem to be connected, so unless someone has a link to the three victims, I think they're safe."

"I don't know any of them." Her eyes widened. "How about you? You knew two of them."

"Yes, I did, but you can only carry the who-knows-who so far, or you'll have to kill the whole country. I mean, we've been talking. What if the killer is watching me and sees me talking to you? And who are you talking to? The chain never stops."

"I guess you're right, but you should still be careful."

"I will," I said.

"I just met you, but I would feel bad if something happened to you." She gave my arm a little squeeze and wandered off to check on her new customer.

Actually, with all that had been going on, I hadn't thought of myself as a possible target for the killer. It still seemed improbable, but I knew I had better pay closer attention to my surroundings for the next few days. I think I usually do a pretty good job of that all the time, but I had to admit I didn't look twice at the customer Konnie had greeted a few minutes earlier. My focus had been on her.

My phone interrupted my thoughts. Rose wanted me to come to the team's conference room and meet someone. I told her I'd be there in a minute, despite my having no desire to meet anyone else in this town.

Chapter 15

A man, about my age, sat next to Rose in one of the side offices. He stood up when I entered.

"Jim, this is Rhett Stahl. He's here to find out what happened to his father."

We shook hands, and I mumbled a hello.

"Nice to meet you, Jim. I understand you knew both Pat and Janice MacCumber. I'm sorry for your loss."

"It's not like losing your father. I'm sorry for your loss," I said.

He sat down, and I did the same. Rose had remained seated.

"Rhett is a retired San Antonio city police lieutenant. He's been filling us in on what he knows about his father's activities here."

"Which wasn't much," Rhett added.

"It helps. We have a number of leads being pursued as we speak," Rose said.

"Did he know Pat?" I asked.

"Yes, and his killing scared him. He never communicated much. Ever since my mom died, he's been wandering around out here. I think he mostly wanted to be left alone."

I nodded. That made sense to me. "Was he a prospector?"

"Not in the serious sense. He thought people like Pat, your friend, were a little nuts. But he liked Pat, and my dad didn't like a whole bunch of people."

"Yeah, we used to be friends," I said.

"The last time I talked to him, it was on the phone a few days ago, I told him to talk to the police about his suspicions. I hoped he would, but he claimed he didn't actually know anything."

"Did he feel like he was in danger?" I asked.

"I've already gone all through this." He looked over at Rose. She nodded but didn't say anything. He looked back at me. "No, he said there was no way anyone could be mad at him. He was scared though. That came through loud and clear. I told him to come back to San Antonio. He said he would."

"I'm sorry," I said again.

"He never met Mrs. MacCumber."

"Makes sense, she had only arrived."

Rose spoke up for the first time since the introduction. "You both have an interest in identifying the killer. Neither of you have an official role, but no one has a problem if you do some digging. Just please keep us informed and don't try to confront the killer on your own."

"I'm not here on a vendetta," Rhett said.

"You two are in the same hotel. You might as well get to know each other," Rose said. She probably sensed that neither one of us wanted to become buddies, so she added, "You don't need to do things together, but each day you could at least talk to each other about what you and we have learned."

"You'll share that with us?" Rhett asked.

"As much as I can, and maybe a little more."

It made sense. However, I already knew there were a few things I didn't like about Rhett. For one thing, he had kept himself in better shape than I had. His hair was a little too perfect, like he went to a salon rather than a barber. Mostly, maybe, because of the way Rose's eyes smiled when she talked to him.

"We could do that, Rose," he said.

She looked at me. "Jim?"

"Yeah, sure, but I got here first, so you buy the first beer."

"It's a deal," he said. "Now, Rose, I need to do a few things."

She grinned at me after he left. "Handsome, don't you think?"

"How would I know?" I grumbled.

"He's going out with one of the deputies to his father's place. It's nearly an hour from here, so you may not even see him again today. He came in with a whole list of investigative steps that needed to be done. We had done ninety percent of them, but he had a few ideas we hadn't. Mostly because he knew more about his father's activities than we did. You didn't think of compiling a list for us, did you, Jim?" She smiled with this last question.

"Why harass me?" I asked.

She laughed. "He did give us some information on his father that may help. Apparently, four or five of these guys would get together every now and then at a place near Lay-By. A small diner that also serves drinks at night. Rhett went there once with his dad."

"You have people out there now?"

"Of course. It's not near here, so none of my people, as you call them, are familiar with it. Never had any trouble there as far as I know."

"Are you heading out there?" I asked.

"No, I've got things here to do. Rhett might head out there later. You could go with him, or I could get you directions."

"I think I'll wait. Any update on what happened to Janice?"

"Initial examination didn't reveal any evidence of anything else happening to her. Broken finger and the blow to head that killed her."

"Guess that was sufficient, but I'm glad she didn't suffer from anything more. The more I think of it, the more ways I can think that someone may have lured her out of the hotel."

"We have verified that a call came into the hotel a few minutes after nine and was connected to her room. We haven't received any information yet on the phone used to call her. We believe the caller got her to come outside," Rose said.

"The killer took a risk."

"One that worked, so far."

"Was Rhett able to give you the names of the other men in the group you mentioned? I'm assuming they were all men."

"That was his impression, too, and no, he didn't have any names. He only learned of Pat's name when his father called him after Pat was killed."

"Hopefully, something will turn up from the visit to the restaurant," I said.

"I'd settle for a few more names. Jim, I need to get to some paperwork. Want to do dinner?"

"Yes, let's do." I left her there with her paperwork. Outside, I put on my sunglasses and went in search of the Italian restaurant I had seen that morning. At the time, I didn't pay much attention to it. Now, no longer looking for Janice, I wanted to see if it might be a place I would like to bring Rose.

The restaurant appeared nice enough. One table was crowded with five young men, college students most likely, sharing a large pizza and a pitcher of beer. An older man sat alone by a table near the window looking out onto the street. He had all the looks of a homeless person. A drink sat on the table in front of him, possibly a soft drink, but no food. The rest of the tables were empty.

"Any table," said a man who looked like he might run the place. He took a step toward me and motioned with his hand toward the tables.

"I'm really just looking. I'll be back later this evening."

"Better buy something. He'll be out of business soon," the old man said.

"Shut up, Bart. Don't mind him."

I glanced from the manager to the old man. The old man laughed. "He tells me I can't sit here unless I buy something. Says he's going out of business as it is." He laughed again.

"I'll have a beer, something on tap," I said.

He listed four or five choices, and I settled for a Modelo.

"Good for you Junior. I hope you're passing through because we have a demon out there killing people," the old man said.

"A demon?"

Chapter 16

"Yes. I'm serious. This isn't the first time either. When I was a kid, a demon killed a bunch of people. Sit down, I won't bite," Bart said.

I didn't really want to, but I had trapped myself by ordering a beer. Plus, his talk of a demon piqued my interest.

"Thanks," I said and said down at his table.

"Name's Bart, Bart Maverick." He didn't offer his hand to shake. From the color of his fingernails, I didn't mind.

"Maverick?"

"Yep, the TV show is long gone, but I'm still alive. Yours?"

"Jim West."

He looked at me for a second and started laughing again. "You even kind of look like that guy on the show."

I wanted to say my name was Jim not James, but didn't. I also wanted to move to a different table. Instead, I asked, "Why do you think it was a demon?"

"This part of Texas has always had demons, devils, and all types of unexplained evil. You roam around a few nights out there, and you'll know. Some people say there are aliens from outer space out there, but I think that's crap. If they came all the way from Mars or someplace, they'd be living on the Riviera or in Acapulco."

"That's where I'd be," I said.

My beer arrived. Bart stared at it like my glass contained a million diamonds.

"Is he bothering you?" the manager asked.

"No, could you bring me another one?"

The manager looked over at Bart and back at me. "One's his limit."

"Just one," I said.

He walked off, Bart's faced twisted into a large smile.

"I ain't got no money," he said.

"That's okay. I can afford one more beer. Why do you think this demon has killed these three people now?"

"Demons ain't got no soul. They don't need a reason, but I think this one is protecting something it doesn't want found."

"Like a treasure?"

"A treasure? No. Demons don't need treasures. Usually, it's a charm or a secret," he said.

"A secret?"

"Yes. Demons have secrets, evil secrets."

"What might the secret be?"

"Hell, I don't know. It's a secret. You know Indian tribes used to live out there. Some disappeared without anybody knowing why. The white man built forts, but they're all gone, too. Cities grew where the mining was good. They're all ghost towns now. People like to say the Indians wiped out the settlers, or the soldiers wiped out the Indians. They was always fighting, yessir, but they didn't wipe each other out. No one really knows why they all disappeared."

His beer arrived. Bart took a long look at it before he gulped down a third of it in a matter of seconds.

"People disappear out there," he looked out the window.

"People disappear in cities," I said.

"Demons live in cities, too."

"Of course they do. Have you seen one?"

"I think so," he said.

"What do they look like?"

He drank some more beer. "I know you think I'm crazy. They all do."

"I don't know you well enough to think that."

"I may be, but I know what I saw. Scared me to death, I don't go out there no more."

He stopped talking, but I waited to let him gather his thoughts. I wanted him to continue talking. He might be crazy, but listening to his story beat drinking alone.

"I saw a demon. It was maybe fifty miles south of here. The sun had not quite set. The wind blowed so hard, I had to hold onto my hat. I squatted beside a pile of rocks to get out of the wind. Suddenly, I saw what I thought was a man about twenty yards away walking across in front of me." Bart dragged his finger from his left to his right. "Then I got a good look at it. It wasn't a man. It had two legs, two arms, it was built like a man." He closed his eyes.

"What was different about it?"

"His skin looked grey, maybe had scales on it. It had red eyes that kind of glowed, and its head wasn't shaped quite right. It may have had small horns, but that may be my imagination working on me all these years." He took a small sip of beer. "I followed him after he passed me by. He never saw me, and the wind was blowing my scent away from him. I made sure of that. I saw him twice more as he weaved in and out of the valley. I always stayed thirty to forty yards away from him and stayed in the shadows."

"So, he never saw you?"

"No. I watched as it approached this car. A station wagon parked on a dirt road. My first thought was what if someone was in the car. I looked at the car trying to see if anyone was in it. I didn't see anyone, but when I looked back at the demon, it had changed."

"Changed?"

"Yes, it was now a man. It had clothes on, too, jeans, boots, a dark shirt. He got into the car and drove off."

"A shapeshifter," I said.

"I don't expect you to believe me. No one did back then. Maybe I am crazy."

"Maybe not. If it wasn't a demon, any ideas who may have killed the most recent three?"

"It could be a demon. They can look like you or me. You need to find out what he's protecting, what he's hiding. You do that, and you'll be able to identify him."

"His secret?"

"Yes, his secret. Could be nothing more than an old Indian trinket, a single gemstone, even just some old bones. Find out what he's protecting, and you'll have your demon."

"Did you know Pat MacCumber or this Stahl guy?"

"No. I keep to myself." He emptied his glass.

"You haven't heard anyone talking about it?"

"Only at Stu's."

"Stu's?"

"Yeah, Stu will give me a beer now and then."

"Is Stu's a bar?"

He smiled. "Not much of one. Only the old guys go there. I knew Stu since school. He knows about demons, too."

I still had half a glass. I looked around and saw the manager talking in his phone with his back to us. I swapped my glass with Bart's, and stood up to leave.

Bart grinned. "Thanks."

I nodded at him and left. Demons. I didn't think he saw what he thought he saw, but I have long believed that some people are so cruel and ruthless that they have to have a demon inside controlling them. One can argue whether God exists or not, but there's no denying Satan does.

Walking back to the hotel, I thought about what Bart had said. Maybe we should approach this investigation from a different angle. How to do that, though, didn't jump out at me, and I couldn't suggest we start looking for demons.

At the hotel, I asked the man at the registration counter if he had heard of a bar named Stu's. He said he hadn't. My phone vibrated with an incoming text from Rose. She would be leaving the office in a few minutes. I sat down on a couch in the lobby and searched the internet for any mention of a bar named Stu's in or around Alpine. I called Deputy Anne Lanier, and she answered on the first ring.

"Anne, this is Jim, are you familiar with a bar named Stu's?"

"It's a dive. The health department has been on the verge of shutting it down for years. Why? Do you want to buy me a drink somewhere where no one will see us?"

"You know I'd only take you to the highest quality places."

She laughed. "Really, not a good place to take Rose on a date if you're trying to impress her. How'd you hear about it?"

"From an old guy I ran into today. Says demons are to blame for the murder."

"That would be old Bart Maverick. He's a little mixed up, but he's not a bad guy. He's semi-homeless. I know him well. We all do," Anne said.

"Semi-homeless?"

"His brother has a good-sized ranch west of the city. He's welcome there and spends some time out there, but always drifts back into town and can be found sleeping in different places."

"You've heard the demon story?"

"We've all heard it."

"Where would I find Stu's?"

Chapter 17

Bart Maverick had left the restaurant before Rose and I arrived for dinner.

"I wish he was still here. He sounded like a fascinating character," Rose said.

"Not sure if fascinating would be the word I would use. I can't help but think, though, his opinion that the killer may be trying to prevent something from being discovered does make sense."

"How and why would our three victims know anything that might threaten him? It would take someone who's both ruthless and paranoid to kill Janice. A normal person would have realized that Janice would've already told us everything she knew."

"I think it's safe to assume that we're not dealing with a normal person," I said.

Rose ordered lasagna, and I went with the dependable spaghetti with meat balls. We decided to share a bottle of chianti.

"We should've invited Rhett to join us," Rose said.

I hoped she was teasing me. Either way, I gave her a half-hearted smile and took a sip of water. "Is he back?"

"I don't know. Don't be so hard on him, he's a highly decorated police officer."

"Okay, okay, enough about him. What do you think of going to Stu's after we eat? It may not lead to anything but it couldn't hurt."

"The way you described the place, it didn't sound very appealing. You want to talk with Stu, don't you?"

"I do. He supposedly has seen a demon, too."

"I'll go with you, but I don't want any mention of any demons in whatever we report on the visit. If we have anything to report, I mean. Knowing you, you want to go there because you think the beer is cheaper there."

"A valid point, usually, but I'm only interested in the demon, and anything he may know about the killings."

The spaghetti was better than I imagined it would be, and Rose ate most of her lasagna. We eyed the dessert list but decided the loaf of garlic bread we put away along with the main course had been sufficient.

The instructions we had to Stu's got us there without a hitch. Once there, we discovered a very old looking, wooden building with a front porch that reached from side to side. The porch had slats that looked like they might not support us. A dilapidated screen door gave us access into Stu's. The door slammed shut behind us thanks to a new spring. The spring stood out as the only new thing in the entire bar, and that included the customers.

"I feel like I need my flashlight in here," Rose said.

Three men in overalls wearing cowboy hats huddled at the far end of the bar. They talked in soft voices, but looked over at us when we entered.

A very overweight woman sat by herself at a nearby table, wearing what looked like a flowered bathrobe. A whiskey bottle and a shot glass sat on the table. Both of her elbows rested on the table with her forearms guarding the bottle. Both fists were clenched. She eyed us like she dared us to try and take the bottle away.

"There's your demon," Rose whispered.

I might have laughed, but the thought had also crossed my mind. We started toward the counter, and I almost stepped on an old hound stretched out on the floor. Rose sidestepped around it. I followed her.

The bartender stared at us as we approached. He didn't appear to be happy that we were there.

"Is your dog okay?" Rose asked.

"Not my dog. What do you want? Directions?"

"A beer. I assume that's what you serve here," I said, not feeling polite.

"You?" he asked Rose.

"The same."

I saw that he had a bottle of Sol beer on the counter with the display of four other American beers.

"Two Sols, please," I said.

He opened two bottles and placed them in front of us.

"Twelve bucks," he said. One didn't run a tab here.

"Thanks," I said and put a twenty on the counter. He looked at me. I pushed the money to him. "Keep it."

He didn't say thanks, but his expression softened. He looked like he hadn't shaved in seven or eight days. I assumed he was one of those men whose beards somehow stop growing after a week. I couldn't imagine how else one could maintain that look.

"What do you want?" he asked.

"Some conversation, if that would be okay?"

"You the police?"

"No," I said. "I'm a friend of two of the people murdered."

"I don't know nothing." He kept his eyes on me. Rose moved a half of a step away and leaned against the bar, drinking her beer.

"Bart Maverick suggested I talk to you."

"You talking to old Bart? Now I know you're not the police. Why did he suggest you talk to me."

"He thinks you know a lot of what goes on around here."

"People talk to me," he said.

I had to fight the urge to look around the room and ask who, but I didn't think he would like me ridiculing him.

"What have you heard about the recent murders?"

"Nobody knows anything. There's been talk, but mostly about the ones who got murdered. They were strangers. A couple folk knew them but not well. They didn't seem to have anything anyone else would want."

"Why do you think they were murdered?" I asked.

"Don't know. Maybe to keep them quiet. Don't know, maybe something someone wants kept secret."

"Like maybe a charm?"

"Could be."

"Bart says you saw a demon, too."

"I don't talk about that anymore. People would think I'm crazy. Maybe it was just my imagination anyways," he said. He finally looked at Rose. Maybe he didn't want her to think he was crazy.

"You don't sound crazy to me," she said.

"I'm not. A charm doesn't have to be a jewel or something you put on a bracelet. It could be something else."

"Such as," I said.

"Bones." He walked away and joined the conversation at the end of the bar. The three men glanced our way. One of them said something that made them all laugh.

Probably something about Rose, I thought.

"Will he come back?" Rose asked.

"When I order another beer. Want one?"

"No thanks, but I don't mind staying if you want one. Why do he and Bart keep referring to bones?"

"I'm not sure, but many civilizations consider their burial grounds sacred. Think someone is buried out there, and our killer doesn't want anyone to know about it?"

"That would make sense, but who and how would Pat or Stahl have learned about it? With Pat's background and Stahl's son being with the police, surely one of them would have mentioned that to the police," Rose said.

"Especially Stahl to his son," I said. I raised my beer when Stu looked at us.

He walked over to us, "One or two."

"One," I said.

He opened another Sol beer and set it in front of me, but he kept a grip on it. "Six dollars," he said.

I gave him another twenty. He didn't make any immediate effort to give any change, but he stood there.

"Think someone is buried out there?" I asked.

He snorted. "I know people are buried out there. Hundreds, if not more, in unmarked graves. If you wanted to hide a body around here, you've got a million good spots."

"Any special areas a demon might use?"

"They don't talk to me, and I avoid them. Listen, it doesn't have to be bones," he said and walked back to his other customers.

He didn't return with change. Rose and I left when I finished my beer. The dog hadn't moved, and the woman still sat guarding her whiskey and watching us until we left.

"That was interesting? Think he really knows anything at all?" Rose asked.

"No. I guess we learned he doesn't know anything. Is that an accomplishment?"

"Part of the process, that's all. That demon stuff is real to him."

"I picked up on that, too. Like you said, that woman could have been one," I said.

Rose laughed.

Chapter 18

Rose's phone woke us up a few minutes before seven. She answered it, mumbled a few words, and climbed out of bed. I stretched and sat up.

"Got a team meeting in thirty minutes. They apparently just realized no one had told me. I need to go back to my room and put on some fresh clothes." Two minutes after the phone call, she walked out of my room.

Twenty minutes later, I walked across the street to the coffee shop. I ordered before I noticed Rhett Stahl sitting at a nearby table.

"Join me, Jim."

His spoke loud enough to be heard outside the café. He knew I heard him. My order hadn't been put on the counter yet, so I couldn't say I needed to run elsewhere. I joined him at his table.

"How's it going?" I asked.

"Alright, I guess. My dad was a mess. His place was a mess."

"Did you learn any more that could help identify who's doing this killing?"

"We picked up a handful of things to follow up on, but nothing of substance. He had a woman he was seeing."

"Good for him," I said before thinking it was no business of mine.

"Yeah. They need to track her down. Her name was Nessy or Izzy."

"You hadn't heard of her before."

"No, no reason for him to tell me anything about her, I guess. The good news is that a neighbor of his gave us names of four people whom my dad hung out with. Five, if you count the first victim. He lived in a room of a strip motel that had been converted into eight apartments. A rundown place, but at least it gave him shelter and a little privacy. Cheap, too."

"The names are good. They need to start unraveling this case and finding some lines of inquiry."

"You used to be in OSI with the air force, right?"

"Yep."

"What do you think of the job they're doing?" he asked.

"The team?" He nodded. "I guess okay. They haven't had much to go on. I haven't seen anything they're not doing that they should."

"Yeah, that's my take, too. I hated these types of cases. We would get them in San Antonio, a body found out in a field somewhere with little or nothing to go on."

"Did you solve many of them?"

"Over time, we did alright, but too many went unsolved. This area out here puts middle of nowhere in a new perspective. You came down here with the first victim's wife, right?"

"I met her here."

"If we're assuming there's the one killer, as far as I can see, there can only be one reason he went after her."

"He thought she might know something," I said.

"That's how I see it. Can't see how it could be anything else, if we're talking about one man doing all the killing."

I nodded in agreement, but I hadn't totally given up on the possibility that two or more people could be in this together.

"I'm still trying to figure out how anyone got Janice out of the hotel. She wasn't very easy to get along with and would normally have me do something she wanted done, or she'd demand I go with her."

"If it was someone she had already met, would she step outside with them?"

"You mean someone on the team, a cop?"

"Yes, that's the easiest solution I can come up with. I don't like it, but it's the most obvious answer. Who all has she had contact?" he asked.

"Rhett, I can't see it."

"It wouldn't be the FBI guys, and gal. They aren't from around here and couldn't have killed MacCumber. The Texas Ranger is a long shot. He's not really local either. We can't discount the local police or the park ranger."

I almost said I'd rather believe it was a demon, but, for obvious reasons, didn't. "I don't buy it. You said yourself that you came up with a list of names. I suggest we let that list be worked before we start any scrutiny of the members of the team."

"It doesn't have to be a member of the team."

"And it could have been someone saying he was."

"Lying is less of a sin," Rhett said. "You like these guys, don't you?"

"Yes."

"I understand you are especially fond of Agent Luna."

"I am. We have a past."

"Okay, let's focus elsewhere to start off with. I don't mean we work this together, but I recommend we meet each day and share what we have learned."

"Okay, but I'm hoping the team will share stuff with us. They'll be way ahead of us, and I don't plan to keep anything from them."

"You shouldn't, but we may come up with a different angle

or two. We can even share dumb ideas that we may not want to discuss with them."

"Like thinking one of them might be involved," I said.

"Don't totally dismiss it. We could meet here each morning at this time. I'll even treat tomorrow."

"Okay." I could always drop out after tomorrow.

We stood up, I noticed a bulge on his hip under his untucked shirt. As a retired police officer, I assumed he had all the licenses to carry a concealed weapon. Of course, this was Texas, and maybe a license wasn't required.

"Your coffee is getting cold," he said.

I looked back and saw my order sitting on the counter. If they had called my name, I hadn't heard them. It made sense to stay in contact with Rhett, and my reluctance, I knew, was irrational. San Antonio is one of the most populated cities in the country, and if, as advertised, Rhett retired as a highly decorated police officer from there, he would be an asset to the investigation.

Deputy Anaya called my phone as I stepped outside. "Jim, I'm heading out to the scene where the two men were killed. I'd like for you to go with me, if you don't mind."

"Sure, when do you want to leave?"

"Right now."

He picked me up in front of the hotel a few minutes later. He had the old jeep that belonged to the sheriff's office. I had seen it before. The dry air felt cool this early in the morning, as it blew through the jeep.

"Some of us have been tasked to take a second look at everything. Not sure why they picked me to go to the scene though, I've been out there a lot already. You can help me. A new set of eyes and a fresh analysis. That's why they wanted you to go with me."

"I don't mind. Gives me something to do," I said.

Tony grinned. "Deputy Lanier is taking Rhett Stahl to MacCumber's trailer, and she'll be bringing him to the scene this afternoon. We'll be gone by then. Agent Luna and Ranger Wilkins will be reinterviewing a number of the people, we talked to early on, before they arrived here to help. The rest will be working the new names we got yesterday."

"I appreciate the update."

"Don't get too excited, they may want to deputize you," he laughed at his own remark.

I smiled and almost laughed, too. "Let's hope it doesn't come to that. You'd be better off deputizing Rhett."

"We know," he said, and then started laughing again. "You stepped into that one."

For the rest of the ride, Tony talked about growing up in the Big Bend. He learned how to ride a horse before he learned how to ride a bike. At different times in his youth, he had encountered a bear, a mountain lion, and a nest of killer bees. Both the bear and the mountain lion were close enough to attack him, but fortunately had not. The bees had, and he had been stung a dozen times before he made it back into his truck. At the same time, he expressed nothing but a fondness for his youth.

"Are there many bears around here?"

"Not here, but deeper into the park, further south there are some. People see them more often than the mountain lions."

"I imagine their coloring helps them blend into their surroundings."

"After we get done out here, we'll be going to Raymond Stahl's trailer. I didn't go out there with the team, so we'll both be a fresh set of eyes. Between you and me, I doubt if they missed anything at either location, but it can't hurt."

"Not at all. They may have missed a neighbor who was unavailable, who knows," I said.

We didn't stop and take the shortcut walking to the scene. Tony wanted me to see the road Pat's pickup truck would have taken. The last two miles were indeed rough and slow.

"I'm surprised Pat would've taken the effort to get out here," I said.

"Makes you think he had a specific reason. That's what we all thought, too, but we couldn't find any signs of recent digging." He parked the jeep in the middle of the dirt road.

From the spot where we parked, I couldn't tell where we were. I didn't see the crime scene, and the area around us looked like everything we had driven by in the last ten minutes.

"Right up there, by the tree is where he parked his truck." Tony said and led me to the spot. "Right here, the front of the truck was right there." He pointed to the ground five yards in front of us. "We scoured this whole area and his truck and found nothing of interest. Some of the equipment in the bed of his pickup had some value, but it was left behind. If something was taken, we don't know what it was."

I walked around the space, looking at the ground and up into the tree.

"You can walk anywhere. This scene has been processed more than once."

From the front of the imaginary truck, I could see the police tape marking off the spot where the two men were murdered. Walking slowly to the police tape, I wondered what I could possibly see or find that the team hadn't. Tony walked beside me, probably wondering the same thing.

"That's where his body was discovered. No sign of a struggle, the remnants of a small campfire near his feet." Tony again pointed out the locations.

"His clothing didn't appear to be disturbed?"

"No. It didn't appear that he was moved at all after he was shot. He would've died instantly, too."

"Any evidence that he had been eating or drinking?"

"Nothing that we found. Of course, the critters out here would've run off with everything. We did find a coke can about twenty-five yards in that direction." This time Tony simply nodded in the direction.

"He wasn't in a sleeping bag and there was no tent, so I guess he was going to sleep in his truck or go somewhere else."

"That's what we think, too. Not being sure of the time, he could've been shot before it was late," Tony said.

"He may have finished whatever he was doing out here and built the fire to watch the sun go down. Who knows?"

"As good of a theory as anything else."

"Who found him?"

"Old Sally Gibbons found him. We discovered Stahl on a return trip."

"What was she doing out here?" I asked.

"She has a small cabin about five miles south of here. Not much of a place, but she seems fine with it. The team has pretty much ruled her out."

"Why's that?

"She was at her son's place in San Angelo when we believed Pat was murdered. We've confirmed that as much as possible. Besides, we can't see that she had any motive. She didn't know

Pat, or so she said."

"She lives by herself?"

"For as long as anyone can remember," Tony said.

"What brought her this far out from her home? Five miles hiking out here, off trail can't be easy."

"She was driving, she has a Bronco, looks as old as she is, and saw the buzzards circling. She said she had a bad feeling. She parked about a mile from here and hiked in. She's wiry thin and walks everywhere."

"The buzzards hadn't gone after the body yet," I said.

"No, but probably would've within a day or so. By then the hogs would've found him, too. I hate the hogs."

I didn't ask him why. I walked around and began to study the ground near the area where Pat had been. Nothing caught my attention. Tony crouched. His eyes studied the ground.

"Nothing."

"Yeah, me too. Let's move over to Stahl's spot," he said and led me to it.

"The killer shot him four times with a different weapon than the one used to kill Pat, right?"

"Yeah, that is a bit peculiar."

"He might have already ditched the weapon used to kill Pat," I said.

"Makes sense."

I walked around the spot where they found Stahl. "No sign that he was moved either?"

"No, we're certain he wasn't. Splatter from the wounds was found in the right spots. He'd been killed less than fifteen hours before we found him. We think the shooter stood right about here."

He stood still and raised his two hands together like he was shooting a handgun. "After shooting him twice, and for reasons we can't explain, he fired two more rounds into him. The first two would've killed him."

"He didn't like Stahl. That or Stahl had made him very angry."

"Or both," he said.

"Besides the emotional side of it, what could be his motive?"

"And why kill them both here?"

"The sixty-four-million-dollar question, and that's before inflation. Did the killer come here with Stahl or Pat, or did he follow them here?

"You're asking all the right questions, Jim, but it's the answers we don't have. Wait a sec."

He stared off to a point on a rocky hill about three hundred yards away. Someone or something was standing there watching us. The sun reflected off the side of the hill in patches of bright light, making me squint.

The figure realized we had seen him or her and hurried off.

"Wait here, I didn't lock the jeep," Tony said and ran off.

I thought his pursuit was a waste of time. The individual, or whatever it was, had a huge lead. If he caught up with him, he couldn't arrest him or anything. As far as I could tell, the person hadn't done anything wrong.

The sun went behind a cloud, and the wind picked up, blowing dust and small leaves by me. I looked back up to where I saw the figure before it ran off. Suddenly, my mind produced a human-like creature with grey skin and red luminous eyes.

"Don't be an idiot," I said out loud to myself. I looked back at the hill and saw nothing. I returned to the jeep and sat on its hood waiting for Tony's return. I waited for ten minutes before wandering back to the crime scene.

He hadn't returned, and I couldn't see him. Looking around, I studied two areas close by that I thought could be good hiding spots from which a person could observe the area around me. I moved closer to one of the spots and realized that while someone could hide themselves among the bushes and rocks, getting to and from the spot would put the person in the open, clearly visible from where Pat had been killed.

The second spot held more potential. An outcropping of rocks and bushes that marked the beginning of a rocky ledge that separated the wide trail that we had taken from the road on my first trip to the crime scene, and the rough, uneven terrain that had bordered it to the left as we went back to the car. The spot gave someone an elevated, unobstructed view, and a person could approach it unseen.

I walked close to this second spot and looked for any traces of someone being here but saw nothing. I started to walk back to the crime scene when I saw it. A very healthy-looking Gila monster watching me. He was perched on a ledge of rock about three feet from me at waist level. I jumped back a step, and it crawled back into a crevice in the rocks.

Enough exploring, I thought, and returned to the jeep. Ten minutes later, I heard Tony call my name. I yelled back that I was guarding the jeep.

"I couldn't catch him. Thought I saw him again, but then nothing. I only wanted to know who he was, why he was out here, and what if anything he may have seen here in the last few days." He wiped the sweat off his forehead with a handkerchief.

"He probably hadn't seen anything," I said, trying to mollify his disappointment.

"I know. We're are not near anything, so why someone would be out here watching this spot or us, is something I wanted to get answered."

I nodded but didn't say anything.

"Ready to go?"

"Sure. I didn't know you had Gila monsters out here."

"We don't," Tony said and looked at me.

"Probably just a big lizard." I knew what I saw, but then a few minutes earlier I thought I saw a man with red eyes, a demon.

Chapter 19

We decided to go directly to Raymond Stahl's apartment before doing lunch. The long drive had me wondering again how people had survived out here in the "old days". As described, Stahl's apartment turned out to be the end unit of a defunct, one-story motel with eight units. A couple older cars and pickups filled spots in front of the other units. A gas station that looked like it had closed some twenty years earlier faced the apartments from the other side of the road. Tony had the key and led me into the apartment.

"Damn, I couldn't live like this," he said. His hand covered his nose for a few seconds.

"Can we turn on the air conditioning?"

"I doubt if it works, but give it a try. We're supposed to tag anything we take, but no one said anything about leaving the AC off."

The air conditioner looked like hundreds of others I'd seen in roadside motels. Situated under a window and vented to the outside. To our surprise, it started right up when I turned it on.

"Makes sense, living in this heat makes the air conditioner something you need to keep in working order," I said.

We left the door open, despite the heat outside and the now running AC. The apartment needed to be aired out. Stahl's place had only one bedroom and a bathroom. All the drawers had been pulled-open and left that way. The closet had no door. The mattress was partially off the bed.

Tony and I went through the room tugging at the corners of the carpet, pulling out drawers and looking underneath them. He even pulled down the shower rod and looked inside it. After thirty minutes, we called it quits.

"I was hoping we'd find something they missed. A note, a map, something that we could use to show off our great searching skills," he smiled when he said this, but I knew he was only half joking.

We left, and Tony relocked the front door. Like the others before us, we turned off the air conditioner before we left. Outside, I noticed a wooden sign that read Shady Meadows had fallen over near the end of the building.

"We're only fifteen minutes outside Alpine, but there's an excellent, cheap Mexican restaurant a few miles up the road. Want to do lunch?"

"Sounds good, can't do better than excellent and Mexican," I said, knowing cheap was also one of my favorite adjectives when it came to restaurants.

A man looked out from two doors down, "I hear they killed Ray," he said. He took a step outside his door. He had on jeans but no shirt or shoes. His short grey hair and grizzled, short beard didn't match his tight abs and well-defined chest and shoulders.

"Yes, someone did," Tony said.

"Same people got MacCumber, too, you think?"

"What do you know about it? We could use some help," Tony said.

"Nothing, it don't make no sense. Ray was harmless, and I only met MacCumber a couple of times, but he seemed to be a simple guy. He was younger than me and Ray and full of questions about the past. He thought he would find gold. Ray and I told him there weren't none or someone would've found it by now."

"Did you already talk to the investigators that were here?"

"Not the first group, I was in Junction visiting my daughter, but I talked to his son and the deputy that came with him. Gave them some names, but I doubt they'll help much. I can't think of anyone who would have any reason to kill either one of them. I felt sorry for his son."

"Can I have your name?"

"Sure, Deputy, it's Wes Banner. I'll be around if you need anything else. I liked Ray. He was a nice man. We used to eat dinner together sometimes."

"You feel safe out here?" I asked.

"Yes, but now when I leave, I take my old six-shooter along."

As we drove away from Stahl's apartment, I noticed a small general store, a barbershop that also advertised haircuts for women, a rural utility office, and a small diner.

"Not much here, and it's unincorporated, but I guess there's enough business in the surrounding area to support what they do have. I've eaten at that diner, and it's not bad. The place of Stahl's ain't much, but we haven't had many calls to come down here for any trouble."

"Banner referred to his six-shooter. That's a term I haven't heard in a long time," I said.

"It's a cowboy thing. Down here a lot of the old timers like to carry a Colt 45 and many of them refer to it as a six-shooter. The younger set likes their semi-automatic pistols. Most any brand will do. You don't carry?"

"No, not usually. In my time with OSI, I had to qualify with a lot of weapons, but since I left the service, my intent was to not get mixed up in matters where I might need one."

"Like this?"

I nodded.

"You seen Rhett's pistol?"

"No."

"It's a fancy one. Brand new, and he says it's the best 9mm pistol he's ever fired. Looks nice, too. You should ask him to show it to you. Whoa! Look at that!"

I saw it. A huge rattlesnake slithered across the road in front of us. Tony slowed down to let the snake cross.

"A lot of people would've sped up to run over it," I said.

"Yeah, maybe I would've when I was younger, but this is a long way from town. He won't be hurting anyone out here."

"That's the biggest one I've seen in a while."

"We have some huge ones down here," he said.

"I'd rather see one of your bears or mountain lions."

"You probably won't. They stay away from people and will know if you're around long before you'd see them."

Tony received a call while we were eating lunch. He grumbled an okay before ending the call. He looked at me and shook his head. "The sheriff wants all of us working the investigation, his people, not the feds, to meet with him. I think that means he's feeling some heat from somewhere."

"Like what? The FBI complaining they're not getting enough support, or the locals upset about the lack of progress with the murder investigation?"

"Could be either. He's not a bad guy, but it seems to me, no matter who the sheriff is, they let politics affect them more than they should."

"You put that more diplomatically than most. For what it's worth, I haven't heard any grumbling from anyone on the team about your support."

"They're an easy bunch to get along with. I know the park ranger, a nice fella, six kids, if you can believe it. I have three and they were too much for me to handle. Never met the Texas Ranger."

"He seems alright, too," I said.

"We better head back."

Neither one of us said much on the short drive into Alpine. When we arrived, Tony hustled into the building, and I walked back to the hotel. He had offered to drop me off, but I knew he wanted to get to his meeting.

Chapter 20

"Want to go see the lights tonight?" Rose asked. She stood in the hall outside my hotel room.

"Come in," I said.

"I can only stay for a second. Joe wants me back at the office. We're having a short follow-up to discuss all the interviews today? We may have made some progress."

"That's good." I might have asked about the progress, but my mind had placed a priority on remembering who Joe was.

"It would be great if things started falling together. You don't look too excited." She arched her eyebrows.

"Maybe I'm not ready for this case to be solved too quickly and for you to leave."

"You're sweet," she said and kissed me for about a nano-second. "Have to run. We'll do the lights tonight. I should be done in an hour or two." Rose left.

I figured the lights she referred to were the Marfa Lights. I had heard about them before. At night, from several vantage points around Marfa, one could occasionally see lights to the south come and go in the distant desert. According to legend, the lights were ghosts or aliens. According to those more practical and bent on ruining all fun legends, the lights were distant car lights. Ghosts, aliens, or cars, it didn't matter to me. I looked forward to it.

Having an hour or so to kill at four in the afternoon limited my options. I left the hotel and took the short walk to Spirits and Sandwiches. Konnie was standing by the table in the corner giggling at something a customer must have said. Two men with beers and empty plates occupied another table. I took a seat at the bar.

"I thought I saw you come in," Konnie said. "Can I get you a Sol? Mack is in the back. He's having a bout of indigestion."

"Yes, thanks. Is Mac the bartender?"

"Has been since I was going to school. Why didn't you tell me you had a handsome friend?"

"What?"

She pointed to the table in the corner. Rhett Stahl raised his finger in a hello. "He says he's your friend."

Lesser every day, I thought. "Now, why would I want to introduce you to the competition?"

"Oh, you're sweet," she said and went around the counter to pour my beer.

"Jim, come here for a sec," Rhett said.

I fought the urge to tell him to come to the bar.

"Go on, I'll bring it over to you," Konnie said.

"Did you discover anything new today?" Rhett asked after I sat down opposite of him.

"Probably not, but we did talk to a neighbor, a guy named Banner. He mentioned he had talked to you."

"That's right. He's the guy that gave us some names of Dad's associates. Have you heard how the interviews went today?"

"Not yet, but I saw Rose for a second before I came here, and she said some progress was made."

"That's good. I know they need a break."

"Here's your beer, Jim, and some snacks, on the house for both of you," Konnie said. She went to greet a new customer.

"Pretty little thing," Rhett said.

"Sure is."

"Why do you think a different weapon was used to kill my

father?"

"Could be there are two different killers, or it could be that the killer wants us to think that."

"It does give us one more puzzle to solve."

I nodded. "I have found that a person who owns guns, rarely owns only one."

"True. There's a lot of motives I think they can disregard: jealousy, money, blackmail, a crime of passion, and a lot more."

"What does that leave us?"

"That's just it, isn't it?" he asked.

"Anger, hatred, fear, but why or from what?"

"Knowledge of something that the killer wants hidden?"

"Well, curiosity killed the cat, you know," I said.

"It's possible they had both learned something that the killer wanted to be kept secret?"

"Or were about to, but what?"

"My dad was in his sixties, and your friend was what, your age. In his fifties?"

Ouch. "No, not yet." I didn't want to say almost. Besides, I thought Rhett had to be close to my age.

"My point is what do men at that age kill over? They weren't two elderly gangsters with a long history of killing and revenge. Best I can tell, both men were harmless. Of course, your lady friend had nothing to do with any of this, and yet, she gets killed."

"She had to be killed by the same person. Too much of a coincidence."

"Yes. I think the two of us need to go to Lay-By, to the bar where my dad and your friend used to gather with a few other old guys. I'm sure the team has looked at it, but we can be a little more direct."

"I'm for it," I said, surprising myself.

"Just the two of us. We don't need to put any member of the team in an awkward position. Besides, that's where my dad usually met his lady friend."

"When do you want to go there?"

"How about late afternoon tomorrow? I'd like to learn what the team has discovered first. That may help us come up with an approach."

"You two doing okay?" Konnie asked.

"I think so," I said.

"You ever been to Lay-By?" Rhett asked Konnie.

"You mean the tiny town south of Marathon? It's more of a ghost town than a real place. I've driven by it a few times. I don't think there's anything there."

"We understand there's an old rundown saloon," Rhett said.

"That could be. You can find a few of those scattered about in the middle of nowhere. Other than some old timers, no one goes to those places. Only the regulars can find them."

"Is there a good steak house here in Alpine?" Rhett asked.

"Sure."

"I'm in town alone, so I'd be happy to treat you to a fine steak. Just dinner, I promise," Rhett raised his right hand like he was swearing his comment was the truth.

"Thanks, but I'm pretty busy this week," Konnie said, smiled at both of us, and walked back to the bar.

"Pretty quick with that one," I said.

"Twenty bucks she'll be eating dinner with me in the next two days."

I didn't take him up on it. Bets like that never appealed to me. We talked until our beers were empty, and then I left.

Chapter 21

Rose and I parked at the official Marfa Lights viewing center. A row of parking spots lined the frontage road on the southside of state highway 90. The parking lot and spaces along the frontage road were nearly full.

"It's getting dark. We got here at the perfect time," Rose said.

"You mean we beat the crowd?"

She smiled but didn't answer. "Think there's anything to them? The lights."

"Could be, I'm starting to believe in demons. Maybe they're causing the lights?"

"No, I'm pretty sure the aliens from some faraway galaxy are out there, studying Earth. How primitive they must think we are."

"If they arrived here from some distant galaxy, we would be very primitive to them. It would be like us studying a colony of meerkats."

"Meerkats," she laughed. "What made you think of them?"

"Something I saw on TV, I guess. They just popped into my mind."

"You know, I like your car, but it's not a very good choice for Marfa Light studying. You can't snuggle in the front, and the back seat is too small."

"I've already thought about that. We should've rented a van."

"Too late now, besides we can't see anything from here. I want to see the lights."

We got out of the car and walked up to the visitors' viewing platform.

"I don't see anything yet," I said.

"Give it time. Want to hear about today's interviews?"

"Yes."

We walked off to the side by the railing.

"Okay, let me start with Vanessa Strickland. She goes by Nessy. She was Ray Stahl's lady friend, and she seems genuinely broken up over his death. She claimed not to know why anyone would want to kill him. She can't remember anyone ever getting mad at him. Claims he was a gentle soul and content with his life."

"Believe her?"

"I do, and she was the one I interviewed. I think his death surprised her."

"Did she know the others?"

"Yes, she knew all the men we mentioned to her, but, interestingly, she didn't identify any new ones," Rose said.

"You would think she'd know someone else who Ray may have hung out with."

"I pressed her on it, but she would only say he knew hundreds of other people, but no one in particular came to mind. She said when the guys were at the saloon, most of the time, the guys would drink beer and start talking about how the country was going to hell. Somewhere, along the line, their conversation would turn to missing treasures. They would talk about old Spanish gold that is supposedly buried somewhere or shipments of gold that never reached an army fort."

"Did she think there is a missing treasure?"

"She said there likely is some type of treasure buried somewhere in the Big Bend, but what it is, or where it is, is a big unknown. The guys were never very specific, but she knows for a fact, she says, that none of these guys had a clue. She didn't think they got together very often away from the saloon. Ray and Pat were buddies. They did things together occasionally, but she considered the others to be loners."

"Any of the guys she didn't like?"

"Good question. She didn't like any of the others. I mean she liked Pat and Ray, of course, but the other three she thought were jerks. I wondered at the time if maybe she holds one of the three responsible for their deaths. If she does, I couldn't get it out of her."

"Who were the other three?"

"A Carl Dunn, a Logan Daniels, and an Alex Karnes. I didn't do them, but I can summarize what I learned about their interviews in one word: nothing. They didn't have any information that could help us. Our guys didn't believe them, but without some way to pressure them, they couldn't get the three to open up."

"Rhett wants me to go with him to Lay-By and try to talk to them."

"You should, but you'll probably only find Vanessa. She said she hadn't seen the others since Ray's murder."

"It's only been a couple of days."

"True, but the way she said it gave me the feeling she wasn't expecting to see them anytime soon."

"They may want to keep a low profile for a while. Maybe they think one of them is next."

"I would. By the way, Rhett let me look at his weapon," Rose said, grinning. "I was impressed."

"His weapon? What was it a derringer?"

"No, silly." She swatted my arm. "He carries one of those new

CZ Shadow Blue nine millimeters. It's got a great write-up, and Rhett claims it's the best semi-automatic he's ever fired."

"What's that?" I pointed at a faint light moving in the distance.

"Oh! I love it, and look, there's another."

We counted five lights that night. One had a slight red glow and looked a little different from the others, but I kept my thoughts of demons to myself. The clear night sky gave us more of a show. Rose saw a shooting star, but wouldn't reveal her wish. We both saw the lights of a few airplanes and what we both believed was a satellite crossing above us.

"I'm not sure how much longer they'll keep the whole team together," Rose said on the drive back to Alpine.

"Any specifics?"

"No, Joe mentioned that he was told to start preparing to cut some people loose. He claimed not to know what timeline is being looked at, but these guys were working for days before I got here."

"So, what do you think? Maybe cut back an FBI person and maybe the Texas Ranger. I imagine the park ranger lives down here somewhere."

"I don't know, but my guess is at least cut back one or two of the FBI special agents within the next week."

"That makes sense and is fine by me, as long as they leave you here," I said.

"I'm keeping my fingers crossed. The other two work here, but they have other fires they need to work on."

"They work here?"

"Yes. We opened two-person office here in Alpine barely three months ago under the SAC, the Special Agent-in-Charge, in El Paso. I know him."

"Why is everything being run out of the sheriff's office?"

"Our field office here is small and not fully finished inside."

"Think the decision-makers back East are worried this could become a black hole that eats up their budget without producing any results?" I knew that's what I would be thinking, if I had the job to worry about the budget.

"Money matters, almost as much as politics. The FBI can back away and leave it in the Park Service's hands. We can take credit for helping, and not lose face by saying we would jump back in if requested."

"That sounds a little harsh. You are with the other team now, you know."

"I know, and I can sympathize with their position better. So, it may sound harsh, but it's not as harsh as the way I use to feel. The FBI is pulled in a lot of directions. We're stretched and not as autonomous as we should be."

"Politics?"

"Yes, it's a cancer. I'm not talking about oversight, either."

I understood her. It didn't matter in what law enforcement agency you served, someone with political power would always try to influence what or who you investigated. It took a lot of courage and professionalism to stand up against it. Nowadays it seemed to me there was too little of both.

Chapter 22

"Forensics has confirmed that Mrs. MacCumber was not sexually assaulted or interfered with in any way, other than the obvious injuries we noticed at the scene," Deputy Anne Lanier said.

She had called me and requested we meet. Rose had left for work a few minutes earlier. I recommended the coffee shop across the street from the hotel, and she agreed.

"That's what we expected," I said.

She nodded. "We're at a bit of a dilemma now. She had come to identify her husband and to help us make arrangements to send him off wherever. We're unaware of any other next of kin."

"As I said earlier, I'm not much help with that. They had a son who died in an accident in college years ago. I think Pat was an only child, and I have no idea about Janice's family. Pat's parents may still be around. I think they live up in Minnesota, or at least they did at one time."

"We have some people working it, but they aren't getting anywhere fast. The sheriff asked me to talk to you."

"Now that you mention it, I wonder why Janice never mentioned anything about telling Pat's mom and dad. I imagine she must have, but I didn't ask her about it. I never met them."

"We'll get there. Between federal records and insurance files, we'll get everything. The boss just wanted to speed things up."

"None of that information was on his phone?"

"We never found his phone. His laptop was password protected. We haven't gotten any results back yet. Same with Janice's phone."

"Well, it's like you said. It's only a matter of time."

"And the less time, the better," she said.

"Anything good come out of the interviews yesterday?"

"Rose didn't fill you in?"

"Actually, she did. You're local, though, you might have picked up something the FBI may have overlooked. Of course, don't tell Rose I said that."

"She'd understand, but no, I wasn't involved with the interviews. What I heard at the briefing afterwards didn't give me any different conclusions. Deep down, however, my money is on one of them."

"How about his neighbor, Banner?"

"He's got a pretty good alibi for the first murder, and a fair one for the second. I know alibis don't always hold up, but at first glance, his appears solid."

"Rhett wants me to go with him to re-interview the four people the team talked to yesterday. Are you all okay with that?"

"Normally, probably not, but everyone's grasping at straws. Rhett is only recently retired. If he wasn't so close to the investigation, the sheriff might deputize him. And you," she stopped talking and grinned.

"Me?"

I could tell she was trying to think of a way to continue. "Rhett wants you to tag along. To be his witness, or maybe, he wants you to back him up."

"Back him up?"

"Not so much to be there if someone attacks him, but to back his side of the story if one of them wants to complain about his tactics. I think that's what convinced Special Agent Rodriquez to let him interview these guys."

I didn't respond. I thought the whole thing was stupid. If they thought Rhett might get physical, then they shouldn't agree to his involvement. If they thought I would lie for him, they were doubly stupid. I also didn't care for this tag-along status.

"You weren't an afterthought. At least not by me and not by Rose. We knew Rhett wanted to reinterview everyone the first day he arrived on scene. At first, Rodriquez put him off, but when the sheriff wanted to let him get involved, Rose and I talked to him."

"Joe?"

"Yes, Special Agent Rodriquez. We, well mostly Rose, convinced him that if he ever did give Rhett the green light, he should insist on you accompanying him. We felt like Rhett was going to end up interviewing everyone anyway."

"Why did you go along with her?"

"Easy. She talked to me a lot about you, girl talk, you know." She grinned. "She also recommended I check you out on the internet. I did."

"Not the damn internet."

"What was there may have glamorized you a bit, but I didn't find anything derogatory. Rose also told Joe that she would know if you lied about anything." Anne grinned again.

"So, I don't exude the tough guy image to you."

She laughed. "One serious thing we don't want to happen. We don't want Rhett pointing his pistol at anyone."

"I doubt he would do that. There's no need. These aren't young men."

"That's the one thing that some of the team is concerned about."

"Have you seen it?"

"His pistol?"

I nodded.

"Yes. He showed it to me," Anne said.

"Why are you women so fascinated with Rhett's weapon?"

She laughed again but didn't give me an explanation. "I better get to the office. Stay in touch."

"Anne," I said as she stood up.

"Yes."

"I like what you've done to your hair."

"Thank you. My friend did it last night. Tried to get it to look like that movie star's. A million little curls. It's not too much, is it?"

"Not at all. Some highlights, too." She had worn her light brown hair short and straight.

"Catch you later." She left.

An hour later, I received a text from Rhett. "Meet me in the hotel lobby at eleven." I felt like saying I wasn't available then. I didn't, because of course, I was.

The lack of a family contact for Pat and Janice occupied my thoughts. It would only be a matter of time before a relative would be identified, but it bothered me I didn't know more. I stacked the feeling on top of the irrational guilt I had for Janice's death and shoved them both to the back of my mind. Hopefully, some black hole in my brain would swallow them, and I would forget them. I knew my brain, like the universe, had black holes. Dozens of passwords, birthdays, and names I had intended to remember had disappeared there over the years.

Rhett and I met in the lobby. He wore jeans and a black denim shirt that did little to cover the bulge on his hip. He had on well-worn boots and carried a cowboy hat in his left hand. I had a silly thought that I should've scuffed up my shiny new cowboy boots.

"Ready? Let's go," he said, not waiting for me to answer.

We climbed into his dusty, black Ford 150 pickup and drove off. I fought the urge to ask him where we were going first, or if he had any plans to how we should handle the interviews. I felt certain his behavior meant he intended to set the ground rules.

Rather than ask him what his plans were, I started asking questions about his past life. Not that I cared about it at all, but I wanted him to think his little game of "who's in charge" didn't bother me. Of course, it did. When he finally got tired of me prying into his life and started talking to me about his plans for the day, I marked it up as a small victory.

"Our first appointment is with Logan Daniels. He has a small ranch near Marathon. He lives there alone. Hell, all these guys live alone. The ranch is no longer being worked, but he has some livestock on it, probably for the tax break."

"Did your dad talk about him?"

"No, he only ever mentioned Nessy. If I met him on one of my visits out here, I don't remember."

"I understand they all claimed to have no idea why someone killed Pat or your dad."

"At least one of them is lying." He clenched his jaw and kept staring straight ahead.

"Are you going to be okay?" I didn't need to explain. He and I both knew if he was still on the force, he would be kept away from this investigation.

"I'll be fine. We're simply going to stir up the hornets' nest. They are all bright enough to know we're outsiders. It's fine with me if they think we can't arrest them. But, I'd also like them to think we might be willing to break a few bones." He grinned, but

I wasn't sure if he was kidding or not.

He had a point. If one of them had killed his dad, that person might be a lot more worried about somebody looking for revenge than the law. Someone out for revenge wouldn't need proof beyond a reasonable doubt. On the other hand, I didn't want to become any part of physical violence against a handful of sixty-year-olds.

Logan Daniel's ranch house turned out to be more impressive than I had imagined. The single story, red brick structure had a large black metal front door. Rhett pushed the old-fashioned door buzzer. The button, part of a built-in, two-way call box, looked like an original part of the house. The security camera fastened to the eaves above looked new.

Despite the security equipment, Daniels opened the door and greeted us without attempting to identify who we were first.

"Rhett Stahl?" he asked.

"Yes. May we come in? I have a few questions."

"Sure, come in. I'm very sorry about your father. He was a friend. You look just like him. I told you on the phone I didn't know anything."

Daniels led us to a large, dark wood paneled room. The interior room had no windows. Despite the bright sunlight outside, two brass table lamps were on in the room. I took my sunglasses off upon entering, but the room made me feel like I still had them on.

"Please sit," Daniels said and motioned towards two leather recliners. They faced a large leather couch where he sat.

"What can you tell me about my father's murder?" Rhett's direct question didn't surprise me, but I could see it threw Daniels off-balance.

"Why, nothing," he said. "I've told the police. I have no idea why your father was killed. It doesn't make any sense." When Daniels mentioned police, he took a quick glance at me. Rhett hadn't introduced me.

"We're not the police," Rhett said.

"Your father said you were."

"I was. I retired some time ago," Rhett said. I thought it had been less than a year.

"Who are you?" Daniels looked at me.

"He's not the police either. We're both retired civilians, like yourself. You can talk to us. No one else will know what you said."

Daniels continued to look at me rather than at Rhett.

"Look at me, Mr. Daniels," Rhett said. He did. "Someone murdered my father. It's possible some drifter did it and is now gone, but the odds against that are huge. No one has noticed any stranger passing through town recently. The police have checked the hotels. I'm a betting man. The odds that one of you four killed him are less than two to one. You know what that means?"

"I didn't kill him." Daniels voice cracked as he spoke.

"That means it's more likely that two of you were involved in the murders than the possibility any one of you didn't kill him," Rhett said.

I didn't think that's what it meant, but it seemed a good way to make a point. Daniels didn't look like he wanted to argue with him.

"He didn't have any friends other than you four."

"He knew a neighbor, Banner, I think," Daniels said.

"The police have confirmed his alibi. Keep talking Daniels, you'll come to the same conclusion I have." Rhett paused for about fifteen seconds, staring at Daniels. I thought Daniels might say something but he didn't. "What do you think? You must have thought about his murder."

"I have, and it makes no sense. No sense at all. He had nothing anyone would want, and he didn't want much out of life. He seemed happy. I mean he was as happy as the rest of us."

"Put yourself in my shoes. How would you feel and what would you do?"

"I don't know."

"Yes, you do. But let me tell you. First, if I find out before the police, I wouldn't kill the person. I'd tell the police. However, I would break a few bones. I would hurt that person very much before turning him over to the police. That's why I brought him along. He can vouch for me that you fell off your horse or down a mountainside."

"How am I supposed to convince you I'm innocent?"

"Tell me who did it."

"I don't know. Carl liked Nessy, too. He was jealous of your father. Talk to him or her. She would know more for sure," Daniels said.

"Carl Dunn?"

"Yes. You should talk to him."

"Where's your bathroom? I need to go before we leave."

"Through that door and to your left," Daniels said.

Rhett left, and Daniels looked at me. "He's crazy. He can't just go around and threaten people."

"I know. The cops wanted me to tag along to try to keep him from hurting someone. Dumb idea because once he has an idea who killed his father, he would return without me. He is a little crazy. My guess is that he would kill whoever he believed killed his father. He's a former cop. He would know how to make it look like an accident. That's if anyone ever found his victim."

"Who are you?"

Good question, I thought. Rhett's behavior in treating me like an anonymous sidekick had irritated me at first. However, I had been around long enough to figure out my role on my own. I also guessed he didn't need to go to the bathroom but wanted to inspect the rest of the house.

"I'm Jim West. I'm a friend of Pat MacCumber's and came down with his wife, widow. She had to identify the body. I'd rather not be here."

"I don't know why someone killed Pat. I didn't."

"I didn't think you did," I said. "What did the two have in common?"

"What do you mean?"

"It seems to me, the person who killed both Pat and Ray likely had the same motive to kill both of them. What could that be?"

"I thought a different weapon was used to kill Ray," Daniels said.

"That's all it means. A different weapon, not a different person. They were both killed at the same location days apart."

"I didn't know."

He lied, and I wondered why.

"You ready?" Rhett asked me as he came into the room.

I stood up. Daniels did the same. Rhett walked right up to him. No more than three inches separated the two men's faces. Daniels tried to take a step backward, but the couch blocked him. Rhett grabbed his shirt, as much to keep him from sitting down as to be threatening.

"If I have to come back, you'd better not hold anything back next time." He let go, and Daniels collapsed back onto the couch.

"I have a feeling he knows more than he's letting on," I said when we were in the truck.

"No kidding, Sherlock," Rhett said. "What did you get out of him?"

"He knew a different weapon was used to kill your father. He was quick to throw that out to infer there might have been a second killer."

"Not common knowledge, but I guess it wouldn't have been that hard to learn about it."

"He didn't comment at all on Janice's death. He's smart enough to know about the second weapon, but is ignorant about the third murder? He had to have known about it."

"Good point," Rhett said. "Not sure how much we can infer by it, but it is interesting."

We drove on, and Rhett remained silent. I fought the urge to ask him why he was being an ass. Besides, I felt like I knew the answer. He wanted me to know he was in charge. He had a plan. My curiosity overruled my frustration. I knew I had to be careful, though, curiosity can get you killed.

Chapter 23

Alex Karnes place better fit my preconceptions. The run-down wooden shack only needed a condemned sign to look complete. A variety of weeds grew in small patches in the dirt yard. The driveway had originally been asphalt. Time and the weather had eroded it to the point that now one might consider it a dirt driveway. An old, empty paint can sat upright on the ground near the driveway.

Karnes met us out front. Dressed in baggy overalls, Karnes looked a perfect match for the house and yard. He kept an eye on us as we got out of the car and approached him but didn't offer any welcome. He spit as we got close, and I saw a lump inside his left cheek. Chewing tobacco, I thought.

"So, you're Ray's kid," Karnes said.

"Yes, and –"

"Who are you?" Karnes asked me, interrupting Rhett.

"Don't worry about him." Rhett walked up to him and pressed a finger against Karnes chest, making Karnes take a step back.

Karnes expression changed, but he tried to hold on to his bravado. "What the hell?"

"I've got a long day ahead of me. Don't waste my time."

Karnes stared at him but remained quiet.

"I want to know who killed my father."

"I have no idea."

"Wrong answer," Rhett grabbed the front of Karnes overalls. He didn't pull Karnes toward him or push him away.

"Let go of me." Fear crept into his voice.

Rhett let go and stepped back. The stern expression remained on his face.

"My dad only hung out with you four. You, Daniels, and Dunn are the only ones left. You either know who killed my father or why. Don't try to tell me some stranger did it."

"I don't know anything."

"How about Carl? Would he have killed my dad over Nessy?"

"Maybe, maybe, yes, you need to talk to him. It was no secret that he was her boyfriend until Ray broke it up."

"Is that why he killed Pat, too," I asked.

Rhett glanced at me. He didn't appear pleased that I had the nerve to speak up.

"Why no, I don't know why he would've killed Pat."

"You telling me that Carl killed all three?" Rhett said.

"Three? You mean MacCumber's wife. I have no idea who or why she was killed. I never even set eyes on her."

"Something isn't right. Did Daniels call you?"

Karnes hesitated but answered. "Yes, he gave me a heads up, but I already knew you were coming. You called."

"Then did he explain to you what I'm going to do when I find out which one of you killed my dad? I'm going to hurt that person. Hurt him bad before I turn him over to the police. You don't want me to guess and hurt the wrong person, do you?" He took a step closer to Karnes.

"No," Karnes said, taking a step backwards.

"When I come back, I'll be alone. No witnesses. You'd better get me some answers by then."

"I don't know anything, but I'll try."

"Don't go anywhere. I'll find you. When I do, I won't be so polite."

We left him standing there in his yard.

"Do you buy this jealousy angle?" Rhett asked me when he turned the pickup onto the road.

"No."

"Me neither. I think we'll go see Nessy next. I want to learn more about it before we go see Dunn."

"Good idea," I said.

One of the deputies had told me that if I blinked, I would miss Lay-By. He was correct. I never blinked and still didn't realize we had driven through it until Rhett brought the Ford pickup to a stop in front of an old rundown building.

An "Open" sign hung on the door, and a light spelling "Budweiser" flashed on and off in the window. The right third of the wooden roof sloped slightly downward. I wondered if a support beam was missing.

"We must have missed the lunch crowd," Rhett said.

"Where would a crowd come from?" Looking back in the direction from which we came, I counted three other dilapidated buildings and one parked, pickup truck.

Rhett ignored my question and walked into the building. Unlike the saloons in the TV shows with swinging doors that you could see over, this door looked like any other door. Disappointed, I followed him.

The place took on a whole different look inside. Whereas Syd's bar had probably never passed a health inspection, this place looked very clean. Rhett approached a white haired, wiry woman. She greeted him with a smile and they briefly hugged.

"Rhett, I'm so sorry about Ray." Her voice, her eyes, her body language all appeared sincere. "He was a good man."

"Thank you, Nessy. I need to talk to you."

"I understand." She looked over at me. "You must be Pat's friend. I'm sorry for your loss, too. I didn't know Pat as well as I knew Ray. Pat was younger, but he seemed to be a nice man. Someone murdered his widow, too. That makes no sense."

"What is this all about, Nessy?"

"Oh, Rhett, I wish I knew. I brewed a fresh pot of coffee. Please sit down, and I'll bring us all a cup. I will tell you everything I know." She left us and walked through a nearby door.

We didn't argue. No one else was in the room.

"It's interesting she knew who you were and brought up Janice's death right away," Rhett said.

"Unlike the other two," I said.

"Here we go," Nessy said. She sat in a chair between us.

A younger woman who looked to be in her late thirties followed her into the room. She carried a tray of coffee cups and a half pot of coffee. After placing the tray on the table, the woman looked at me a little longer than what I thought natural.

"This is Angel. She was friends with Pat. I thought she might be able to help you, too."

"Hi, I'm Jim West."

I could tell Angel's appearance and interest in me had thrown Rhett off track. At the same time, he looked more intrigued than irritated.

"Do you know why anyone may have killed Pat or my dad?" Rhett asked.

"No, but I know a tension developed among all of them. It started after Easter. I'm not sure why, but I think it had something to do with a map Pat had purchased on the internet," Angel said.

Her broken English made me think it wasn't her original

language. She had long straight black hair which contrasted with her short height.

"What map?" Rhett asked.

"I never looked at it. Pat just said the others wanted it."

"A map to some long, lost buried treasure, I suppose," Rhett said.

"It was stupid, and I told him so. If someone knew where a treasure was buried, why sell the map. Why not come find the treasure yourself. He told me the map only cost ten dollars. What a fool," Angel said. Her anger seemed genuine.

"He did bring a map here a few weeks before he was murdered. Angel was off that day. He showed the map to the four others. They all laughed at him. I didn't think much of it at the time. I didn't look at it. Ray later told me it was nothing, a silly fraud," Nessy said.

"Why do you say a tension developed among them," I asked Angel.

"I felt it. They met three times here after the mention of the map and before Pat was killed. The atmosphere around them became different. I sensed the presence of a hostile spirit at the table. It scared me."

"Like a demon?" The word popped out of my mouth without thinking.

"Yes." Angel looked at me, turned, and hurried out of the room.

"Don't mind her. She is very superstitious."

"I'm not sure where you are trying to go with the demon statement," Rhett said, looking at me, "but it is possible she sensed tension among them. Did you?" Rhett addressed the last half of his comment to Nessy.

"Not at the time, but I've had time to think about it. Imagination or not, I felt a change, too."

"Did they have arguments over the map?" Rhett asked.

"Only once, the time Pat brought the map here. They all started picking on Pat. Ray said that since Pat was his friend, he would give him five dollars to share the map with him. Pat refused. Alex pretended he was going to tear the map up and everyone laughed, but Pat got mad."

"Did he?" Rhett asked.

"No. Alex was only teasing Pat about tearing it up."

"Did you see the map again?" Rhett asked.

"No, he never brought it back, and I don't remember them discussing it again while they were here. Your father didn't want the map. I don't think any of them did."

"Jim, I have a personal question to ask Nessy. Can you give us some space?"

"Is it alright if I go in there and talk to Angel," I asked Nessy and motioned to the door Angel left through.

"Yes. It leads to the kitchen. She may not be in there. If she's not, I'd rather you not go searching the house for her."

"Sure," I said and went into the kitchen, carrying my cup of coffee. I saw Angel emptying a large dishwasher. I could tell my entrance surprised her.

"What?" she asked.

"Sorry to bother you again, but Rhett wanted to talk to Nessy about her relationship with his father, and he didn't want me there." I sat down at a small table in the corner of the room. "Pat and I were old friends. We were both in the air force."

"He talked about his air force," she said.

"You must have liked him a lot."

"Yes. He was very nice and kind to me."

"Do you know where he kept his map? I don't want it, but it might help the police to capture his murderer."

"He kept it in his truck. He was stupid. He kept so many things in his truck but never locked it. I don't think he believed in the map either, but he wanted to find something. He didn't want to fail. That's what he said."

I thought I understood. He had given up his family and most of what was his world to follow this crazy idea of prospecting for treasure. Failing would be hard on him.

"How long had you known him?"

"Almost a year. We became friends right away. He was lonely."

"Did you meet him here?"

"Yes. I am a poor woman. Most men think I am someone they can take advantage of. I am not. I am a good woman, a Christian. From that first day, Pat treated me with respect. He was a good man. He knew I was poor."

"Did he feel threatened by any of the other men?" I was happy to hear she considered Pat to be a nice man, but I wanted to get back on topic.

"No. The others were older. Pat used to be a special agent, and he had a gun. He was never afraid."

"Did one man want the map more than the others?"

"I don't think so. He never said that."

"I'm glad he had you as a friend," I said.

"I am too. My Mary misses him."

"Mary?"

"My daughter. She's nine. Pat would buy her presents and candy. Her father never knew her."

"Can you think of anything that might help us find his killer?"

"No, but Jim, you must be careful. You are hunting for an evil thing. Be careful."

I thanked her and walk back out to Rhett and Nessy. Rhett stood up when he saw me. We said our goodbyes to Nessy and left. A stiff breeze blew dust off the porch but did little to fend off the heat from the sun.

"She says that Carl would never have killed my dad over jealousy. She and Carl had been an off-and-on again item for thirty years. She even confessed to asking Carl twice to marry her. Carl had gone through two divorces before he hit thirty and told her he would never marry again. Since then, they have been friends with benefits. That was her expression. I suppose that meant they slept together on occasion."

"Believe her?"

"Yes, but we'll be at his place in a few minutes. We can ask him. She did say she would have stopped seeing my dad if Carl asked her to marry him. That kind of irritated me."

"If she gave your father some comfort, and he liked her, then that's all that matters," I said.

"Maybe. What did Angel tell you?"

"She didn't know, but she thinks Pat was killed because of the map he had. All five of them knew about the map. So did Nessy and Angel, but I don't see them as suspects."

"I don't either. The map does give us a link, but it's such a stupid one," he said.

"One other thing, she said Pat had a gun. I didn't follow up but I don't recall the team mentioning anything about finding a weapon that belonged to Pat."

"Everyone carries out here. You should, you know."

Chapter 24

We drove the next ten minutes in silence. The map was a common thread. Despite how little value we gave it, one of the three men still alive may have highly valued it. Years ago, I investigated a brutal assault of a young man by his brother over a plastic, model airplane that wasn't worth ten dollars. That never made any sense to me either, but it happened.

We drove down a long dirt driveway to Carl Dunn's house. It may have been a private road, winding around rocky hills and dry creek bed. A woman wearing white shorts, a light blue tee shirt, and a dark blue scarf on her head leaned against the front porch railing. Once out of the car, I heard the sound of a lawn mower in the distance.

"That's probably him," Rhett said looking at a man on a riding lawn mower about a hundred yards away.

The woman left the porch and walked out to greet us. "Are you here to talk to my dad?"

"We're here to talk to Carl Dunn," Rhett said.

"That would be him. Are you Ray's son?"

"Yes, I'm Rhett."

"Sorry for your loss." She looked at me and back at Rhett.

"I'm Jim West. I was a friend of Pat MacCumber." I could have told her Rhett had the manners of a horse fly, but she would figure that out herself.

"I liked him, too. I'm Lucy. Dad wanted me out here since I also knew them. Please have a seat on the porch while I round him up."

She jogged off in the direction of the lawn mower.

Rhett swore. I imagined he was thinking, like me, that playing the tough guy now might be counterproductive. I left him standing there and found a wooden rocking chair on the porch. He stubbornly stood in the sun the full five minutes it took for Carl to arrive, driving his riding lawn mower to the house. Lucy jogged up behind him.

"Let's go into the house, gentlemen," Carl said and walked up to and through the front door without any other comment.

I followed him and looking back, I could see Rhett's face flush. Not too happy, I thought. We followed Carl inside. To our immediate left was the kitchen. Rhett entered with Lucy. Carl was already sitting at the kitchen table with his back to the wall. Lucy took the chair to his right. A shelving unit with dishes and cookbooks prevented anyone from getting to him by going around the left side of the table. They had obviously planned this out. I played along and took the chair across from Lucy.

"Sit down," Carl said.

"This is not a social call," Rhett said.

"I know. I hear you've been an ass today," Carl said.

"Please everyone, let's be civilized and maybe we can answer all your questions without anyone getting hostile," Lucy said.

"We're looking for answers," I said. I knew Rhett would need a few seconds to settle down. He had been outplayed.

"Let's start with me," Lucy said. "My husband is a truck driver. He runs stuff all over the country. He's gone a lot, so I spend most of my life here helping out. I've met both Pat and Ray dozens of times. Daddy makes the best barbeque in Texas. When they're here, I'm the bartender." She smiled like it was an inside joke among the group.

"Why do you think someone killed them?" I asked.

"I haven't the slightest idea. They did seem a little uncomfortable around each other the week or so before Pat was murdered. I didn't see them after that."

"What made you think they were uncomfortable?" I asked. Rhett remained silent.

She hesitated. "It's hard to say. They were always kidding each other and happy when they were here. This last time they were quiet. They seemed different. I have to admit, it could be my imagination now that the murders have occurred."

"Were you aware of any animosity between any of them?"

"No."

"How about you, Carl. Did you kill my dad because he had stolen Nessy from you?" Rhett said. His tone signaled to me he wanted to take over. Unfortunately for him, Lucy snorted and laughed.

"Yes, daddy, answer the question."

"I like Nessy a lot. I always have, but I made it clear to her and to everyone who asked, we were not an item. We were good friends. I neither had nor wanted to formalize my relationship with her," Carl said.

"And you know that's stupid and childish," Lucy said. Despite the harsh tone of her voice, she reached out and put her hand over his.

"That's the way it is," he said to his daughter.

"Then you tell me a motive for someone to kill two of your friends," Rhett said.

"I wish I knew. They didn't have any enemies. None of us do. We don't have anything anyone wants. I've never heard someone threaten anyone of us," Carl said.

"You need to understand my dad may be the next victim.

We'd love to be able to tell you and the police who killed your father, Rhett. We would. We feel threatened," Lucy said.

"She's right, so we don't need your tough guy act on us. I won't be bullied."

"Carl, do you think it could be over this map that Pat bought online?" I said to try to calm things down and get refocused.

"The map? That's crazy," Carl said.

"Your father and Pat were discussing it the last time they were here. They were hush-hush about it, but I heard them. Something was bothering them," Lucy said.

"When was that?" I asked.

"Two, maybe three days before Pat was killed."

"Lucy, what are you talking about?" Carl asked.

"I didn't think much about it at the time. Haven't since until this moment right now," Lucy said, looking at me.

"Were they arguing over it?" Rhett said. He had calmed down.

"No. It was like it was a secret between them. Like they didn't want the others to hear."

"Could they have been talking about one of the others?" Rhett asked.

"Maybe. At the time, I thought it was some secret about the map. But it did seem like there was something different that afternoon."

"I didn't notice anything. That map was trash," Carl said.

"You were too busy drinking and grilling. Besides, you never notice anything," Lucy said. I wondered if that comment had anything to do with Nessy.

"Listen, if the two murders ---"

"Three," I said, interrupting Carl.

"You think the same person also killed Pat's widow?" Lucy asked.

"We do," Rhett said.

Lucy's hand shot up to cover her mouth. "My God, you've got to catch him."

"We hope to," I said.

Carl's expression made me think he hadn't linked Janice's murder to the other two.

"Did you see the map?" Rhett asked.

"Just a glance at it as we passed it around the table," Carl said.

"Do you remember where the map said the treasure could be found?"

"The general area, maybe," Carl paused a few seconds. He looked up at Rhett, "but it was in the area where Pat and Ray were killed. Right at the edge of the park."

Carl couldn't remember anything more specific and after another five minutes of discussion, we started to leave.

"Wait a second," Lucy said after she led us to the front porch. She went back in and returned with a pound of brisket wrapped in white butcher paper. She gave it to me. "It's barbequed brisket. It's for you, Jim. You come back with a nicer attitude, Rhett, and I'll give you some, too." She turned and went back inside.

Rhett swore, and we left.

"They had that all planned out," Rhett said once we were back on the road.

"I bet she planned everything, too. She impressed me."

"Me, too," he said, shaking his head, "Think they did that to throw us off track?"

"No, I think she did that to protect her father. I mean, they were willing to talk to us. She wanted to set the boundaries. I'm starting to think this was all about the map. Sounds crazy, but there must be more to it."

"The police never found a map. I can't see people killing each other over an unproven treasure map. These guys weren't stupid. I can't believe any of them would even buy such a thing."

"Pat was new at this. Maybe he didn't know better," I said.

"The rest of the guys had lived here for a long time. They would have already gone through their treasure map years as teenagers, if they ever went through them at all. My dad grew up here. He moved to San Antonio for work when he was in his twenties. I was born there. We often came here to visit my grandparents. My parents moved back here nearly twenty years ago."

He didn't mention his mother, so I didn't bring it up.

"I think your father was killed because he was a closer friend to Pat than the others. Janice's murder still makes no sense."

"None of it does. There has to be a major piece of the puzzle we're missing."

Lucy's scolding of Rhett must have been more effective than I first thought. On the ride back to town, we discussed the investigation as equals. He no longer treated me as a subordinate on a ride along.

Chapter 25

"Ever hear of any treasure maps for sale around here?" Konnie set my beer down on the counter in front of me and smiled. "I can sell you one for five dollars. Three for ten."

"So, someone buying one would be a fool."

"And someone selling one should be sent to jail for fraud. Don't tell me you bought one," she said.

"No, not me. Do you believe in demons?"

"How interesting. What legends and lore book have you been reading? We have the chupacabra, the Marfa Lights, well they could be something. Let me think. We have old Indian burial grounds and, some say, demons. The Chamber of Commerce would like me to encourage those stories to drive up tourism, but between you and me, no."

"A practical woman."

"Well, I do have my beliefs. I believe in saving the whale, preventing forest fires, cleaning up the planet, and free love." She brushed my fingers with hers.

I left my hand on the counter. Not that I wanted to encourage her, but I did want her to continue considering me a close confidant.

"Have you seen a demon?"

"No. If I have, I didn't know it. I've had a couple people refer to them when discussing the murders," I said.

She leaned in closer. "What have they said?" Despite the place being empty of customers, she whispered the question.

"That the killer is a demon or possessed by one. They believe demons exist."

"Oh, that's different. I do believe that a person who is usually normal can snap and become incredibly evil. How else can you explain people killing babies or their parents? Maybe a demon does possess them. It wouldn't be the scientific explanation, but I can see the rationale."

"Good point," I said.

"I'm intelligent. That's how I got this job."

"Don't pick on yourself. There's nothing wrong with this job, and you do it well."

"I need to move on, though. If I keep working here much longer," she paused for a moment. "You think a demon killed someone over a treasure map?"

Her remark caught me off guard. "Can you keep a secret?"

"Of course," she said.

"I do. Not so much the demon part, but definitely a very bad person."

"It would have to be a stupid demon. There's no buried treasure out there."

"That does seem to be the sticking point," I said.

"What if the map is to something else, like an Indian burial ground or something else?"

"I don't see how that could justify killing someone."

"But if you think the map is the key, then there has to be something about it that the murderer wants for himself or wants to keep secret," Konnie said and smiled.

"What are you grinning about?"

"You're sharing this with me."

"Why wouldn't I? You're bright, you know this city, and I'm a private citizen. There are no rules telling me who I can and cannot talk to."

"Can I go with you when you interview someone?"

"Unfortunately, I've been paired up with Rhett Stahl."

"Oh, I like him."

"Konnie, now you're giving me the idea you'd rather be his partner."

"A girl needs her options," she laughed and walked off to take care of two men who entered the bar.

I had considered the possibility that the map didn't lead one to a buried treasure but to something the killer wanted to remain a secret. However, that too seemed a little far-fetched. My phone rang.

"Hey, Jim, where are you?" Rose asked.

"At Spirits and Sandwiches, want to join me?"

"I'll be there in a minute," she said and ended the call.

Rather abrupt, I thought, but she hadn't sounded upset. When Konnie returned to her spot behind the bar, I ordered a whiskey sour for Rose.

"For you?" Konnie asked when she placed it next to my beer.

"No, Rose will be here in a minute."

"So, I better behave?"

I didn't get a chance to answer her as four more customers walked in. Konnie left to welcome them. An older woman I hadn't seen before entered through the door behind the bar that led to the kitchen.

"Are you okay?" the woman asked.

"Yes, perfect," I said.

She started rearranging a few things behind the bar.

"Konnie, you know these go over here," the woman said to Konnie when she returned to the bar counter to punch an order into the register.

"Yes ma'am. I moved them to clean a spot off and then got distracted."

I wondered if I was the distraction.

The door opened, and Deputy Anne Lanier entered the bar. She saw me and waved. "Join me at a table?" she asked.

I followed her to a four-person table by the front window. "Rose will be here in a minute," she said.

"Rhett briefed us on what you two learned today."

"Not much."

"No, but it does seem we need to dig deeper into this map and do a more thorough background on our three possible suspects. Is that for me?" Anne said and reached for the whiskey sour.

"If you want it."

She took a sip. "It's good. Better order another. Rose just drove up." She grinned.

I looked around and saw Konnie watching us from behind the bar. I motioned with my hand for another whiskey sour.

"Are you hungry for anything?"

"Thanks, Jim, but I need to head home in a few minutes."

We both watched Rose enter and head toward us. Konnie came around the end of the bar behind her, carrying a new drink. She placed the whiskey sour in front of Rose when she sat down.

"Thank you," she said and looked at me.

"I stole yours," Anne said and raised her glass.

Rose took a sip. "Thanks," she said to me.

"Anne said Rhett briefed everyone on the little new stuff we may have discovered today."

"Yes, why weren't you there?"

"Rhett said he wanted to do the briefing, and that I didn't need to be there."

Rose studied me for a second.

"That was rude of him. You should have come anyway," Anne said. Rose continued staring at me.

"Yes, you should have. He may have left out something important."

Rose sounded a little angry with me.

"We have all night to compare notes. Did you hear the weathermen are saying a big storm may be heading our way tomorrow?" I didn't want to get into a discussion about Rhett with Anne there.

She seemed to understand me, as did Anne.

"We need the rain. They say this one could be quite violent. While we need rain, we don't need any flash flooding," Anne said.

"Is that a problem here?" I asked.

We talked about the weather and then about the local college. When Anne finished her drink, she left.

Chapter 26

"Now tell me, what's going on," Rose said.

"Nothing is going on. Rhett didn't want me around today. He didn't want me at the briefing to the team. I'm playing the hand I was dealt rather than head butt with him. My story of what happened today may also differ a little from his, and we don't need that conflict either."

"What do you mean?"

"Exactly," I said and thought about not saying more. Her glare and the clamping of her jaw, convinced me to continue. "Okay, but I don't want anyone running back to Rhett to tell him he needs to be a good boy."

"Towards you?"

"No, towards our three suspects. Don't worry about me."

"Well, he did call you a light foot, and then later, he described you as all hat, no cattle. It made me mad."

"Good for you, thanks." I grabbed her hand. "He did his best to physically intimidate the three men. He got outsmarted by Carl Dunn's daughter, but his approach today was to get close and personal, and threaten to break bones if he found out they held anything back. He didn't harm anyone today, but I think if I wasn't there, he might have done some shoving and slapping. Despite the lack of fun being with him, you all need to ensure he doesn't go out alone."

"He thinks the map Pat had might be the key."

"It's the best thing we have. The map's existence seems to have affected the relationships within the group. They won't admit to it, but Dunn's daughter, Lucy noticed it."

"Lucy?"

"Yes. If no one has talked to her, you should. Also, there's a woman who works for Nessy. Her name is Angel. You all should talk to her. Didn't Rhett mention these two?"

"No. He talked about the information he picked up, which wasn't much, but didn't mention anything specific about the people. Although, he did say that the jealousy motive with Carl Dunn was a weak one."

I nodded. "By the way, Angel told me that Pat kept a handgun of some sort in his pickup. He also kept the map there. My understanding is that the team didn't find a weapon or a map. To me, the map's disappearance makes it even more likely that it is the key behind this whole series of killings."

"Good point. He didn't mention that to us. How dare he call you a light foot," Rose said and squeezed my hand.

"Yeah, and what's this all hat, no cattle business?"

She laughed but didn't explain.

"Do you really think he would hurt those old men?"

"I don't know. He was pretty convincing to me, but maybe that's what made him an effective cop."

"And it was his father someone killed. His anger is probably real."

"Justifyingly so."

"Did anyone mention anything about Janice's murder?" Rose asked.

"Not really. The universal response was that it didn't make any sense. I know you don't need my advice, but I recommend you grab Anne and the two of you interview Lucy and Angel. They might give you a new perspective for all this."

"I'll need to double check the file. I'm surprised no one has already interviewed them."

"It's an easy miss. Unless Nessy or Carl brought them to the team's attention, it's easy to miss them."

Rose nodded, "And people being interviewed by the police rarely get names volunteered to them."

"I think Pat's relationship with Angel wasn't something he talked about. That may be why she's still alive." I hadn't thought about it that way until I said it. "We need to be careful with that bit of information."

"Yes, we do. In the morning, let's the two of us go talk to her. You've already met her, and she talked to you. It will make it easier for her to open up with me. How serious was their relationship?"

"I didn't get into that, but I think it could have been serious. He bought presents for Angel's daughter."

"That serious," Rose said.

"She might have been a reason why Pat stuck it out as long as he did down here. Having a friend would've made it easier to stay."

"He wasn't leading an extravagant lifestyle. You would think his retirement alone wouldn't have taken him far. He must have split it with his wife, too."

"True, but he was barely living above the poverty level here. He might have done a few things to help with his expenses," I said.

"Now that you mention it, I think I heard someone say that he did some stuff around the trailer park where he lived in order to cut down on his rent."

"Makes sense."

"Want to get a sandwich here for dinner? I'm not that hungry.

Afterwards we could take a bottle of wine back to the room."

"Sounds like a plan," I said.

Konnie came by a minute later to check on us, and we each ordered a sandwich. Throughout dinner we talked about the different people on the team. Rose seemed to like everyone. When the bill came, Rose insisted on paying. I offered to run next door to buy the wine.

The convenience store didn't have much of a selection of wine, but I located a decent bottle of chardonnay. When I turned to head to the cashier, I nearly bumped into old Bart Maverick.

"I've been looking for you, West."

"Why is that?"

"I saw another one?"

"Another one?"

"Yeah, a demon. It was prowling around where them two was killed."

Bart looked sober, but it was hard to tell. He definitely looked like he had spent the last few nights on the streets.

"Was it the same one you saw before?"

"No, this one looked like you or me. Another old fool roaming around, but then I saw his eyes. Red eyes, evil eyes, he looked right at me like he could see me. He couldn't cause I was too far away and behind some bushes."

"If you were that far away, how could you see his eyes?"

"With my binoculars, don't be stupid. When he looked right at me, I almost froze. Demons can do that."

"Make you freeze?"

"Yes, but I ran. It didn't get a chance, but I wanted to tell you something."

"What?"

"When he looked at me, and I ran, I think he was looking for you," he said.

Maverick stared right at my eyes. For a moment, I thought his eyes might turn red. I shook off the strange sensation.

"Me?" I asked.

"Yes. That surprised me, too. I knew I needed to warn you. Don't go back there. He's marked you." His hands were shaking. His eyes remained fixed on mine.

"Can you better describe him?"

"No. I only saw him for a second. He knew I was watching. I had to leave, but I know it was a man at first."

"At first?"

"Before it was a demon," he said. "It wasn't no woman."

"Let me pay for this, and then I have someone I'd like you to meet," I said.

I left him in the aisle and paid at the register. After paying, I turned around but didn't see him anywhere.

"Did he leave?" I asked the middle-aged man working the register.

"You mean old Bart? Don't pay him no mind. He's harmless."

Rose walked into the store and approached me.

"Did you see the old man who just left?"

"Nobody left while I was out front. I was there for a minute or two before coming in."

I looked down the few aisles not clearly visible from the register but didn't see him.

"He left out the back door. He helps out taking my boxes down to the dumpster. Like I said, pay him no mind," the clerk said.

"Let's get back to the hotel. I need to get out of these shoes," Rose said.

"The old man, Bart Maverick, you know, the one who claims to have seen a demon –"

"What about him?"

"He was in the store. He said he was looking for me. He claimed he saw a demon down at the crime scene."

"When?"

"Good question, I was thinking today."

"You didn't ask?"

"No, I was going to bring him to you, but he disappeared."

"Like a ghost?" She grinned.

"No, come on, you need to hear his story."

"So tell me."

We discussed what Bart told me on the short walk back. I told her that I believed he saw someone, and that was the interesting point, not whether the person was a demon or not. She had some of the same questions I had asked Bart. Most for which I didn't have answers.

"Well, I guess you stay with me tonight. I'll keep those demons away from you," Rose said, poking fun at me as we entered the Cattle Rustlers Hotel.

Chapter 27

The bright blue, early morning sky didn't give any hint of an oncoming storm. Even the wind had died down to a light breeze. Rose turned down breakfast, saying she wanted to get an early start. We planned to get back together before noon and go to Lay-By to talk to Angel. Rose wanted to brief Special Agent Rodriquez before we did and let him know about our concern for her safety. She also asked me to call Nessy to make sure she was available.

I decided to kill an hour or two by visiting the Museum of the Big Bend at Sul Ross University. I didn't know much about it but it had good reviews. It didn't disappoint. For such a small town, the college and the museum impressed me.

Shortly before noon, I met Rose back at the hotel. She seemed all excited about something.

"Any new breaks with the investigation?"

"No, unfortunately not," she said.

"You seem to be pumped up. What's got you in such a good mood?"

"Rhett asked me out to dinner." She tried to keep a straight face.

"Did he really?"

"Yes. Said something about me wasting my time."

Before I could think of a good response, she started laughing. We had reached the parking lot. "I'll drive," she said.

"Why are you harassing me like this?"

"Oh, I can't help it. I told him no. I'm very happy wasting my time with you." She punched my arm.

"Two hands on the wheel. You're driving."

"He is an interesting character. He's very self-confident, too much so. I think he looks down at everyone," she said.

"Let's talk about something else."

"Like what?"

I told her about my visit to the museum and some of the stuff I had learned. She seemed interested, and it did me good getting my mind off Rhett. We talked about how difficult life would've been out here a couple hundred years ago. Then we debated how someone two hundred years from now would look back at life today. Would they, too, wonder how we survived?

Both Nessy and Angel were waiting for us. Nessy guided us to a table that had a pot of coffee, four cups, and a tray of cookies on it.

"I've already talked to you all, and while I'm willing to answer any questions you may have for me, I know you're here today to talk to Angel. If you don't mind, she would like me to stay while you're talking to her," Nessy said.

"That's fine. We're looking for more background. In particular, I'm trying to get a better understanding for what motive anyone would have for these murders," Rose said.

"But I don't know," Angel said, interrupting Rose.

"I understand, and you are not in any kind of trouble, Angel. However, you may have known Pat better than anyone else. You two were close, right?"

Angel hesitated for a moment and looked at Nessy for support. Nessy nodded, encouraging Angel to respond.

"Yes. I loved him."

That surprised me, although I wasn't sure why it did.

"He was good to you," Rose said.

"Yes, and to my Mary."

"Your daughter?"

"Yes."

"What was your relationship with the others? Dunn, Daniels, and Karnes, were they nice to you?" Rose asked.

"I had no relationship with them," Angel answered. "I saw them when they were here, but I never saw them away from here. Never!"

"She doesn't associate with customers," Nessy said.

"Except for Pat," Rose said.

"That surprised me, too," Nessy said, looking at Angel.

"It surprised me. He was different. We would visit and talk sometimes after the others left. He came back alone now and then, and we would just talk. I knew he was a good man before I agreed to go with him."

"Go with him," Rose said.

"Yes, to dinner in Marathon and then in Alpine. He was a gentleman."

"He never said one of the others had threatened him?"

"No, never, but he was nervous the last time I saw him. I asked him what was wrong, but he didn't say."

"Were one of the others jealous of your relationship with Pat?"

"What? No, why would they be jealous? I never went anywhere with the others," Angel said.

"How about Ray Stahl?" Rose asked.

"What about him?"

Rose didn't answer.

After a few seconds, Angel said, "He was Pat's friend, and he liked Nessy."

Nessy smiled and said, "He liked you, too. He thought you were pretty."

"He never said anything to me."

"Ray was shy, and he knew you and Pat were a couple. He was happy about that."

"Do you think the map could have caused the tension you sensed in the last few weeks?" Rose asked.

"Yes, but that is also stupid. Pat was new here, and he was like a child with a dream. The others lived here. They knew better. They had to have known the map was not worth the ten dollars Pat paid for it."

"That's true, Agent Luna. Only the foolish believe in treasure maps. Those men were not fools. Yet, as I said earlier to you, Jim, I think the map was a source of tension among them. It makes no sense, I know, but I can't think of anything else that may have happened. Those men had been coming here for years. Pat was new, but the rest had been coming for a long time. None of them have been back since," Nessy said.

As if someone gave a signal, we all drank a sip of coffee in silence for about a full minute.

"Angel, do you have an old boyfriend who might have become jealous?" I asked to get the conversation going again.

"No, no old boyfriends, only Pat."

"Were you sleeping with him?" Rose asked.

"Yes. He was going to get a divorce." She answered without hesitation.

"He would have," I said. I wanted to support her. Like everyone should know treasure maps bought on the internet are scams, people ought to know the phrase "I'll get a divorce" is usually a lie. However, I also believed his divorcing Janice would have been a good decision.

Angel smiled at me, and I saw the beginning of tears form in her eyes.

"What do you think?" Rose asked me when we got in the car to drive back.

"I think both women are being honest with us."

"Me, too. Not sure what we gained today."

"I think it's safe to rule out the jealousy angle with Pat's murder, like we did with Ray's. Since we don't seem to have a real motive, maybe we should let Rhett beat a confession out of one of them."

"Don't be silly," Rose said.

Chapter 28

He watched the two leave the building. He recognized West but not the woman. The FBI agent, he wondered. His plan had been to talk to Nessy and see if she might tell him what the police knew. A younger woman worked with her, and she might know something, too. He didn't want to kill them.

Killing Pat had been necessary. The map had to be destroyed. Pat and Ray spent time together, so Ray may have seen the map more than that once at the table in the diner. No one seemed to give it much interest when Pat showed it to everyone that day. However, Ray may have seen it again later.

He had slowly come to dislike Ray over the years. He had gotten smug and full of himself ever since he had started dating Nessy. It was easy to see where his son got his manners.

He made a mistake killing Pat's wife. He knew it the minute he smashed the hammer into the side of her head. She had resisted getting into his truck, and he had panicked. He had only wanted the blow to knock her out. It had, and she had come to, a few minutes later but she refused to answer his questions. She cursed at him and even spit on him. He grabbed her hand and broke her fingers. Rather than cooperate, she died.

At first, he thought she had faked being unconscious again. It only took a few seconds for him to determine she had really died. He thought leaving her in the field would make her almost impossible to find. He hadn't thought about the planes overhead.

The police appeared to be running around in circles, interviewing and re-interviewing the same people. Rhett Stahl did worry him. Not because he might solve anything. Rhett had no clue either, but Rhett might hurt him the next time he came and demanded answers. He did not want to get slapped around by Ray's damn son.

Maybe he should kill Rhett. Yes, he thought, kill the bastard, and then become a model citizen again. The other guy, West, didn't seem to pose much of a threat. In fact, he believed if Rhett returned to talk to him, he would come alone. Rhett wouldn't want any witnesses.

Killing the three hadn't bothered him. He had killed before. That had been a long time ago, and he had not broken any laws since then. Well, maybe a few minor ones, but nothing serious. His secret needed to be kept. After he killed Rhett, he would have to become a model citizen again.

He thought about Nessy and her young helper again. He wouldn't bother them. They might mention to the police his showing up and being curious about the map. No, he needed to stay out of the frame for a while.

Chapter 29

Rose received a call within minutes of our leaving Nessy and Angel at the diner. She listened for a few minutes with the occasional responses of yes, what, where, and finally will do.

"Another body," she said.

"Oh, no, do they know who?"

"Not yet. It's deeper in the park. I'm the closest team member at the moment, so they want me to respond."

"How about the park ranger on the team?"

"Mack? He's heading down, too, but he's at least forty-five minutes behind us. It'll be the two of us from the team, and, of course, my dependable sidekick." She grinned at me.

"Don't you mean your handsome and dependable sidekick?"

"Maybe."

Good enough for me, I thought.

We entered the park through the official entrance south of Marathon and drove towards the mountains. Large flat-top mesas rose above the ground around us. The terrain appeared desert-like with rocky, hard looking soil. Other than the rare car heading out of the park, I didn't see anyone.

"How did people cross this land in the old days?"

"It would've been hard. You know, thinking about that. I bet this poor person we are going down to see isn't related to our case. Too far away," Rose said.

"Might not be a bad place to dump bodies, but none of the others were brought out here. Why would the killer change his routine?"

"Does he have a routine?"

"Good point, but with what we know so far, why would he suddenly bring a body way out here?" I asked.

"He probably wouldn't. Most likely, he didn't even know that he killed Ray and Pat in the national park. A hundred yards further west, and he would have been outside the park. There's no fence."

"You mean, Pat may not have known he was in Big Bend National Park," I said.

"That's right. Unless he had some kind of sophisticated GPS equipment, he would have had no idea. Prospecting in the park is illegal. You aren't allowed to remove a rock, a stick, anything from the park."

"Interesting." Looking out the window, I didn't see anything anyone would want. "That makes sense, though. I think it's the same rule at all the national parks. Where would you start?"

"Start what?"

"There are millions of acres out there and no real landmarks. Unless you had a very sophisticated GPS location, you'd never find anything. I can't imagine what Pat thought he could find," I said.

"That's what makes all this so stupid. Prospectors usually search river or stream beds, and even then, they usually search areas where gold or silver had been found before. You don't prospect for some hidden treasure. That's more like what the guys do who walk along the beach with metal detectors."

"At least things wash up on beaches. Nothing is going to wash up out there."

"Maybe he simply needed to get away from his wife for a while," Rose said.

"That does make a lot more sense to me, too, but then why all this hype over the map?"

"A map everyone says is junk, too."

"Let's talk about something else. Tell me about your place in D.C."

We drove to the visitor center where a park ranger met us and drove us in a jeep to the remote site where the body and the surrounding area were still being processed.

"Sorry you had to come way out here," an older park ranger said to us when we arrived and introduced ourselves. "I think it's someone who came across illegally and thought he could walk somewhere. That's simply my guess from his clothing. The critters have got to him pretty bad. He had some money with him, not much, but no identification."

A temporary awning provided shade to those working close to the body. Only one man wearing jeans and a Dallas Cowboys tee-shirt remained crouched near the body. The ten yards separation from the scene didn't prevent the foul odor from reaching us.

"That's Doc Regalio. Got here about fifteen minutes ago. He's got the thankless job to see if he can get a first look at what was the cause of death."

The medical examiner, I thought, or whatever they call them here in Texas.

"We're being extra careful due to the interest in D.C. with your ongoing investigation. Once we received the report of a body being found, it only took a few minutes for headquarters to tell us to call you."

"Do you find many bodies in the park?" I asked.

"Thankfully, no, but it does happen. It happens throughout all the border counties," the old ranger said.

"Any missing person reports?" Rose asked. We had already checked with the team and had been told no.

"No. Here comes Doc," the ranger said.

Fortunately, the medical examiner didn't offer to shake hands. "Sorry they made you come out this far. Although I can't be definite until we do a proper autopsy, my best guess at the moment is that the poor guy died of exposure. He's pretty messed up, but everything I could see was post-mortem. Did you notice the tattoos?"

"No, we only made certain he was dead and left him for you," the ranger said.

"Not sure, but they look like Mexican prison tattoos. We see a lot of them up here," the medical examiner said to Rose.

"Did you get a picture of them?" Rose asked.

"Pete, come over here," he called to a young man standing nearby and looking pale. "Show these people the pictures of the tattoos."

Rose took a close look and them and nodded. "I spent a number of years with the El Paso Sheriff's Office. I think you're right about them. Could be gang related."

They all murmured in agreement as another jeep pulled up. Mack, the park ranger assigned to the team, climbed out of the driver's seat. Rose went to meet him. The two stood by the jeep for a minute before the small gaggle of individuals at the scene all walked over to them.

Now alone, I walked a circle around the dead person, staying about five yards away from the body. I didn't spend much time looking at him. I could see why the scene affected the young photographer. The hard ground left no prints or anything else which might indicate from which direction the man had come.

Although I was not about to inspect the body, I agreed with the medical examiner's suggestion that the man had died from exposure.

"Not a very nice place to die," Rose said. I hadn't noticed her approach me.

"Is there any?" I continued looking toward the ragged peaks of the nearby mountains. "This is a long way from nowhere. Why would he be out here?"

"Your guess is as good as mine. If he planned on meeting someone, he definitely took a wrong turn somewhere. At sunrise this place is beautiful, even out here. At sunset, I've always thought it was a little spooky. It's the vastness. If you're alone, you really feel alone."

"Are you speaking from experience?"

"Yes, but not from right here. This would be a terrifying place to be alone at night. I was at a campsite. They have a number of campsites in the park. Well, not exactly at the campsite. I had hiked an hour or so away from the camp with someone whom I thought was a friend. We argued, and he left me. I sat on a large rock, and I can remember feeling relieved that he was gone. He was a jerk, but then it started to get dark."

"And you needed your big strong man ---"

"Screw that, you guys need us more than we need you."

"Okay, so what happened when it got dark?"

"I had this awful sensation that I hadn't paid attention on the hike away from camp. There was this trail, but I didn't recall if we had stayed on the main trail. I also remember feeling like the darkness was rushing in on me."

"I guess you did make it back," I said.

She rolled her eyes at me. "Of course I did. Once I started

walking, I settled down, but I've never forgotten that feeling."

"You notice those guys are still circling this spot." I pointed upward.

"The buzzards? Yes, I noticed them. You and I have been cut loose. We can head back. I'd like to spend a few minutes in the visitor center where we parked, if you don't mind."

I didn't. We spent a good twenty minutes walking through the small building studying the exhibits. Outside I saw a roadrunner that had already attracted the attention of some small children.

Chapter 30

We discussed doing a little more sightseeing before we returned to Alpine, but Rose decided she better head back. We did stop in Marathon to visit the Gage Hotel. The hundred-year-old hotel is registered as a historic building and was still operational.

"This had to be the place to stay in the old days," I said once we were back in the car.

"Before the interstate highway system, Highway 90 was the route through Texas to the Pacific, or Atlantic, whichever way you were traveling. Took you right by here, as did the railroad. Today it's a destination hotel with access to the park."

"Been reading up?"

"The guys talked about it when we discussed the hotels in the area. Alpine has several of the national chain hotels, but the Cattle Rustler has history and is centrally located."

"I imagine Marfa has a few, too."

"It does, but not like Alpine. Having the college makes a difference."

Rose dropped me off at the hotel. She continued on to the office. I considered a nap, but after a brief stop in my room, I decided to go to what I considered my office, the Spirits and Sandwiches deli.

Konnie sat on a stool at the counter.

"Alone?"

"Yes, no one's been here for the last thirty minutes. I'm glad you showed up," she said, getting off the stool and moving around to the other side of the counter.

"I thought I'd come here and do some thinking."

"I'm glad you did." She poured me a draft beer and sat it on the counter in front of me. "On the house."

"Thanks. I've had a rough day." I told her about the dead man in the park.

"That's sad."

"Yes. It was."

"By the way, do you know an old man, Bart Maverick?'

"Yes, a little," I said.

"He came here at lunch time and was looking for you. I think he had already been drinking. He said to warn you not to go back there. He wouldn't tell me where 'there' was. He said something about you being in danger if you do. I asked him to be more specific, but he wouldn't say anything more. He seemed scared and mentioned something about dreams."

"For some reason, he's worried about me."

"I've seen him before. I think he's a bit crazy. Why would someone want to hurt you? Do you think he means the same person who's killed the others?"

"You're full of questions today. I wish I knew who he meant, too. He told me it was a demon."

Her eyes widened. "You're kidding me."

"Not really. That's what Bart Maverick has told me."

"Maybe you shouldn't go back to wherever it is. I don't believe in demons, but I wouldn't press my luck either. I watch too much scary stuff on television as it is. I don't need to be out looking for real life demons."

"Don't worry. If I go back out there, I won't go alone."

"By the way, I saw your friend a little while ago."

"Who, Rose?"

"No, Rhett. He still wants me to go out with him. Think I should? I mean he seems nice, but he scares me a little."

I wanted to tell her Rhett was a jerk, and she shouldn't waste her time with him, but I didn't. "I'm not a good judge of who should go out with whom."

She smiled. Maybe she knew my non-answer was an answer. "I actually have a guy I like already. He's the son of a rancher and will be taking over the ranch one day. He's nice, but the whole idea to me is so boring. Please don't tell him."

"How can I? I don't know who you're talking about."

"I know. I need someone to whisk me off my feet and take me somewhere exciting for a few days."

"Where?"

"New York, Chicago, Paris, and that's Paris, France, not Paris, Texas. Maybe Las Vegas," she said and grinned.

"Won't your rancher's son?"

"No. I've asked him to, but he has no interest."

"Is that why Rhett appeals to you?"

"Maybe, but only a little."

We talked for a few more minutes. I knew I couldn't solve her life's problems, nor did I want to try. When I left, I walked straight to the pizza place where I had first encountered Bart. He wasn't there. I didn't know what he could tell me, but I was curious. I took my time walking back to the hotel, but didn't see Bart on the streets either.

The storm never materialized, but the weatherman on my hotel room's television said we had another chance for rain tomorrow. I dozed off in the middle of a report of another forest fire in California.

Rose knocking on my door brought me out of one of those

deep sleeps that leave you feeling drugged when you wake up.

"You look like you've been sleeping."

"Didn't mean to, but I was really out." I went into the bathroom and rubbed some cold water onto my face.

"Everyone's getting frustrated," she said.

"That's only natural."

"I know, but the discovery today of that body reminded everyone that we're still stuck with little or nothing to go on."

"Things will change tomorrow," I said, not believing a word of it.

"You want to bet?"

"Why don't I take you out for a steak dinner. I recently found out this little town has a great little steak house. We need some cheering up."

"I knew there was a reason I put up with you," she said and pushed me back onto the bed.

Later, over dinner, I told her about my conversation with Konnie. I thought she'd be more interested in Bart, but she focused her questions on Konnie. When I told her I thought Konnie could do better than Rhett, and I felt a little sorry for her, Rose's face lit up.

"I've got a super idea," she said. She didn't elaborate, but she did reassure me that I didn't need to be involved.

"They finally got into Pat's laptop," Rose said while we walked to the hotel.

"Anything interesting?"

"Not yet, he did a lot of bouncing around. The guys say it will be a while, but they should find the website that he accessed to buy the map."

"Not on something simple like eBay?"

"Apparently not. He had dozens, if not hundreds, of contacts who were involved in these fringe nut groups. You know, conspiracy theorists, UFOs, get rich quick scams, etc."

"Janice said he went a little nuts. Hard for me to believe, but I know it happens. I didn't see any of that in him."

"I knew a couple of level headed girls from home who got sucked willingly into a crazy cult. They got really messed up. I never understood the attraction."

"With all the social media now, it's got to be worse."

"On another subject, Rhett wants to go out again and reinterview our three main suspects."

"How does the team feel about that?"

"Mixed feelings," she said.

"He's got a temper."

"We know, and he's as frustrated as we are. Joe was going to talk to him tonight. I think he's going to insist that Rhett take you with him. My fault."

Chapter 31

Although I wasn't thrilled, I knew my involvement with Rhett wasn't over. It only made sense. His phone call came at eight in the morning.

"I saw your lady friend leave the hotel, so I figured you were awake," he said.

"Up and dressed and ready for this fine day. What can I do for you, Rhett?" What I really wanted to do was smack him across the head with a baseball bat.

"Meet me across the street again. We need to talk."

"When?"

"Now."

"Be there," I said and ended the call.

Five minutes later, I sat across from him at the same table we used before. This time I angled my chair so I could watch for my cappuccino.

"I need to go talk to those guys again. Joe tells me you're supposed to go with me."

"Okay. I guess they want a witness in case one of these guys say something incriminating."

He looked at me for a moment. I wondered if he hadn't thought about that as a reason for their insistence in my tagging along. He probably thought they didn't trust him, and he'd be correct. He didn't need corroboration, but the court would. I wanted to give him something to consider to lessen the tension between us.

"Maybe," he said. "But you need to give me some space today."

"What do you expect to happen?"

"The more I go over this in my mind, the more I'm convinced one of these three killed my dad."

"I agree with that, but how do we prove that?"

"That's why I need my space today. I don't carry a badge anymore. I don't have to be so polite."

"Rhett, I understand. I really do, and I don't have a real problem with you breaking a few bones that belong to the murderer. Two of those men, however, are innocent. Maybe they're withholding something, but they didn't pull the trigger."

"If they know something, they're guilty, too."

"Yes, but what if they don't. Two of them may only be guilty of being your dad's friends."

"You don't have to preach to me. I know the rules."

"They don't just apply to the police."

"They killed my dad. The rules don't apply to me." He stared at me so hard, I felt like he might jump over the table and take his anger out on me. If I had one, I would've been gripping my baseball bat really tight. He desperately needed to hit something.

My cappuccino showed up on the counter. Relieved, I stood up and retrieved it.

Rhett stood up when I sat down. "I'll call you when I'm ready to go. Be ready, or I will leave you." He left the coffee shop.

I called Rose.

"Miss me already," she said.

"Always, but I also need to vent. I met with Rhett. He called me. I'm not sure it went so well."

"He doesn't want you to go with him?"

"You guessed it. He's also got quite upset with my telling him he couldn't try to beat a confession out of each of them."

"Well, he didn't need to be told that. He knows it. I'd be upset if you thought you had to tell me that, too."

"No, Rose, you don't understand. I didn't tell him that until after he said he wanted me to give him space today so he could do just that."

"He told you he planned to beat a confession out of them?"

"Not exactly, no. He's not stupid. At least, not that stupid. He didn't say anything to me he couldn't rationalize away, but believe me, it's something he's considering."

"Think you can keep him from going too far?"

"I'll try."

"He's a private citizen. We can tell him not to interview anyone, to stay out of the investigation. We can threaten him with obstructing, but he knows all that, and he knows we can't physically restrain him at this point. He also knows until he crosses the line, there's not much we can do to him."

"And, we all want to solve these murders," I said.

"There is some of that, too."

I knew they were playing a delicate game. The pressure on the team had to be significant. They could claim all day that they didn't know Rhett intended to physically hurt someone, but if he did, the blowback would still damage careers.

"These old timers he wants to intimidate can be dangerous, too. Even if they had nothing to do with the killings, they may greet us with a weapon in hand. I imagine none of them want Rhett to get close to them," I said.

"I'll talk to Joe. This is a bad idea."

"You sure you want to? He knows all this already. He may not want to admit it, but he didn't strike me as a fool."

"Him and me both."

"Don't say that. You've been mesmerized by my charm and superhero abilities."

"Well, maybe I have overrated you," she said. In my mind's eye, I could see her grinning.

"Let's let this hand play out. Like I said, I needed someone to whom I could vent. Thank you, I can handle him."

"To whom, the king's English is it now?"

"The better to charm you with."

"That's more like it."

"I'll stay in touch once Rhett and I leave."

The call ended. I sat there sipping on my cappuccino. A large grackle sat on top of the fire hydrant outside the window. It stared in at me. I wondered if it believed in demons.

Chapter 32

He ended the call and looked out over his property. On the phone, Stahl's son had told him he'd be coming out today to talk to him again.

"Damn him," he said to himself. Rhett had the gall to threaten him over the phone.

He knew killing one more person, maybe two if Rhett brought along the other guy, would only increase his chances of being discovered and arrested.

It was all MacCumber's fault. Him and his dumb map, he thought.

He had lived here in peace for eighteen years. He thought about the day he buried his wife and her boy out there. Eighteen and half years it had been. The tramp had fooled around on him. She didn't know he had discovered her secret.

They left their rental apartment in Artesia, New Mexico, for a short vacation in the Big Bend. Neither of them had family in Artesia. She had run off from California at a young age and hadn't stayed in touch with her family. She never admitted knowing who her boy's father was. Looking back, he wondered why he ever married her. She was easy, getting married was easy, and maybe back then, he had some idea living with her would be easy.

He spit at a large grasshopper on the ground.

He had brought them to the Big Bend with the plan to kill them both. He had no plan after that. She needed to be punished, and the teenage boy, what was he, thirteen, well that he did with pleasure. The kid had shown him no respect from the day he showed up with her in Artesia.

The plan was simple and until recently had been amazingly effective. They went camping out in the middle of nowhere, and in the morning, he drove away alone. For a year, he worked with an oil service company, saved his money, and lived in Alpine. Then, he found a better paying job and purchased his current house, south of Marathon.

Life became simple and the years passed. He left people alone and they left him alone. He had few friends. MacCumber came along and screwed everything up. First, Ray started out hanging around MacCumber more than with him. That irritated him but wasn't too bad. Then MacCumber showed up that day with a map he believed would lead him to a buried treasure.

Initially, he simply thought MacCumber was an idiot, but when he looked at the map, he almost gasped. He had to fight the surge in emotions that raced through him. The map led right to the spot where he had buried them. He only handled the map for a few seconds, and later doubt did try to mollify his fear.

He had tried to see the map again, but MacCumber refused. The fool actually thought it might lead him to a buried treasure. None of it made sense, the scale of the map wasn't small enough to pinpoint the exact spot, but the map also had GPS coordinates. He needed to get those coordinates. After a couple of weeks, his fear and anger overwhelmed any rational thinking. MacCumber had to die.

Killing MacCumber was easy, but the search of his person and his pickup didn't reveal the map. The spot where he did the killing was a good hundred yards from where he had buried his wife and her kid. Too close for comfort, he thought. Besides, the ground wasn't flat at the burial site, MacCumber may have chosen his campsite because it was flat. The GPS coordinates may have led him closer to the site.

When he didn't find the map with MacCumber, he wondered if he had shared it with Stahl. Those two were close.

He had not planned his encounter with Stahl. It happened by chance when he went out to see how far the police search had gone. He had stayed hidden on his approach to avoid being seen by any police presence. He hadn't seen any; however, Stahl showed up a few minutes after he did.

Stahl's arrival at the spot where he had killed MacCumber angered him. For some reason he couldn't understand now, he confronted Stahl and shot him four times. He didn't regret it. Stahl needed to die, too, but he wondered why his memory of leaving his hiding spot and walking up to Stahl was so fuzzy.

He had the same muddled memory about his killing of the woman. He had wanted to question her about the map. He had to be sure she didn't have a copy. He didn't regret killing her either, but he couldn't clearly recall the events of that evening. That troubled him, and none of the killings got him any closer to the map.

Now, Rhett Stahl had shown up, wanting to discover who killed his father. He didn't believe Rhett could prove anything, but what if Rhett carried through with his threats? Could he remain silent if Rhett started breaking his fingers? He didn't think it would come to that, but what if it did?

He spit again at the grasshopper. This time he hit it, and the grasshopper leapt away.

He thought about killing Rhett. He couldn't do it at his place and couldn't think of a way to lure him elsewhere. Time to plan an ambush, he thought. There were only so many ways a person could drive out here. After opening a can of Coca-Cola, he made two phone calls and confirmed that Rhett had plans to see all three of them today. His main suspects, that's what Rhett had called them. He also learned the times each expected Rhett to show up.

Picking the right spot for the ambush took some time. There were so many good choices. After running through scenarios for twenty minutes in his mind, he settled on what he believed would be the perfect one.

If Rhett was alone, his task would be a simple one. If he brought that other fellow, he would try to kill him, too, but he needed to ensure Rhett was dead first. He opened his gun safe and took out one of his hunting rifles.

The rifle would give him a leg up on anything Rhett might be carrying, but he knew surprise would be his real advantage. He would target Rhett first. Yes, he would kill him and then anyone else who might be with him.

He started humming to himself.

Chapter 33

I debated whether or not to wear my cowboy boots. After wearing them the one day I was out with Rhett, my feet hurt, and I thought I had the beginnings of a blister. But I didn't think my soft-sided, croc loafers fit the image I needed to portray.

"You're an idiot," I said to myself but put the boots on anyway.

My phone rang.

"Jim, this is Anne, Rose wanted me to call you and let you know the person discovered in the park yesterday did die of simple exposure. Too much sun and too little water will do it to you every time. Their best guess is that he had recently crossed the Rio Grande. That's a little harder to determine, but his cloths and everything else indicates that. Either way, no one believes he has anything to do with our investigation."

I thanked her for telling me, and we made non-specific plans to get together for a drink later on. The news wasn't unexpected. That's what we all believed at the scene.

Not knowing when Rhett wanted to leave, and not wanting to wait in my room, I decided to take a short walk. Situated less than a half mile away, a hundred-year-old church mentioned in a local tourist brochure seemed to be an appropriate destination. Dark clouds appeared to be growing and getting closer in the western sky. The breeze even felt a little cooler than it had the last few days. I wondered if the rain the weathermen had been forecasting might finally make it to Alpine.

As I neared the old church, my phone rang.

"Meet me in the lobby in twenty minutes," Rhett said.

"I'll be there."

He ended the call. I shook my head. This would be my last day dealing with Rhett. He would get his chance today, but then I would be done with him. I chuckled to myself, thinking how similar Rhett and Janice were. Both expected others, me in this case, to jump at their every whim. Maybe Rhett would be different in different circumstances, but I had little desire to find out.

"Want me to drive today?" I asked, knowing the answer.

"In your little ladies' car? No thanks."

We got into his truck and drove off. A gust of wind pelted sand against the side of the vehicle.

"The rain may finally get here today," I said.

"Doubt it. We're going to Dunn's place first. Lucy should be at work, and I didn't give him enough time to get her back home. We'll see how he does without her skirts to hide behind."

"He may shoot you when he sees you."

"Oh my," Rhett said and patted his pistol through his shirt, "how I hope he tries."

"Which one do you think is the killer?"

He glanced over at me. "Why? You know who it is?"

"No, but I've been thinking, and I don't think Dunn did them."

"Why?"

"The body language between Dunn and his daughter, and his eyes when he answered your questions."

"You that good at this stuff?" he asked, grinning in a way that said he thought I wasn't.

"No, I'm no expert. It's my impression of him. My money is on one of the other two. Evenly split, I'd say."

"We'll find out today. I don't make predictions on who the guilty party is, but I feel in my bones that we'll find out today. My money is on that. My bones are rarely wrong."

"More of a reason to be careful."

"That's why I have my little buddy." He again patted his pistol. "A cute little blond in north San Antonio where I go practice recommended this to me. It's a great pistol. What I aim at, I hit. If it gets hot, stay behind me, I'll protect you."

He had a point. What was I doing out here with him, going to interview murder suspects without a weapon of my own?

In my mind, of course, the answer was obvious. I shouldn't be out here doing this. I spent twenty years carrying a weapon and putting myself in dangerous situations. Since my retirement, my plan was to stay away from all that stuff. Take life easy and live forever. That was the plan. I had carried a weapon for twenty years and never shot at anybody. Pat and I used to joke if we had to shoot someone, it would be best to shoot ourself. Less paperwork and less painful in the long run.

Since my retirement from the air force, I had unintentionally entered a world full of mayhem, death, and now maybe demons. I looked out the window and once again wished I was back home playing fetch with Chubbs.

"Are you awake?"

"Yes, just day dreaming," I said.

"About Rose? How is she?"

"She's good. She'll be a great FBI agent."

"Not what I meant. Seems a little cold to me."

I looked back out the window and grinned. "She can be that way. She puts her job first. Depending how you look at that, it can be a good thing."

"I wouldn't mind getting to know her better, but none of us will likely be here long enough for that to happen."

"Your bones telling you things are about to come to a head?"

"Yes, they are."

We turned off the main road and drove down a long, narrow one that led to Dunn's driveway. The terrain became hilly, and the road curled back and forth following a dry creek bed. The sky outside had become darker.

Suddenly, the front window fragmented with a thousand small fractures. A hole the size of a golf ball appeared and Rhett screamed in pain. He jerked the steering wheel to the right, and we drove off the road. Our right front tire dropped two feet into the ditch. The truck's momentum carried us further, and the right front of the truck slammed into the bank of hard rock and dirt.

The scene unfolded in my mind in what felt like slow motion, but, in reality, took less than a few seconds. A high-powered round had blasted through our windshield, busted through the steering wheel, and tore into Rhett's right shoulder. Fragments from the window and steering wheel had cut into his face. A few shards had torn into the side of my face.

He looked at me with wide eyes that asked what happened.

A second shot tore out most of the windshield on the driver's side. This one I heard. Rhett's head jerked, and his eyes rolled up into his head.

"Come on! We need to get out!"

I opened my door which hit solid ground after it opened barley wide enough for me to squeeze out. Crouching in slow-moving, ankle-deep water, I turned around to get Rhett. He fumbled with his seat belt, which surprised me as I thought he might be dead. The belt popped open, and he fell in my direction.

Then he stopped moving. I tugged at him and managed to pull him to the door. The downward slope helped. I leaned in further to get a better grip.

The windshield on my side of the truck exploded, and the loud blast from what I believed to be a rifle erupted again from somewhere in front of us. At the same time, I felt something whiz by my left ear. Ducking and looking at the car seat, I saw the bullet hole. I yanked Rhett, and he slid out of the car into the ditch. As he did, I saw his pistol.

I pulled it out of the holster and looked back to where I believed the shooter had hidden. I saw him. He had leaned over a large boulder on the side of a small hill to get better support to aim his rifle. At the moment, his head was upright as he tried to see what damage he had done to us. I stood, aimed, and squeezed off two rounds. Despite the distance, maybe fifty yards, I saw the impact of the rounds on the rock in front of him.

At this range, I hadn't expected to hit him, and the accuracy of Rhett's handgun impressed me. My goal was to scare the shooter away. I ducked back down as he fired two more rounds at us. Both shots tearing through the open passenger door but missing us.

When he paused, I raised up enough to aim and fire two more rounds at him. I aimed a little higher this time to compensate for the distance. I expected him to return fire but he didn't. I peeked above the car frame and saw a figure running up the side of the hill.

I fired three more times at him, but he dove for cover and disappeared along the top of the ridgeline. Following him was out of the question. I could tell that Rhett was still alive. Getting help here now was imperative.

The first drops of rain hit my head.

Chapter 34

The air turned cold. Low clouds raced in and more rain fell. A shadowy twilight replaced the bright sunshine.

I fought the urge to crawl back into the truck. I also resisted the desire to start running. The fear that our shooter may be maneuvering for a better shot angle tried to overwhelm me.

We had to move, to hide, if only for ten or fifteen minutes. I looked around, keeping my head as low as possible and still using the car door as a shield. I didn't see any place suitable for hiding behind us for a hundred yards on my side of the road. The hill on the opposite side would have a number of options, but I didn't like the option of going towards the shooter.

"Rhett! Rhett!"

He gurgled a response that I couldn't understand. His eyes didn't focus. Blood streamed down the left side of his face. I gripped his chin to inspect the head wound. Fortunately, it appeared the round scraped off several layers of skin and the top part of his ear but nothing more. His shoulder injury was more serious.

It took all my strength to maneuver him around in the ditch into a sitting position against the bank. I noticed water was now streaming down the ditch from the direction where we had come.

I leaned close to his face. "Rhett, you need to wake up. I don't want to have to drag you out of here."

His eyes opened but didn't focus. I wondered if the head wound had knocked him unconscious, or if he had entered some level of shock from the shoulder wound. I looked around again for any sign of the man who attacked us but saw nothing.

The rain started pouring down. The running water in the ditch began to tug at me. As I watched it, I could see it get higher. I remembered the dry creek bed and realized this ditch either fed into it or out of it. Either way, we didn't need to be here if the rain caused any flash flooding.

I looked around again. The heavy rain made it harder to see into the distance.

"Damn! This is no good, Rhett."

I grabbed his good arm and tried to drag him out of the ditch. He barely budged. I figured he weighed over two hundred pounds. In the cramped space, two choices were all I had. Get out of the ditch and try to lift him out from the other side or drag him sideways until he was stretched out in the ditch.

Neither option looked feasible. I had placed his back against the bank, so picking him straight up and over the edge of the bank from the other side would take more strength than I thought I had. Dragging him sideways until he was lying lengthwise in the ditch would put his whole body and me in four inches of running water.

If someone was watching, what followed would have been a comedy skit with a bit of terror built-in. I gripped the back of his shirt and his good left arm near the arm pit and pulled him sideways as hard as I could. The inertia held him for a moment. Suddenly, his body slid rapidly toward me, and I fell over backwards into the cold running water. His head and shoulders rested on my legs up to my knees. The cold water rushed over and around me. I struggled to get my feet free of him.

The water swirling around, and at times over his head, didn't revive him. I squatted by his head and picked and pushed him up into a sitting position. This time, his back was against the flow of the running water. Wrapping my arms around him as low on his torso as I could, I forced myself to stand up with Rhett still held against me. Knowing I couldn't climb the simple two feet to get onto the road, I did the next best thing. I backed against the bank. I intended to sit down and then slide Rhett off me onto the road.

As I started to sit, my left foot slipped on the wet ground, and to prevent complete disaster I yanked Rhett backwards with me. We fell onto the road. Rhett wasn't centered on me and rolled off landing on his bad right shoulder. That got his attention.

Rhett screamed and said something unintelligible. Somehow, using his good arm he maneuvered himself around to where he was on his back. Then he started cussing.

The back of my head had hit a small rock when I fell. I barely noticed it in the excitement, but rubbing my hand against it, I saw blood on my fingers when I pulled my hand away.

"Where are we?" he asked.

"Near the Dunn's."

"Bastard, I knew it was him. Help me get up."

I helped him into a sitting position. He groaned and instinctively supported his right elbow with his left hand.

"What happened?"

I told him about the attack and the man with a rifle.

"Where's my gun?" he asked after glancing at the empty holster.

"Back on the car seat. I used it and about seven of your bullets, maybe five, I'm not sure."

He looked at me, his eyes still a little out of focus. "Did you hit anything?" Despite the pain and his situation, his tone told me that he doubted if I could hit the side of the hill.

"He was too far away. I mostly wanted to scare him away."

"Where is he now?"

We were right behind the truck. I stood up and looked over the truck at the hillside. I took a good thirty seconds to study the hill. Despite the heavy rain hampering my vision, I was certain he was gone.

"Not there. We're safe behind the truck." Circling behind us would be a tedious task, and we would be able to see him if he wanted to get within a few hundred yards of us.

"I need my pistol."

"I'll get it, but I'm going to hang onto it. You're in no shape." I started to go around to the passenger side but stopped when I saw the water was now a foot high and moving quickly. I estimated the ditch to be four feet across. The road had been built up where it was six or seven inches higher than the bank on the far side. When the ditch overflowed the water would run towards the creek bed.

I went to the driver's door, all the time watching for movement on the hill. The truck slanted downward towards the right front, so opening the door turned out to be more like picking the door up. I managed and stretched across the front seat to reach the pistol. I did feel a degree of increased confidence when it was in my grasp.

I didn't think I could get the truck out of the ditch. The frame under the passenger door had dug into the ground as well as the front right fender. Time to call for help, I thought. My phone was wet from my fall into the ditch trying to move Rhett. It appeared to want to work but didn't. One small bar showed I had some coverage, but whether it was the storm, or the wet phone, nothing happened when I dialed Rose.

"I need to lay down," Rhett said and did.

The rain poured down on him, but other than closing his eyes once he was fully prone, he didn't move. The blood on the side of his head continued to stream down to the road, the rain making it a light pink by the time it spread out on the thin layer of water on the road.

The headlights of a car driving toward us appeared in the distance. I tightened my grip on the pistol. The vehicle approached us from the same direction we had come, so I didn't think it could be our assailant. Still, the hairs on the back of my neck were dancing. Who would be out here?

Chapter 35

A small, white Ford sedan pulled to a stop about twenty yards from us. The windshield wipers operated at full speed.

It took me a few seconds before I realized Lucy sat in the driver's seat. She made no effort to get out or drive around us. I clicked the safety on and tucked the pistol into the back waistband of my jeans. Raising both hands to indicate I was no threat, I walked to her car door.

The driver's window rolled down. She stared out at me with a poker face. I noticed her right hand was positioned under a blanket on the passenger seat. "What's going on?"

"Someone shot at us and hit Rhett, twice. He needs help. The truck's stuck."

"Where's my dad?"

"I haven't seen your dad. You think he did this?"

"No, no way. He wouldn't have called me to come home if he was planning to ambush you. No way."

That did make sense to me, too.

"Does your phone work? Can you call 911?"

"This is a dead spot. We need to get closer to the house," Lucy said. She opened the car door and got out. "Is he alive?"

"Yes, at least he was a minute ago. I think the shooter has left, but we need to be careful." I looked around as I spoke.

Lucy hurried past me to Rhett. She knelt over him and gasped. She stood and walked to the side of the pickup that was stuck in the ditch. As if she was running the scene through her mind, she stared at the hillside from where the man had shot at us.

"Did you see him leave?"

"Yes, I shot several rounds at him, and he fled over the top of the ridge."

"There's a trail on the other side. Did you hit him?"

"I doubt it. All I had was a pistol. It's too far to be accurate."

"It wasn't my dad. Can we get him into my car? My dad's house is less than a mile from here. A helicopter can land near it. Fastest way to get help to him."

"Pull your car up close. He's not light and likely won't be helping us."

She ran back to her car and drove it as close as she could.

"We'll have to lay him flat on the back seat," she said.

Lucy opened the door and together we picked him up to the point where his feet dragged behind him while we maneuvered his head and shoulders onto the back seat.

"Keep him like this, while I go around and pull him in." I ran around to the other side of the car and stretched in far enough to get my hands under his arm pits. I looked up at Lucy. The heavy rain pelted her and streaked down and across her face.

"Pull!" She yelled. I did. She grabbed his belt buckle and lifted. Between the two of us we wrestled Rhett into the back seat. She forced his feet in and slammed the door. I closed the car door I had opened and walked around the rear of the Ford.

Lucy wiped mud from Rhett's boots off her hands onto her soaked dark slacks.

"Thanks," I said.

"Don't get in until after me, and I say it's okay." She hurried to the driver's side and climbed in.

I watched as she rolled up the blanket that had been on the passenger seat. Something was definitely in it. She placed it on the floor immediately in front of her seat.

"Get in!"

I did, and she maneuvered the car around the pickup and drove toward her house. The rain, and perhaps the overall situation, kept our speed down.

"This is going to ruin my car," she said.

I thought it was a petty thing to say at this point with Rhett dying in the back seat, but I also thought she needed to say something.

"Rhett's truck is likely totaled," I said.

"Yeah, probably so. You know your face is bleeding."

"Just scratches. Hopefully, the rain washed them off well enough to keep any infection away."

"How long were you out there?"

"I'm not sure. It couldn't have been more than ten minutes before you showed up, but I really don't know. He's lost a lot of blood. The first shot got him in the shoulder, and the second creased his head."

"Part of his ear is missing," Lucy said.

"I know. I don't think that's the serious wound, although it may have something to do with his staying unconscious. The shoulder wound may have also busted up his collarbone. The round went through the windshield and the steering wheel. It didn't come out the back of his shoulder, so it's still in there."

"That's not good, is it?"

"None of it's good."

"I didn't mean it like that."

"I know," I said. A round from a rifle should normally go right through a person. The damage to the round prior to its impact with Rhett could cause much more internal damage than a clean round would have caused.

We rounded a bend in the road and nearly ran into a man standing in the road holding a rifle.

Lucy hit the brakes hard, and I reached for the pistol.

Chapter 36

"No!" Lucy shouted and put a hand over on my chest. "It's my dad."

I didn't care whose dad he might be, but I did notice he had not raised the rifle to a firing position. He walked at a fast pace toward us, angling to Lucy's side of the car. The rain affected his vision, and he raised his left hand to protect his eyes. He noticed me when he neared Lucy's window. I thought I could see him tense up.

Lucy had her window down. "It's Rhett. He's been shot bad, Dad. We need to get him to the house and call for help."

"What? He's been shot?"

"Yes, hurry home. I'm fine." She drove off, leaving her dad. The house was visible to us now. She parked in the garage.

I tried calling again. This time my call went through and Rose answered.

"Rose, you need to get an ambulance out to the Dunn's house right away. Rhett's been shot, and I'm not sure if he's going to make it."

"What? Are you okay?" Rose asked.

"Yes, I'm fine. Listen, it wasn't Dunn, so we don't need an armed response."

"Thank you," Lucy said.

"And Rose, they'll pass the scene where we got ambushed as they near the Dunn's property. We're not there anymore, we're at the Dunn's. Rhett needs medical help as soon as possible."

We ended the call, and I looked at Lucy and then out the back window at her father. Although he was still thirty to forty yards away, I could see the strain in his face as he jogged toward us.

"Lucy, you need to get that rifle from him. It will help diffuse the situation, and we'll have to have it checked."

She leaped out of the car and sprinted to her dad. He hugged her, then they both looked at me as I stood by the car. The scene could have been a tense one. I knew it would only take a second for him to raise his rifle and shoot me. However, everything I saw indicated Lucy had been correct.

She said something to him, and he gave her the rifle. She gripped it in her left hand and took his hand in her right hand. They started walking toward me. He wore an awkward looking rain hat and a waterproof poncho. His face was wet and flushed from his jog. He looked like I felt, worn out and wanting to be left alone.

Dressed in her dark slacks, light blue blouse, and soaked to the bone, Lucy no longer sported her poker face. A small smile had appeared. She stood as tall as her dad, both a couple inches shy of six feet. As I watched them the rain stopped.

"What happened?" Carl asked.

"We were ambushed by a lone man with a rifle. It happened less than a mile from here while we were driving to see you."

"Wasn't me. I went out there when I heard all the shooting. I knew Lucy was on her way, otherwise I would've bunkered down inside and waited," he said.

He walked over and looked into the car at Rhett.

"He's peaceful right now. Should we leave him be?" Lucy said.

"I think we need to get him inside and do what we can to slow or stop the bleeding. The loss of blood may kill him if we don't," I said.

"Yeah, you're likely right," Carl said. "Looks like he lost a lot of blood already. May be too late. Is he still alive?"

"Let's find out," I said. I opened the back passenger-side door and started to reach in.

"Wait one second. Dad let's bring that old mattress out here. It'd be easier to plop him down here than try to carry him inside and to a bedroom."

"Yeah, you're right," Carl said.

"Lucy, please put the rifle against the corner over there before you go."

She did, and they both went inside through a door in the garage. Fifteen seconds later they muscled a mattress back into the garage and placed it next to the car. We pulled Rhett out by his feet. Once he was halfway out, I grabbed him around his chest to support his upper half. We managed to get him out and onto the mattress.

"My God," Carl said after getting his first good look at Rhett's wound.

Rhett groaned and his legs started moving. Lucy knelt down and started talking softly to him. Rhett calmed down.

"She's good with the ranch animals," Carl said.

My phone rang.

"They're sending out the helicopter. Radar indicates the storm has passed you by, and it's the only way to get someone there in the next twenty minutes. Joe is sending most of the team out to where he got shot."

"Good," I said.

Rose had me confirm the location of Rhett's pickup. She also wanted me to stay with the Dunn's until the helicopter arrived with the medical team and a deputy. I told her I would.

"A helicopter is coming for him?" Lucy asked after the call ended. She still kneeled next to Rhett and had her hand on one of his.

"Yes, they'll be here soon."

"Put this on the wound and press down," Carl had gone into the house during the call and had returned with a clean bath towel. "No, on second thought, I'll do it. You go in and change into a different blouse before everyone gets here."

Lucy looked down at her blouse. Rhett's blood had gotten on it, but I believed she knew that wasn't what bothered her father. Her drenched, light blue blouse had become transparent. She had on a bra, so she wasn't entirely exposed. She stood up and stepped away.

Her father took her position and pressed the towel down on the wound. Rhett groaned.

"If it was me, I would have shot you in the head," Carl said.

"I'm sure he was trying to," I said.

Carl didn't look back at me. "It hurts him. I think he's lost so much blood his body is shutting down. Did the round come out the back?"

"No."

"Both Logan and Alex called me today and wanted to know what time he was coming out to my place."

"No one else would've known," I said.

"That's right. I guess I knew it, too, but I can't figure out any motive. It makes no sense. Neither one of them have done anything wrong since I've known them. That's been at least ten years."

"The map?"

"No way. It was trash. We all knew it. We even felt sorry for

Pat wasting his money. No, it couldn't have anything to do with a dumb map."

"This okay, Dad?" Lucy asked when she reentered the garage. She had replaced her blouse with a Dallas Cowboys tee shirt. Her tone carried with it a little frustration.

"Better," Carl mumbled.

Lucy looked at me and rolled her eyes. I could sympathize with Carl. He was her father. Despite all the stress and activity going on around me, I had noticed how nice she looked in the wet blouse.

"Let me clean that face of yours. You're still bleeding, and there's something stuck on your face."

Lucy had a wet washcloth and, without waiting for a response, reached up to my face.

"I'm fine."

"No, you're not. What are these things?"

I let her clean and inspect my face. Every couple seconds, she would stop and pluck something off the left side of my face. I felt a minor sting each time she did.

"What are these from?"

I had to think for a second. "Glass from the windshield?"

"A couple, but the rest look like something else?"

"Maybe pieces from the steering wheel."

"Ah, yes, I bet that is what they're from. Let me get something," she said and went back into the house.

Carl twisted his head around to look at me. "She should have been a nurse."

"She's gentle."

"Don't get her mad."

Lucy returned with a bottle of hydrogen peroxide.

"The medics will be here in a second," I said.

"You want to take some of their focus away from Rhett?" she scolded me. "Don't worry it won't hurt, much."

I didn't feel anything.

Rhett made a loud gurgling sound that got all our attention.

"That's not good," Carl said. "Maybe we should turn him on his side."

We did, rolling him onto his good side.

Then the sound of an arriving helicopter got our attention.

Chapter 37

Deputy Tony Anaya climbed out of the helicopter followed by a three-person emergency medical team. Carl and I met them and led them to the garage. When we reached the garage, Tony tugged at my arm and pulled me to the side.

"How certain are you Dunn wasn't the one who ambushed you?" He spoke soft enough to not be heard inside the garage.

"Ninety percent. It's possible but highly unlikely. His rifle is in the garage, in the corner. You should take it as a precaution and to eliminate him. They want you to take it, too."

"Okay," he said, and we both entered the garage.

The medical team had already cut open Rhett's shirt, had a monitor of some sort attached to his arm, and two of them were working together to hook him up to an IV. The third member of the team studied the wound to his head. One of them said something, and all three repositioned themselves, picked Rhett up, and placed him on a stretcher.

"We need to move him now," the oldest looking member of the team said to Deputy Anaya.

"Do it. I'll be staying here."

The three hustled to the helicopter with Rhett.

"They were certainly quick and efficient," Lucy said.

We all watched as the helicopter lifted off seconds later.

"He's an ass, but I hope he makes it," Carl said.

"Oh, Dad," Lucy said. "What now?" She addressed her question to Tony.

"I need to get a preliminary statement from each of you," Tony said.

"That's easy. Only Jim saw what happened. We don't have any idea," Lucy said.

"Then this won't take long. A bunch of people are heading to the scene right now. They should be there in twenty minutes or so. I'd like to get this part wrapped up by then. Carl, let's you and I talk first."

Carl agreed, and Lucy offered to make coffee for everyone. I imagined she wanted to be within earshot of what her father was saying, too. Tony spent less than five minutes with Carl and a little more with Lucy.

While Tony was with Lucy, Carl came out to the porch where I was sitting in the sunshine trying to dry out.

"It's going to get awfully hot today with all this humidity. We got at least an inch of rain, and we needed it," Carl said. He sat down next to me.

"It was heavy."

"Why did Rhett have to come down so hard on us. Not only me, but the others, too. He drove one of them to do this."

"I can't explain his behavior. You know, I think one of your two friends has something big he's hiding."

"Something big and bad in his past?"

"Yes," I said. "Any ideas?"

"No, not at all."

"What brought you out in the rain with your rifle?" I thought he may have told us before, but I wanted to be sure.

"I heard the shots being fired, a lot of them. I knew Lucy was driving home, and I was worried about her. No offense, but if she wasn't on her way home, I would never have come out to check on you two."

I grinned. "Don't blame you. You didn't see anyone?"

"No, it started to rain as I was leaving the house. Went back in to get my slicker. By the time I got to where you saw me it was pouring. Couldn't see much of anything. The shooting had long stopped, and I imagined whoever had been doing it was long gone. How far down the road were you?"

"Not far, maybe a half mile past where we met you, maybe not that far."

"He used that small hill, didn't he? The one that runs right up to the road."

"Yes, I think it's the last one before everything levels off in front of your home. He hit Rhett with his first shot, and we drove off into the ditch."

Carl nodded. Lucy and Tony came out and interrupted our conversation. Tony was on his phone and walked about ten paces away from us.

"I think it's the sheriff, and he's not too happy," she said.

"I hadn't thought about that, but I imagine a lot of people are going to react the same way. I wonder how many higher headquarters will be sending their rep on the team a 'What in the hell is going on down there' message today."

"Jim, can you come over here for a minute?" Tony said. He walked away from us, and I followed him to a spot about ten yards away for the others.

"Are we all fired?" I asked.

"I wish it was that simple. The sheriff's pissed, to put it politely. Do you still have Rhett's weapon?"

"Yes."

"Let me have it. It will need to be inspected and comparisons made."

I handed it to him. I knew it was a normal step in the

investigation, but the timing and the way Tony asked for it caused me to wonder if the sheriff had told him to get it, because I could be the person doing all the killing. An asinine assumption but not impossible I thought.

"We need to get back to the scene. He wants us there when the team arrives. How far is it?"

"Not too far, but the road is muddy, and it's hot out here again. Let me ask Lucy to drive us. They may want to ask her a few more questions, maybe take pictures of her bloody back seat," I said.

"Lucy, can you drive Jim and me back to the scene?" Tony asked.

"Of course. Let me get a towel for you to sit on."

I ended up in the back seat. My clothes were already a mess. I stayed close to the door where mud covered the seat but only a little blood. We drove in silence until the truck came into view.

"That's going to cost a fortune," Tony said more to himself than to us.

"Lucy, stop here," I said. We were still a good thirty yards from Rhett's pickup. "I don't want your car to interfere with the line of sight between the hill and the pickup."

She stopped, and Tony didn't object. The team had not arrived yet.

"Should we wait in the car?" Lucy asked Tony.

"No, we can walk up closer. With all the rain and the fact that the shooter was nowhere near the car, it probably doesn't matter, but let's play it by the book."

"This is the hill right here?" Tony motioned with his hand to the hill on our right as we faced the pickup. The hill came close to the road here and didn't seem very tall. Going back to the house it fell off gradually to level ground. In the direction of the pickup, the hill became much higher and the base of the hill moved further from the road.

"Yes," an obvious answer since it was the only hill around. "I'd have to get a better angle from where we were, but I would guess he was up there by the rocks near the top. He shot down at us."

Tony nodded, but I doubted if he knew exactly where I pointed. He started walking toward the pickup. Lucy and I followed him. We stopped about ten yards from Rhett's vehicle. The water in the ditch still ran high and fast in the direction of Carl's house.

"Yes, those rocks," I said and pointed back up the hill.

Both Lucy and Tony turned around.

"That's close. With a rifle he should've had an easy shot," Tony said.

"He did. We got lucky, if you could say that, the bullet hit the steering wheel. That impact deflected it a little and slowed it down," I said.

"The round must have been messed up when it hit him. That can cause a lot more damage around the impact area," Tony said.

"The second round creased the left side of his head. The windshield was messed up then which likely through his aim off a little. The third round missed my head by an inch. There may have been another round or two that struck the vehicle. It's all kind of a blur in my mind."

"Here they come," Lucy said.

I turned and looked down the road and saw two vehicles with lights flashing heading our way. We moved to the edge of the road away from the pickup and started walking again. The two vehicles, one unmarked and the other a sheriff's SUV stopped about ten yards from Rhett's pickup.

Rose and the younger male FBI agent stepped out of the unmarked car. Anne and Caleb Wilkins, the Texas Ranger, stepped out of the other car.

Rose hurried to me while the rest paused to take in the scene.

"You look a mess," Rose said with a slight smile.

"I'm okay. Lucky, but okay. Any update on Rhett?"

"No. A forensics van should be here momentarily."

The others arrived, and Tony introduced everyone to Lucy. I knew all the names except for the younger FBI agent, Sid Lukens.

"Now, Mr. West, walk us through what happened," Sid said.

Once again, I told my story. This time I could point out things as I talked. They all had questions, even Lucy. Sid walked us around the side of the pickup where everyone could see the open car door, still jammed into the muddy bank. The ditch water at one time had been high enough to create a wet and muddy line across the bottom four inches of the door.

"Did you have to drag him out of the car?" Rose asked.

"Yes, and it wasn't easy."

Sid led us around to the front of the car. We remained several yards away from it. He turned around and looked at the hill. "Where was he?"

"Behind those rocks." I pointed. All of them moved in closer to me to get a better line to where I pointed.

"Think you hit him?" he asked.

"I hit the rocks. It made him scramble up to a higher point over to the left. We exchanged rounds again, and he dove over the top."

"Dove?"

"Jumped, whatever, he looked to be in a hurry to get away."

"It doesn't drop off there. It's a slight decline, and there's a trail on that side," Lucy said. "A four-wheel drive can handle it, but it's rough. It's been there forever. No one knows its purpose."

Sid nodded but didn't ask any more questions.

"Want me to take a look up there?" Caleb asked.

"Yes."

"I'll go with him," Tony said.

"Okay, take pictures and mark anything at all that looks interesting."

Chapter 38

Rose's phone rang. She walked a few steps away from us and took the call. After less than a minute, she ended the call and came back to us.

"Neither of the other two men are at home. If they are, they aren't answering their door. Someone is going to remain at each house until they return."

"Love to catch them returning and maybe have them make a run for it," Sid said. "It looks like we're down to two possibilities, but it's still a crap shoot." He looked at Lucy. I thought he might be considering whether to put her father back on the list of suspects.

She must have felt the same way. "Well, it wasn't my father. You have his rifle, his only rifle. He was walking toward the scene from the house, and he was glad to see me, us. He had no apprehension about Jim being with me."

"I'm not accusing him," Sid said.

A county crime scene van drove up and parked. Sid had me explain what happened to the new arrivals. He then told them to do their magic and to take a lot of pictures.

I heard one of them mumble to one of the others that if the suspect wasn't anywhere near the pickup there wasn't much they could do.

"When you get done here, we'll need you up where the shooter had positioned himself. With all the rain, I know it's a long shot, but you may find something," Sid said.

"You should find shell casings," I said.

Lucy and Rose walked about ten yards away and started

talking. The rest of the team followed and watched the crime scene technicians. I decided to climb up to where the shots came from.

Caleb signaled me when I got close. "Come over here."

I did and saw four shell casings scattered close to each other on the ground. "This was the spot."

"Some more are up here," Tony said.

We joined him and saw two more on the ground. They had marked the location of each casing with small plastic flags.

"I took pictures," Tony said. "Look at this." He walked the short distance to the top of the hill and pointed at a rough looking, old trail about ten yards away. It led away from the house and down the slope.

"I've heard there's a number of these old trails that simply lead to observation points used long ago by the Indians, the Spaniards, the soldiers, and so on. It's higher up there, but it's hard to get there, and this is high enough." Caleb pointed to the top of the hill some distance away.

I walked the few steps to where I could see for miles in almost all directions. "This would work," I said.

Caleb's phone rang. "Yes, send them up." He ended the call. "The experts are on their way."

He sounded a little critical, and I imagined he thought that gathering a few bullet casings was something he could have easily done himself. He could, no doubt, but with all the scrutiny this investigation was going to get, I understood why Sid wanted to do everything by the book.

"You have to be uncomfortable," Caleb said to me while we waited. "You got caught out in the rain?"

"Worse than that," I said and told them both about falling backward into the flooded ditch while trying to move Rhett.

They both laughed.

I walked down the hill with Tony, and we returned to the gaggle near the pickup. I saw Rose huddled off to the side with Sid. She nodded a few times as did Sid, so whatever they were discussing, they both appeared to be in agreement.

She started walking toward the car she had arrived in and waved at me to join her. I did.

"They don't need us here, and both Joe and the sheriff want to hear the whole story from you. The guys here are in the process of sending all the photos to them," Rose said.

"Okay. Do I have time to change and clean up?" Every item of clothing I had on felt damp.

"Sorry, no. I did ask that question, but they insist they won't keep you long."

"Famous last words."

"I know, but look at it this way. Your boots no longer make you look like some kind of urban cowboy." She tried not to grin but failed miserably.

I looked down at my scuffed and dirty boots. "I think the blood stains on my shirt and jeans help out, too."

She smacked my arm, "That's more like a serial killer look. Not a good one."

Joe and the team ran me through the entire day's events and had me brief them on the ambush twice before they let me go. They had pictures of Rhett's truck and the view from the truck up to the spot where the shooter had ambushed displayed on a large television screen. I referenced them as I went through my briefing. They recorded everything.

When they started discussing theories and were finished with me, I slipped out and walked to the hotel. Outside, a few people stared at me, most likely bothered by the blood stains, but no one spoke or bothered me. In my room, I tossed the jeans and shirt in the small trash can, showered and tried to nap.

Visions of the shooter kept me from falling into a deep sleep. He appeared larger now in my imagination. He stood straight and tall and smiled as he shot down at me. His eyes glowed red, bright, bloody red.

Chapter 39

After thirty minutes of tossing and turning I got up, left the room, and walked to Spirits and Sandwiches. For the first time since I had started coming, a noisy crowd filled the place. They occupied half the room, but the stools at the bar were open.

Konnie carried two pitchers of beer to them while I sat down. Both the woman, whom I had met before and thought managed the place, and the older male bar tender worked behind the bar, pouring wine or making mixed drinks. They placed the drinks on a tray. A second tray filled with drinks already poured sat next to it. Konnie returned, gave me a wink, and grabbed the full tray.

I watched her carry the drinks to the crowd. I always wondered how one developed the skill to carry a tray with a dozen drinks on it with one hand without spilling anything.

"That should be everything," the manager said to the male bartender. She spoke loud enough to be heard over the noise from the front of the room.

The male bartender sat down. He looked tired.

"You tell them that if one of them touches you inappropriately again, I'm kicking the whole group out," the manager said to Konnie when she came for the second tray.

"I can handle them, but if they get worse, I will," Konnie said and left with the second tray.

"They've been drinking since lunch time. I can use the business, but this could get rowdy. I don't need no fights, or people taking clothes off," the manager said to me.

"Think they might go that far?"

"It's happened." She turned around and started cleaning the

counter behind her, putting the bottles back where they belong as she cleaned.

Konnie returned with the tray now full of empty glasses.

"Beer?" she asked.

"Yes, that IPA on tap, please. You're getting a workout today."

She poured the beer into a frozen glass and brought it to me. "I heard what happened today. Are you okay?" She studied my face, looking at the damage from the ambush rather than my eyes for the truth.

"I'm fine."

"Is Rhett going to be alright?"

"I don't know. He's strong, but I know he lost a lot of blood."

"How can you just be here, like it was no big deal. I'd be home hiding in my closet. Aren't you afraid?"

"It bothers me. I tried to take a nap a few minutes ago and couldn't fall asleep. I may have a hard time sleeping tonight, but it's over. You have to move on. Look at me now, drinking a delicious cold beer with the prettiest girl in Alpine talking to me. This makes it all worthwhile."

She smiled and put her hand on mind. "Oh, Jim, there are plenty of girls prettier than me in this town."

"Konnie," the manager said and pointed to the crowd when she had Konnie's attention.

A man had taken a couple steps toward the bar and was signaling.

Konnie shot over to him. They talked for about five seconds and Konnie returned.

"He wants to pay the tab," she said to her boss.

"Good, I get nervous when they drink this much and stay this long. It's hell if we have to divvy up the tab or track down who's paying." She said it as much for me to hear as Konnie.

Konnie turned back to me as her boss tallied up the tab. "My friend's boyfriend was on the helicopter that went out to pick up Rhett. My friend asked him about you. He said you looked terrible, but you claimed you were okay."

"I was covered in Rhett's blood."

"Oh," Konnie grimaced and put both hands to her face.

"Rhett was his target, not me." I didn't add that after he shot Rhett, he fired a few rounds at me.

"Why did he want to kill Rhett?"

"I think this killer is not thinking like we do." I didn't want to get into the whole story with Konnie or anyone else at this point. I took a sip of my beer.

Konnie scurried off with the bar tab. She made a couple round trips to the crowd, giving the man a receipt and collecting more empty glasses. A few in the group left, but the majority stayed.

"It's breaking up," I said to Konnie when she leaned against the counter next to me.

"Thank heavens. That group is here every once in a while. When Mr. Sullivan is with them, he always pays. He's a good tipper, too. When he doesn't come, we've learned not to run a group tab. Seems like they can never remember who asked us to do so. Then they argue among themselves who ordered what. It's a pain."

"Is Sullivan their boss?"

"It's not really like that. A few of them work for him, but the others are loyal customers or friends. I'm not sure. They're not bad, except for the couple guys that keep touching me. I know who they are and keep my space."

"Sullivan one of them?"

"Oh heavens, no. It's two of the younger ones. What really makes me mad is that both are married." She shook her head. We watched two more of the group leave.

I received a text from Rose asking me where I was. I replied and received a response asking me to stay for a few more minutes. I assumed she was on her way, but a few minutes after the text, Deputy Anne Lanier entered the building.

"Rose asked me to come talk to you," she said. She looked at Konnie, who excused herself and went to collect more glasses and an empty beer pitcher from the group.

"She's okay," I said.

"I know, but still."

I nodded. "How's Rhett?"

"That's one reason Rose sent me over. They're now saying he's in serious but stable condition. They've taken him off the critical list."

"Good."

"He'll have to be nicer to you now. You saved his ass," Anne smiled as she said this.

"Did they locate either of the other two?"

"Not yet, and that has everyone worried."

"Jumping to conclusions, are they?"

"It's only natural. You know, are they both involved and so on."

"Yeah, I thought of that, too."

"How are you, Jim? Seriously, no lies."

"I'm shook up a little, but otherwise I'm fine. Unfortunately, I've been through this before. In another day or two, I'll be over it." I lied, and she likely knew it. Deep down this would stay with me.

"Can I get you something?" Konnie asked Anne. She had offloaded the dirty glasses on the counter next to the sink.

"How about a vodka and seven, Konnie, and you can stick around."

"How are the bosses taking all this?" I asked Anne.

"I'm not sure, but nobody is looking forward to the after action review we're sure to be going through in the near future."

"Rhett brought this on himself," I said.

"Maybe, but no one told him to stay away from the investigation. He should have been told to go home."

"If he dies, and hopefully that is off the table, I'd say people would be fired, transferred at a minimum. If he lives, I'm sure he'll say he insisted, and that you would've had to have locked him up to keep him from looking for his father's killer."

"At this point, I'm not sure that would help."

Konnie returned with Anne's drink.

"What's the feeling around town? Is everyone shook up?" Anne asked.

"That crowd isn't." Konnie motioned toward the group. They slowly made their way to the exit and left the building.

"Looks like they enjoyed themselves," Anne said.

"But it's all over social media. Of course, the two men running for sheriff against our current sheriff are playing it up like crazy," Konnie said.

"That's to be expected, but it doesn't do anyone any good," Anne said.

"I think you need to get both men in and separately interview them until one of them makes a mistake," I said.

"We're already working on search warrants, too," Anne said.

"Good. It may be nothing, but the more I try to remember more details, I'm starting to think I may have winged him with one of my last shots."

"That would have been a lucky shot at that distance," Anne said.

"I know. It's the way he jumped and I lost sight of him. It's more like he stumbled or fell. He may have simply tripped over a rock, but it happened less than a second after I fired that last round. I initially said he dove. That's what came to my mind. He wasn't trying to land on his feet. Who knows, really, but if I winged him, that would sure help us identify the right one."

"They didn't find any trace of blood."

"It poured rain out there for a good ten to fifteen minutes after all the shooting ended. Maybe longer, I don't know. Any blood would have been washed away."

"I can't believe you're letting me hear all this," Konnie said.

"You're officially helping us out in this investigation, Konnie," Anne said.

"You are desperate," Konnie said, smiling.

"No, Konnie, we need people outside the department to help us. To be our eyes and ears in the community. People we can trust," Anne said.

"I'm surprised they are talking to me," I said.

Konnie seemed to be confused for a second, then she appeared to understand. "Like Rhett, too."

Both Anne and I nodded. "You know, he tried to take me out on a date," Konnie said to Anne.

"Rhett or Jim?"

"Rhett. I don't think I want to go out with him. I want him to be okay, but I don't want to be alone with him, if you know what I mean."

"I do," Anne said.

"Now, Jim, I'd drag him back to my apartment in a minute if I wasn't afraid Rose would shoot me."

"She'd shoot us both," I said.

Chapter 40

I looked out my hotel room window. The bright sun turned the few clouds in the horizon a vivid red. Yesterday's storm had driven all the dust out of the air and made the early morning sky amazingly clear.

Rose didn't show any signs of waking up. She didn't get back from work until ten. I had a bottle of wine open and waiting for her, but all she wanted to do was go to bed.

Despite my concerns about having trouble sleeping, Rose's presence comforted me. I had slept well. Even as I stood there, staring out the window, the events of the day before had somehow been pushed to the back of my mind. I kept thinking about Rose and our relationship. I dreaded the fact that in a few days we would once again be heading in different directions. The two of us had discussed it a number of times, and I knew, at least for the near future we would have to settle on a long-distance relationship.

I didn't have any plans for the day, but finding a cup of coffee sounded like a good way to start. I put on my last clean shirt, thinking about how to get my clothes washed when Rose's phone rang.

She sat up, looked at me with bleary eyes, and reached for her phone. "Good morning, Joe," she said. She listened without speaking for a good minute. "Okay, I can do all that," she told Joe. The call ended a few seconds later.

"Trouble?" I asked.

"No. What were you doing? Getting dressed to sneak off? Is that what you do, take advantage of an innocent woman and then sneak off in the morning?" She smiled and rubbed her left eye.

"Guilty," I said. "Actually, I was running out to get us both a cup of coffee."

"Did you get much sleep last night?"

"Once you left me alone, I slept like a puppy."

She laughed. "Good. The call was from Joe. Rhett is stable and talking. They want me to get a statement from him now. The doctors want to do surgery on his shoulder this afternoon, and they'll be taking him to San Antonio for that."

"You want me to go with you?"

"Yes. I think one of the deputies will be there, too."

"Sounds good."

"So does the coffee, if you go now, I'll meet you down by my car in a few minutes."

She was standing by her car when I got there.

"That was quick," I said.

"No makeup and messy hair. I hope Rhett doesn't mind."

We arrived at the hospital a few minutes later. Deputy Tony Anaya met us and took us straight to Rhett's room. A young city police officer sat in a chair outside Rhett's hospital room.

I was surprised to see Rhett sitting with the bed propped up behind him. His shoulder was wrapped and his right arm was in a sling. A wide bandage circled his head and covered his left ear. I could see where they had shaved his head and stitched him up along the trail the bullet had taken. He looked pale, but his eyes were alert.

"I guess I owe you my thanks, Jim. If I was alone, I imagine I would be dead by now," he glanced down at his shoulder. "They've got me on a lot of pain meds."

"I was worried about your blood loss."

"Do you feel good enough to give us a preliminary statement? I'll record it," Rose said and held up her phone.

"Yes, but my mind is kind of fuzzy. Jim could tell it better."

"I know, and he has, but, as you know, we have to hear it from you, too," Rose said.

"What I do remember is the loud sound made when the round struck the windshield, and the glass cracking in a thousand places. I remember feeling a sudden, sharp pain in my chest, but I know now it must have been my shoulder. I didn't see where it came from, or who shot at us. I know I jerked the steering wheel to the right. It was a reflex, but that's all. I also have a fleeting vision of you trying to get us out of a river, but I'm not sure about that."

"Let's go back before you left to go out there. Did you phone each of the three men?" Rose asked.

"Yes. I remember all that. I talked to each of them, and scheduled Dunn first. I wanted to get to him before his daughter could get home."

I almost told him that she helped save his life, but I didn't want to break his frame of thought. As it turned out, he didn't have much more to offer.

"Do you remember driving off the road and into the ditch?" Rose asked.

"I think I remember my truck going off the road, but it's not clear. The doctor said this one is what caused me to black out." He touched the side of his head. "Even though it's a shallow wound, it put a couple small cracks in my skull. He said they should heal themselves if I take it easy for a few weeks."

"In your phone conversations with the three men, did any of them give you any idea that you might be in danger?"

"No, Rose, they all called me a few choice words, but no one said anything to alert me I was in danger."

Tony followed up with a few other questions but Rhett couldn't add anything to what he already said.

"Do you suspect one of them more than the others?" Rhett asked.

"No, but we're close to excluding Mr. Dunn," Rose said.

"Hmm…" he hesitated. "What happened to my weapon? I hope you all didn't leave it in the truck."

"We have it, but we'll be done with it later today. What do you want us to do with it?" Tony asked.

"Keep it somewhere safe. No, wait a second, give it to Jim. He can keep it for me for now. Besides, he's probably the next target. You were dumb to get involved without one anyway, Jim."

I didn't argue. He was right, but I had my reasons. I came down here to help Janice with her dealings with the authorities while she identified Pat's body. That was all. Nothing else was supposed to happen.

"I'll get it back to you," I said.

We talked for a few more minutes before the three of us left Rhett.

"He'll be leaving soon. They needed to bring him here to stabilize him. They also gave him some blood. The nurse told me the doctors were as worried about the head wound as the shoulder. Hard to believe as she also told me the shoulder and collarbone are a mess. Part of his ear is gone," Tony told us as we walked out of the hospital.

"Are they taking him to San Antonio by helicopter?" I asked.

"Yes. Driving would take four or five hours, and that's without traffic problems," he said.

Rose and I thanked him and walked to her car. He stayed at the hospital.

"We didn't learn anything we didn't already know, but I guess we had to do the interview anyway," she said.

"He looked better than I expected."

"Think he has ever been shot before?"

"No idea," I said.

"If not, he can join the club."

My eyes went to the top of her forehead. A little over a year ago, I was with her when a bullet nearly took off the top of her head. She had a permanent scar, but her hair covered it.

"What did you think of his pistol? He seems to like it a lot. Like you and your Mustangs."

"I'd never heard of the brand before. A CZ Shadow Blue, I think I have the name straight. It felt solid, and at the distance I was shooting, it was accurate. I could barely take time to aim, yet I hit the rock he was perched behind. If I had to give it a preliminary grade, I'd give it an A."

"Think Rhett would care if we took it to the range?"

"No. Why would he?"

I planned to spend as little time as I could with the team, but when we reached their bullpen, my day took a different direction. Both Lucy and her father were being interviewed separately, and everyone else I saw had their eyes glued to their computers or talked on their phones.

Texas Ranger Caleb Wilkins came up to us. "You should have stayed away," he said to both of us. "Seems like the whole country and the state are after us today. They all want to know what the hell is going on. An FBI supervisor is driving in from El Paso later today. I have a video conference call in about an hour with our deputy director. The sheriff is holding a press conference this afternoon or evening and won't coordinate it with us."

I nodded but stayed quiet. This was bound to happen.

"Special Agent Rodriquez wants to reinterview you, Jim. He doesn't want you in the room when he does, Rose. Sorry."

"Grasping at straws?"

"That's right, Jim. It doesn't smell right," Caleb said.

"They need some thing or someone to point at, even if only for a few days, to get the pressure off," I said.

"Maybe," he said.

"No way. I'll talk to him," Rose said.

"No don't. Stay out of it, please," I said.

She didn't look too happy, but just then I heard my name being called. I turned and saw Joe waving me to his office. I went, and Rose grumbled but stayed behind.

Chapter 41

Joe did his best to act like he and I hadn't talked at all since my arrival. He had a sheriff's deputy I had seen but not met with him to assist in the interview. The deputy played the "bad cop". The whole thing was a laugh. As the interview progressed, I realized my theory had been correct, Joe must have thought it would be good if they could find someone to point at even if only for a few days. They needed something to use to deflect some of the pressure they were feeling.

Near the end of the interview, the deputy became angry. We had retraced my steps since my arrival. I believe Joe felt a little embarrassed about the whole thing.

"Focusing on me is a waste of time. It's like the end of the game hail Mary pass, actually it's worse," I said.

"We had to try, you're the only outsider, and you have links to three of the victims," Joe said.

"It's one or both of the other two. It has to be," I said.

"We have the whole state looking for them. I need you to stay away from the investigation," Joe said.

"I'll be happy to," I said and meant it.

It may have dawned on him then that he had wanted me to tag along with Rhett. Doing so was never my idea. I didn't mention it as Rose had played a part in that decision. He sent me on my way.

I didn't see Rose in the large outer room. No one paid any attention to me. I walked out to the street and had taken a handful of steps toward the hotel when I heard someone call my name. I looked around and saw Bart Maverick across the road. He waved at me to join him.

"Jim, I saw it again this morning," he said when I got close.

"The demon?"

"Yes. He was close to where those two men were killed. He was looking for you. He was digging you a grave."

"This morning?"

"Yes, early, before the sun came up. I couldn't sleep last night and knew something was wrong. I realized it was pulling me there, so I borrowed one of my brother's trucks and drove there."

"How did you know where the two men were killed?"

"I knew. I saw you and the deputy there a couple days ago. He ran after me, but I hid. I wasn't doing anything wrong."

"No, you weren't. Why were you there?"

"I go there sometimes. It's where the demon buried its secret," he said.

"You mean where the two men were shot?"

"No, Jim, where I was when you saw me."

"West!" I looked over and saw Deputy Tony Anaya signaling for me to return to the other side of the road.

"Will you take me there?" I asked Bart.

"In the daylight, but he has dug you a grave."

I appreciated his concern. "We'll be careful. I'll pick you up at the restaurant where I bought you a beer. Say, in about an hour?"

"I'll be there," he said and scurried off.

I crossed over to Tony. He was watching Bart leave.

"You know that guy is a flaky," he said.

"I do. What's up?"

"I have Rhett's pistol for you. We're wanting to get rid of it, and he said to give it to you. Come inside and sign for it, please." He accentuated the word please.

"Sure." I followed him back into the building. He led me to a side room off the entrance area.

"Here it is. A nice looking pistol, I like the blue on it." He handed me the holster, the pistol, and the magazine. "It's not loaded but there are still some rounds in the clip. I didn't count them."

"Thanks, I'll make sure he gets them back."

I signed the receipt and started to leave but stopped. "Tony what are you doing today?"

"As you know, I've been taken off the case."

"No, I didn't."

"The boss is putting in a new team to help out on the investigation. Anne and I and the others have been fired. Not from the job, from the investigation. You know, the blame game."

"That's crazy," I said, and Tony lifted his palms in a "what can I say" way. "If you're free, why don't you come with me today. I'm to stay away from the case, too."

"What do you mean?" Tony asked.

"Bart Maverick wants to show me something. I think it's a fresh grave."

"Where?"

"Remember when you saw someone watching us the other day out by the murder scene?"

"That was Bart?"

"Yes. That's where this alleged grave is. At least that's my understanding. It may be nothing, but we can safely tell everyone we didn't go out there to do anything related to the case."

"But you think it might be?"

"It's admittedly a long shot," I said.

"But it's better than sitting here shuffling someone else's paperwork. When would we be going?"

"In about forty-five minutes."

"I'll drive," Tony said.

"Do you have something unmarked? I don't want to spook Bart."

"I have just the thing."

We agreed that he would pick me up at the hotel and go together to get Bart. I walked to the hotel and had a half hour to change clothes into something that would at least partially cover the pistol. Open carry is allowed in Texas, but I felt better having it tucked away.

Tony pulled up in front of the hotel in an oversized white pickup truck that must have been twenty years old. A winch fastened to the front of the truck looked strong enough to pull Rhett's truck out of the ditch, but I knew we weren't going there.

"Watch your step getting in," he called out the window.

I had no trouble climbing in, but wondered if old Bart would need help with the extra height of the truck's body.

"Does this belong to the department?"

"Yes. We use it when we need to get people out of rough areas. It's four-wheel drive, and the diesel engine will run all night."

"Did they use it to rescue Rhett's truck?"

"No, we used a local service for that. This brute is for places the service doesn't like to go. You know, where there ain't no roads," he said.

I told him where we were meeting Bart.

"Two minutes away, you know he's a bit of a nut."

"I know, but I'm curious."

"Curiosity killed the cat."

"I've heard that more than once since I've been here," I said.

Tony parked on the street about twenty yards from the

restaurant. I hopped out and went inside. He sat at the same table, drinking a cup of coffee.

"This your spot?"

"Yes, I can see out the window. He would only give me coffee. Can you buy me a beer?" Bart motioned with his eyes at the manager.

"Not now, our ride is waiting."

He looked at me suspiciously.

"Trust me. We're birds of a feather."

He grinned. "Yes, we are. Two from the wild west."

As we started to leave, the manager hustled over to us. "That'll be two bucks, Bart. You know the rules."

I handed him the three dollars, and we left.

"I'll buy the next time," Bart said. I highly doubted it. "It's good to see you're packin'." His eyes glanced at the bulge under my shirt where I had holstered the pistol.

"We're not going to let anything happen to you."

"Me? He wants you dead."

Bart said it with such conviction, a small shiver ran through me. "Front or back seat?" I asked him when we reached the truck.

"Back seat," he said and climbed in with ease. "Deputy Anaya, you get to be my chauffeur again today."

"Yes, Bart, and amazingly we're headed away from the jail not towards it."

Bart laughed.

I thought he might be hesitant with Tony along, but he appeared to genuinely enjoy his presence.

"Jim, I knew Deputy Anaya when he was in diapers. All the trouble he caused as a teenager, I never imagined he'd become a lawman."

"It surprised me, too, Bart. Now explain to me where we're going."

"Where are we going?" Bart asked.

"I want you to take us to where you saw the guy digging my grave?"

Tony glanced at me, "What?"

I held my hand up to let Tony know I'd answer him in a minute.

"You mean where the demon plans on planting you." Bart said.

I saw Tony's eyes roll, but he kept looking at the road ahead of us as he drove.

"Yes."

"You know, Deputy Anaya and the rest think I'm full of bull."

"You should also know, I don't. Help us find the spot. I'd rather not let him bury me there. Maybe we can outsmart it."

Bart's eyes twinkled, "Maybe we can at that. You and me working together can get the jump on him."

"That's the plan, but we need to see where he wants to bury me, so we can make our plan to trap him."

"It's not far from where he killed the others."

"Did you see him do the killing?" Tony asked.

"No. I don't know if he did, but I know he wants Jim here. You want to get to it from the other side."

"The other side?" I asked.

"Yes, from the other side of the hill. It's harder to see you coming, and there's a dirt road that takes you up part of the hill."

"Show me the way," Tony said.

I couldn't tell if there was any enthusiasm in his voice. He may have already started regretting his decision to come.

Chapter 42

Alex Karnes answered the door but didn't offer to let Logan Daniels in.

"What's going on? You been playing in the rain? You're soaked," Alex said.

"They're going to frame us. Ray's boy is going to frame one of us. You know that."

"He's going to try."

"Let's talk a little further from the house. They may have bugged us all," Logan said.

"You're crazy they can't do that. Besides they wouldn't hear anything but the TV at my house. There's no one here to talk to."

"Except I'm here now. Let's get closer to my car." Logan started walking toward his old Subaru wagon.

Alex shook his head but followed him. "Don't play games with me, Logan."

"Why not? You're it," he spun around and shot Alex in his chest with his large revolver. Logan watched him fall. He looked dead, but Logan leaned closer and studied Alex's open eyes. He then double checked the location of the wound. The shot had hit his heart.

"Now they'll blame you, Alex, for all that nasty killing." Logan chuckled to himself. He was really getting quite good at this. Before the blood could spread too much, he lifted the body into his trunk and placed him on the shower curtain that covered the trunk space and the two rear seats that had been folded down. "Good thing you're a little guy," Logan said to Alex after struggling to get him in and positioned on the shower curtain.

Logan pulled the rest of the curtain over him to wrap him sufficiently, so no one could look in the window and see the body. He laid a black blanket over the shower curtain and pulled the edges of the blanket to each side of the car.

No one would get the chance anyway he thought. He had the perfect plan. Although he didn't know if he had killed Rhett, he knew he had shot him. Odds are he would be dead before anyone could get to him. He was surprised the other guy, West, was that his name, was able to hit him from that range in the rain with a pistol. Lucky shot for sure, and Logan felt a little lucky as the round only grazed his leg. It still stung like the devil, but he was able to stop the bleeding and treat it himself.

He would bury Alex by the others. His body would never be found. The police would be looking for both Alex and him. Their disappearances would be suspicious; however, he would only be gone a day.

He planned on driving straight to Terlingua and have a late lunch, using his credit card. After that he would kill a few hours at a bar he liked, before checking into a cheap hotel. He would leave in the middle of the night, and drive straight to where he would bury Alex. Only then would he return home. Logan followed his plan. He felt confidant anyone looking into his whereabouts for the day would think he spent the entire day down by the Mexican border.

The police would be suspicious of him, but it would look like Alex had fled. That would put Alex as the number one suspect.

An hour before sunrise, he was back near the edge of the Big Bend National Park and digging a grave for his old friend. Logan sweated and cursed as he used a pick ax to break up the hard soil. He didn't remember the ground being so hard years ago when he buried his wife and her son here. Even the rain hadn't done much to soften the ground. Maybe, he thought, he had gotten old and weak.

Logan buried Alex with the shower curtain still wrapped around him. The grave was shallow, but deep enough where he hoped nature's scavengers wouldn't dig him up. He buried his rifle with Alex.

He didn't see any obvious signs that the police had been to his house, but he felt certain they had been. He showered and shaved. After drinking a cup of coffee, Logan thought about his situation. Something didn't feel right. Suddenly, he thought of Alex's blood. Did he get any of it on his clothes? Rather than inspect them, he gathered everything he wore the day before, except his boots, and placed them in a black, plastic trash bag. No time to lose he thought.

Logan peeked out his front window, and after ensuring no police were around, he hurried to his car. He drove to a nearby gas station where he placed the trash bag with his clothing into a dumpster. He routinely dumped his trash there.

Not ready to go home and possibly have to face the police, Logan decided to drive to a nearby diner he liked in Marathon. He could rehearse his alibi over an early lunch. Overall, he felt pretty good with how everything turned out. At lunch, he sat alone at a table by a window that faced the street. He ate a bowl of chili that he spiced up with a large helping of hot sauce and chased it down with a cold beer.

Outside on the street, he watched as a large pickup truck stopped for the one stoplight in town. Rhett's sidekick occupied the front passenger seat. Logan stretched his neck but couldn't see the driver. He started to stand when the vehicle drove off.

"Damn," he muttered to himself. Was Rhett driving the pickup truck? He couldn't be, but who else would be driving West around? Curiosity got the better of him. After leaving some money on the table, Logan hurried out to his car.

Traffic was near non-existent. Within minutes, Logan saw the large pickup in the distance. He saw it turn south, and worry began to gnaw away at his optimism. He watched as the truck carrying West turned south toward the park.

It doesn't mean anything, he tried to tell himself. He stayed nearly a mile behind. The road had few bends and fewer turnoffs. At seventy miles per hour, he was more worried about driving up on them, if they decided to take a side road somewhere, than losing them. After twenty minutes, he saw their brake lights come on. He slowed.

When they turned off onto a dirt road, Logan felt his stomach knot up. The road they took led to his secret. How could they know about it? It was possible they were simply returning to the crime scene, but there was a better way to get there. Why take a route that would require them to climb up over a rocky hill?

Logan pulled his car over to the shoulder of the road and stopped. He had to think. He didn't want them to see him out here, but if they did, he knew he could come up with some explanation. What he couldn't allow was their stumbling across a fresh grave. That would be disastrous. He would have to follow them and at least ensure they didn't find the gravesite.

He gave them five more minutes before he started his car and drove after them. He knew where he needed to go, and if they weren't there, so much the better. He placed his old reliable six-shooter on the seat next to him. If they discovered the gravesite, he would show no mercy. Both would die this time.

For the first time since following the large pickup truck, Logan wondered who might be driving it. He wondered why he was so willing to believe Rhett was the driver. He had been certain he had shot Rhett. He didn't miss. He even thought he saw Rhett's reaction to being hit.

West lived elsewhere and didn't know the area. It made sense for someone to be driving him, but why would they be out here. It could be one of the new FBI agents, but the pickup truck certainly didn't look like any FBI vehicle he had ever seen.

Chapter 43

"It's just a little further," Bart said.

The large pickup clawed its way up the steep grade. I wondered if it was going to make it to the top.

"Here, pull over here," Bart said. A small, mostly flat piece of land opened up next to the trail.

"I'm glad I grabbed this old thing to get us out here. I'm not sure a regular sedan would have gotten us up here," Tony said.

"Not a chance," Bart said. "But now we're a mere spitting distance from where we're going. Hurry now, we don't want him coming back and finding us here."

Tony rolled his eyes at me. Bart started hiking up the last fifty or so yards to the top, and we followed.

"You owe me," Tony said to me.

"I know."

Despite his age and appearance, Bart made better time to the top than we did. "It's right down there. You can see it."

We couldn't. At least not until we reached a spot next to him. Tony didn't say anything but after a brief pause, continued on to what looked to me as a freshly dug grave that had been filled in. It could have been anything, of course, but out here in the middle of nowhere, I was certain it was a grave.

"Hell, Bart, you weren't dreaming," Tony said as reached the site. "Stay back a few yards. I better call this in."

"This was done after the recent rain storm. Couldn't be more than a day old," I said.

"It's fresh," Tony said, nodding. He worked his phone. "Hey Dwight, it's Tony, I need you to contact Deputy Lanier and have her come to me with a couple of shovels –" he paused, "Yes, shovels and see if she can't bring Hoss with her. We may need his muscles. We found what could be, and let me repeat, could be a fresh grave out by the park." Again, he paused, listening to Dwight. "Yes, I know we're off that case, but this has nothing to do with that investigation. I'll drop you a pin for Anne to follow to get her here. Tell her to hurry."

"A pin?" Bart asked.

"Our GPS location," Tony replied.

"She needs to hurry. It's not safe here."

"We're okay, Bart. Both Deputy Anaya and I are carrying and reinforcements are on the way."

Despite my reassurance, Bart kept walking back and forth, watching for whatever he thought might appear.

Tony took some pictures of what we believed to be a grave and the immediate area around it. I walked a wide circle about fifteen yards from the grave studying the ground for anything out of the ordinary. I didn't see anything.

"Bart, come over here. You're making me nervous. Now tell me your whole story, demons and all," Tony said.

"My whole story?"

"What did you see? When did you see this grave being dug? Why were you out here? Why do you think West was going to be buried here? Since it wasn't Jim, who do you think it was?"

Bart looked at me.

"Tell him everything. It's okay. I believe your story," I said.

Before he could start, Tony's phone rang.

"Hey Anne, let me put you on speaker. I'm with West and Bart Maverick."

"Bart? Are you okay?"

"Yes, everything is fine. Did you see the pictures I sent you?"

"Yes. I've got shovels and Hoss. We're on our way. You know you're right next to where the two were killed. It's not our case anymore."

"There's no reason to think this has anything to do with that matter. We're simply checking out something peculiar reported by one of our citizens. That's all, understand."

"I think so. Dwight said he wasn't informing anyone else until he hears back from you. Is that okay?"

"Yes, that's perfect. See you when you get here."

The call ended. Tony looked at Bart. "Okay, tell me your story."

"This is my land. I grew up only a few miles from here. I –"

"No, Bart, how did you come to see someone digging here and why were you here? We don't need your life story."

Bart looked at Tony and then me. "That's what I'm trying to tell you. I come out here all the time. The rangers know it, and my family, of course. I saw him come here and start digging this morning."

"Who?"

Bart looked hesitantly at me.

"I believe you, Bart. The person was indeed a demon. I have no doubt of that. But for Deputy Anaya, let's refer to it as a man. Do you know his name?"

"No, it was too dark, and I was over there." Bart pointed to another rocky hill about three hundred yards away. "I heard the digging at first, but then I saw him. It was light enough. I knew it was for you, Jim. He dug the hole and left. That's when he saw me."

"He saw you?" Tony asked.

"Maybe not. I was crouched down and behind some rocks, but he looked my way. I could see that. When he walked away, I skedaddled back to town looking for you, Jim. I needed to warn you."

"Where did he go?" I asked.

"I don't know. He must've parked where we did."

"So, you don't know if he came back?"

"No, Deputy, I don't, but he must of. Who else would know to put something in this hole?"

"Good point," Tony said and wiped his forehead with the back of his hand.

"Ohhh, no!" Bart gagged the words and pointed behind me.

Chapter 44

Logan's panic almost caused him to stop breathing. They had parked right below his secret spot. The pickup was visible, but he didn't see any people. His car struck a large rock, and Logan cursed.

"Pay attention," he hissed at himself, steering the four-wheeled drive Subaru back onto the narrow dirt road. He knew he had to fix this obvious problem and do so quickly. He drove past the nearly invisible track that led to where the large pickup was parked. He knew another spot about two hundred yards down the dirt road where he could park the car. From there he would climb up to where he suspected West and his driver were. He would come at them from the side and start shooting as soon as they noticed him.

He wondered if they heard his car. It didn't matter. He had to end this now. Kill the two and figure out how to get rid of them and the pickup later. He felt confident with his large revolver in his hand.

A large rattlesnake slithered away from him as he approached. He took that as a good sign. Often a rattlesnake would coil up and dare you to come close. This one fled, and Logan took that as a sign that he was a top tier predator. He breathed deep and forced himself to relax. Stay cold, he silently told himself.

From his angle of approach, he knew he could take advantage of the terrain to get in close before they would notice him. They might also have weapons, but Logan would have the clear jump on them. If Rhett was there, he would take him out first. Then he would kill his sidekick. He remembered the name, West. He wouldn't talk to them. If they didn't die right away, he would shoot them again and again. He had stuffed extra bullets into his pants pocket, but he believed the six in the gun would be sufficient.

He heard their voices first. They weren't trying to be silent. Good, he thought. They were unaware of his presence and their impending deaths. He maneuvered around some large rocks and alongside the rock face of the hill that climbed another twenty feet.

Three of them, he didn't expect that. West, a deputy he recognized, and old Bart Maverick. So, Rhett wasn't here. He did get him. Logan grinned. Take out the deputy first, he thought. Then he would shoot West and finally Bart. The presence of the deputy worried him. He would be the biggest threat. He had to kill him quickly. They moved around the grave as he watched.

Luck again seemed to be on his side. After only another minute, both West and the deputy positioned themselves with their backs to him. Only Bart faced him. Logan wondered if the old man was even sober.

He stepped out and started walking toward the three. He raised his arm and aimed at the deputy. Patience, get closer, he told himself. Then Bart noticed him. He fired as the two others turned. He saw the blood spray off the deputy.

Chapter 45

Time slowed down. What happened in mere seconds seemed to take much longer. I saw Bart's expression change before he said anything. His eyes told me something behind me had terrified him. I barely heard him as I spun and stepped sideways away from the other two. Trying to remember it now, I'm not sure I even heard Bart's warning.

Logan Daniels walked toward us. A large revolver appeared to be suspended in air in front of him. Its aim moved to my left, and my focus broadened to more than the six-shooter. A good fifteen yards separated us. Despite the distance, I sensed, if not saw, Logan squeeze the trigger. Tony's head snapped back, and a I heard him grunt. I heard Bart start running.

Logan shifted his aim toward me. In my peripheral vision, I saw Tony collapse. The sound of the second shot kicked me into automatic. There's no other way to explain it. I didn't think about my reaction at the time. I pulled out Rhett's semi-automatic pistol, dropped into an awkward kneeling position, and started shooting back. Later they told me I had fired four rounds, all of them hitting Logan in a tight circle in the center of his chest. The first one likely killed him.

I stood up. My adrenalin had kicked in, and I took a few seconds to calm myself before moving toward Logan. I could see where the rounds had entered his body. I knew he no longer posed a threat. Despite his condition, I slid his revolver a few feet away from him with my boot.

"Is he dead?" Bart shouted. He had stopped running but still appeared hesitant to return.

"Yes. Get back here."

Tony shoved himself off the ground, but after trying to stand, he sat down on the hard ground. He looked a mess with blood running down his face.

"How are you?" I asked and walked back to him.

"I feel like I've been hit on the head with a hammer."

"Let me look," I said and bent over to take a closer look.

"I think I'm okay," he said.

"You should be. You're lucky, it looks like it barely nicked you as it went by."

"Feels like more than a nick," Tony grumbled.

"Maybe a graze," I said and grinned. "Here." I offered him my handkerchief.

He either didn't hear me or understand me. He stared past me at Logan's body.

"Did you see 'em?" Bart asked me when he finally reached us.

I knew what he meant. I didn't answer. I didn't want to.

"He's dead now," I said.

Bart looked at me, then at Tony, and finally at Logan. "He's dead," Bart said.

"Help me up," Tony said.

Both Bart and I grabbed an arm and helped him to his feet.

He took some unsteady steps toward Logan. I walked with him concerned he might fall. Bart stayed behind.

"Who do you think he buried out here?" Tony asked me.

"I have no idea. But, I'm thinking he has been behind all the killings."

"Me, too. I better call this in. Maybe get the whole team out here." Tony tried to wipe the blood away from his eyes with the back of his hand.

"Here, use this. It's clean." I handed him my handkerchief.

This time he took it and blotted and rubbed at the blood. Finally, he pressed the handkerchief against the wound and pulled his phone out of his pocket with his right hand.

"You might have some of them go to his house," I said.

"Good point."

He punched a pre-set on his cell phone.

"Sorry I ran," Bart said.

"Don't be. It was the smart thing to do," I said. I could hear Tony talking but didn't listen.

"I should've have done something to help," Bart continued.

"What could you have done?"

"I dunno. I'm glad he was a bad shot. He missed you and just nicked Deputy Anaya."

I had forgotten about the second shot.

"Me, too."

"It was him who shot at you yesterday. He missed you both days, but you sure didn't miss him." Bart walked closer to Logan's body.

I followed him. I didn't think he would touch anything but wasn't sure. He stayed a good ten feet away from Logan and slowly circled the body.

"I wonder if it died with him or has already moved on?"

"Don't know," I said. I knew what he was talking about, but I didn't want to talk about it. Logan no longer posed a threat to any of us. Whether or not he was possessed seemed irrelevant now. Still a little shiver went through my body.

"They're sending the cavalry," Tony said. "Interestingly, there's been no sign of Alex Karnes since the day before yesterday. What are the chances he might be in that grave?"

"As good as anyone else, but why?" I asked.

"Maybe he knew something. Who knows?" Tony said.

"Makes as much sense as anything else. You know, while I can't see any motive for any of this, I keep thinking it's obvious."

"Obvious? Well, if this obvious motive pops into your mind please share it with me. In the meanwhile, stay here and protect the scene from the critters. I need to get the first aid kit out of the truck." He started to walk away.

"Bart, go with him," I said. I didn't think he'd have any trouble walking to and from the truck, but I didn't want him to get dizzy and trip.

Bart got the message and hurried after him.

I watched them as they walked down the hill and out of sight. Thinking about what Bart had said made me wonder what was wrong with me. I may be lucky, but it also seemed I brought a lot of bad luck to anyone being with me. I promised myself to never get involved in something like this again.

My phone buzzed in my pocket.

"Jim, are you alright?" Rose asked before I could say anything.

"I think so. Tony got shot, but he'll be fine. He'll have a scar like yours but much smaller." I instantly thought I shouldn't have said that. "And, no one can even see your scar."

"Ha! So it was Daniels."

"I think so. We have a fresh grave out here."

"But why bury this one when he didn't bury the others?"

"Who knows, but it has to be him. Nothing else makes sense."

"None of this made or makes sense," Rose said.

"Unfortunately, Logan won't be able to explain it all to us now either."

"You had no choice, Jim."

Tony must have told them in his last phone call. Of course, he had to, but still, a part of me wanted no one to know I had killed him.

"He did shoot first," I said.

"Don't dwell on it right now. Has Anne arrived?"

"No, but I think she should be here any minute."

"Okay. I called because I wanted to talk to you. I'm glad you're okay and that this thing may be coming to an end."

"Me, too," I said, and Rose ended the call.

Emotions are a funny thing. I didn't feel any guilt over shooting Logan. I didn't feel any remorse that he was dead. I didn't care anymore about why he tried to kill us. I felt like crawling into bed and sleeping for as long as they would let me.

Chapter 46

"Jim, Anne will be here in a minute. You can see their car." Tony pointed, but I couldn't see it from where I was. "I'll wait here. Do you want to see if you can locate his car? Bart says he thinks he knows where Logan must have parked."

"Sure," I said, despite not wanting to do anything at the moment.

"Are you okay, Jim?"

"Yeah, sorry Bart, my mind was elsewhere for a few seconds."

"Hell, Jim, my mind is most always elsewhere," he chuckled to himself. "Come on. I'll show you where."

I followed him around the side of the hill and down a mild slope for about fifty yards. The sight of an old Subaru helped me refocus my mind.

"I knew it," Bart said. "When I didn't see his car by the truck, I knew that it would be here."

"Very good." I didn't believe it would disappear, but I snapped a few pictures of it in case. "We better not touch it. The crime scene people will want to go over every inch of it. He must have transported the person or the body up here in the car."

"Think he was behind all the killings?"

"Yes, I do, Bart, but I don't understand why."

"Cause he's nuts. People think I'm nuts. And I might be, a little," Bart giggled. "To kill a bunch of people, you have to be really nuts. There may be no logic to all this."

"You're right." I put my hand on his shoulder and he smiled back at me.

"Told you we'd make a good team," Bart said.

"That's where the other two were killed. Isn't it?" I asked and then wondered why I was asking Bart. I thought I could see the police tape about a hundred yards away.

"Yeah, it sure is."

"Let's go tell Tony we found his car." On the hike back, I saw the Gila monster sunning himself on a small ledge on the side of the hill.

Bart saw it, too, and instinctively took a step back. "Look at that. I've never seen one of those."

"He's been hanging around here. He probably wanted to see how this case turned out, too."

By the time we returned, Deputy Anne Lanier and another deputy were walking into view. Tony had already walked a dozen or so yards toward them. They greeted each other, and all three approached Bart and me.

"We left the shovel and other tools in the jeep," Anne said as they approached. "They're sending the first team up here to check out the grave. Let me look at that wound."

Without arguing Tony leaned forward and allowed Anne to inspect it. He had already taped some gauze over it. She peeled back the tape. "A few stitches, nothing more." She pressed the tape back down. It looked to me the tape and gauze would fall off at any moment.

Tony grinned at her. "She's our designated medic," he said to me in way of an explanation.

"Ha! I trained to be an EMT before joining the sheriff's team. How are you doing, Jim?" She asked me, but her eyes went to the body on the ground.

"I'm okay. Better than him. Wish he was alive, so we could ask him a few questions. At the time, though, I didn't think about that."

"What I hear was he was already shooting at you."

"That's true. We're lucky he wasn't a great shot, and that Jim was," Tony said.

"Bart located his car. It's an old Subaru down that side of the hill about a minute's hike," I pointed in the direction to the car.

"Mack, want to head down there and keep an eye on it until the team gets here. Don't touch anything," Anne said.

"He's a big guy," I said as Mack lumbered off.

"A rookie. He'll make a good deputy if he sticks with it," Tony said.

"You know, we're right next to where Ray and Pat were killed," I said.

Tony and Anne both looked around. "It should be out here somewhere," Tony said.

"You can see it from right over here," Bart said and took a dozen or so steps away, pointing to the original crime scene.

Both deputies followed him.

"This can't be a coincidence," Anne said.

I didn't think so either. "But why didn't he bury the other two?"

"He didn't want to drag them back up here. It's too far," Bart said.

At first, I thought he didn't make sense. Then it did, but I kept my thoughts to myself. I looked at Bart. He was staring at me.

"It may not be my place, but I recommend you have the experts check around here for other bodies buried long ago." I moved my hand in a circle, indicating the area around the new grave. I tried not to look back at Bart, but in the corner of my eye I caught him nodding.

Anne finally convinced Tony to wait in the air-conditioned truck. She asked Bart and me to go along to "keep him there," until the team arrived. Once we got the air conditioning going inside the truck, keeping any of us there was not a problem.

The team arrived in a caravan of four vehicles and parked next to us. They came prepared. I saw the medical examiner climb out of the crime scene van. In all, I counted thirteen men and women. Some carried briefcases, a few had digging tools, and two had rifles. Both of the local FBI agents and the Texas Ranger had shown up.

Special Agent Joe Rodriquez approached us and after taking a quick look at Tony's wound, instructed him to lead them to the scene. Everyone followed Tony up the hill. Bart and I tagged along behind them.

After pointing out Logan and what we believed to be a grave, Tony briefed the group on the day's events. I thought he did a thorough job.

"Anything to add?" Joe asked me when Tony had finished answering a few follow-up questions.

"Only that if there is a body down there," I motioned to the grave, "I suggest you try to find out if any other bodies have been buried nearby."

"Any reason you think there may be?"

"It's the only way this makes any sense. Why bring the body here? Why kill the two down there?" I pointed in the direction of the original crime scene.

"What's over there?" Joe asked.

"It's where the first two were shot," Tony said.

"Damn," Joe mumbled and shook his head. "Okay, let's get to work. West, take Deputy Anaya back to Alpine to see a doctor. We've got it from here. Take him, too." By him, I knew he meant Bart.

Chapter 47

Tony insisted we go back to the office first. It made sense, we each had statements to get down in writing. He also had Logan Danels' revolver to log into evidence. They kept Rhett's CZ Shadow Blue 9mm, too. I doubted if I'd see it again.

"They're insisting I head to the hospital now. Come on, I'll drop you off at the hotel," Tony said after my interview finished.

"How about Bart?"

Tony smiled, "They can't shut him up long enough to finish his statement. He may be a while. Don't worry, he's not in any trouble. We gave him to a rookie. It'll be good experience for the kid, but it might take him all day."

As we walked out of the building, a delivery guy entered carrying a McDonald's bag and a soda.

"Bart's lunch," Tony said and grinned.

I smiled, too. "Good for him. He was a critical piece to all this." I meant it but doubted many would agree with me.

Once at the hotel, I sent Rose a text asking her where she was. I didn't get an immediate response, so I showered and stretched out on the bed. My goal was to do some deep breathing exercises while telling myself that everything was fine. Somehow, I dozed off for about twenty minutes before my phone buzzed on the nightstand next to me. It vibrated a second time, and I reached for it, seeing it was from Rose.

"Still at the house. Going through everything twice. They found our third guy where you were earlier today. How are you??" I read her text twice. So, it was Alex Karnes' grave we found on that hill.

"I'm fine, no need to worry about me." I replied in a text.

The motive behind all the murders seemed to get more complicated. Logan had to be the killer. He had to be, but why? I didn't dwell on it very long. The team would piece it together over the next few days. What they couldn't didn't really matter anyway.

I didn't have anything left to do. Hopefully, my involvement in the investigation had come to an end. I did wonder about Bart's comments and whether there might be another body or two buried up there.

Outside, I put on my sunglasses and took a short walk to the Beef and Beans restaurant. I sat by the window and watched people go up and down the street as I munched on a hamburger. Konnie happened to walk by, so I rapped on the window with my knuckles.

She looked at the window and saw me. She reacted like she had been looking for me and hurried into the restaurant.

"Jim, how are you doing?" she asked and gave me a hug.

"You've heard?" I guess I wasn't surprised.

"Yes, but only bits and pieces. You got shot at again and you had to …." She let her words trail off. Her eyes looked like they might tear up.

"I'm fine," I lied.

"No, you aren't. How could you be."

"I'd rather not discuss it right now. How has your day been."

She took the hint. "My day has sucked, too."

"What happened?"

"I think I officially broke up with my boyfriend."

"Oh, sorry."

"Don't be. Rose said she wants me to meet someone. I told her

I had already met you. To that she said hands off," Konnie grinned at her own sense of humor.

"She's playing matchmaker, is she?

"I hope so. She also told me that if I see you today to buy you a couple beers. She's paying. I think she's a little concerned about you. She didn't say why, but the gossip mill has filled in most the gaps."

"Has the gossip mill given you any clue why Alex Karnes may have killed anyone?"

"Not yet, but give it time. By tomorrow, I'm sure theories will start popping out all over the place."

"Hopefully someone will have a theory that pans out," I said.

"After you finish your hamburger, come over to Spirits, please. Rose said everyone will be working until real late. She wants me to help out by keeping you company until she shows up."

"Okay, I'll be there.

"Thanks. Gotta run," Konnie said and left.

Rose's concern was understandable. I didn't think it was necessary, but I knew a few beers wouldn't hurt me. Konnie must have texted her right after she left me, because a text from Rose showed up on my phone a minute later.

"Things are going crazy here. I'll be really late. Glad you are having a beer. I told K that I would pay for them. I also told her to behave." She finished the text with a smiley face emoji.

By the time I finished eating, I had mixed emotions about going to the Spirits and Sandwiches deli. A large part of me didn't want to talk to anyone. If I hadn't already told Konnie I'd come, I probably would've gone back to the hotel. If I was free to leave town, I'd get in my car and head home.

The happy hour crowd had filled most of the tables in Spirits. Konnie motioned me to come to the bar. I sat on a stool, and she placed a waiting beer in front of me. I glanced around the room and realized most of the customers were looking at me.

"Well, this is awkward," I said to Konnie.

"Ignore them. They won't bother you. Everyone in town has heard by now. You're kind of a celebrity right now."

"I don't feel like one."

"Did Rose text you?"

"Yes, she said they would all be working late tonight. Did you know Alex Karnes?"

"No. He lived out of town, and he was a lot older than me. I can't remember if I ever met him," she said.

"You may not have."

"Why did he kill everyone?"

"That's the one thing they'd like to find out. They know the who, when, where, and how. It's the why that remains the mystery."

"Someone said they saw a helicopter going out there. It supposedly flew in from El Paso with some experts at finding buried bodies."

"How in the world do you find out things like that so fast?"

"You know I can't divulge my secrets." She grinned and winked at me.

It didn't surprise me. Many small towns have a very efficient, informal information sharing network. Social media has made it a science.

No one bothered me, and Konnie kept me company talking about how the mayor and the sheriff had been bragging all day about solving the case.

"Hey, Jim," a woman's voice came from behind me.

"He doesn't want to be bothered," Konnie said.

I turned and saw Lucy. "She's okay," I said to Konnie. "Lucy, what can I do for you? Is everything okay with your dad?"

"Yes, for the most part. He's really mixed up right now. He doesn't want to believe what has happened, but he'll be fine."

"I think everyone knows that he wasn't involved in any way."

"It's not that. Everyone in his group of friends is now dead. They were killed by one of the others in his group. He's like the lone survivor."

"He is," I said.

"He also believes Logan was trying to frame him when he tried to kill you and Rhett yesterday."

"I think he's right," I said, wondering if that was only yesterday.

"Rumor has it that you had to shoot him?"

I nodded.

"Are you going to be okay?" she asked.

"I'll be alright."

"Well, I won't bother you anymore. A friend of mine told me you were here. I wanted to come by to thank you. I also wanted to make sure you were okay."

"I am," I said. She surprised me by hugging me before she left to sit at a table with three other women.

"Do I need to warn Rose?" Konnie asked.

"No, she's Carl Dunn's daughter. The lone survivor in the group of five. Her dad was a possible suspect at one time. Now, he's the only one left alive."

Konnie looked like she didn't fully understand what I meant.

"She's married, and you know if I was going to breakup with

Rose, I already have a replacement in mind." I tried to give her my best conspiratorial smile.

"You know I can't wait forever, Jim," she said, teasing me back.

I spent another hour sipping on beer and listening to Konnie tell me the latest gossip about half the men and women in the deli.

Rose didn't get back to the hotel until nearly ten o'clock. I was still awake, watching an old movie on television. She told me they had found two more graves but didn't know the details. We both believed the discovery could be the break we needed to get to the motive behind the killings.

Chapter 48

"Jim, Jim, wake up," Rose said.

"What, what happened?" I mumbled still half asleep.

"You were having a dream. I think you were having a nightmare. You were talking and started thrashing about."

I sat up. "Sorry if I woke you up."

"I'm fine. Anything you want to talk about?"

"Not now, besides my dream was a blur."

"About being shot at?"

"You are a persistent one," I said and kissed her.

She gently pushed me away. "Well, was it?"

"Yes, but it didn't make any sense."

"Roll over and go back to sleep," she said. I did, and she snuggled up against my back.

"You know how it is," I said. She didn't answer. I felt her kiss the back of my neck. We'd both been here before, getting shot and shot at.

Her alarm woke us both up. She suggested I come in for the morning briefing scheduled for ten. By then, the team would've been able to compile all the results from the day before into one succinct briefing. I told her I'd be there.

My breakfast consisted of a cinnamon roll and two cups of coffee. The lone person behind the counter kept looking at me as though he wanted to ask me something. Finally, as he refilled my coffee cup, he asked, "Were you involved in that stuff yesterday?"

"Yes, briefly."

"I heard they found three graves. Is that right?"

"I'm not part of the investigative team. What I know is limited and unofficial."

"So?"

His question made me smile. "So, I can only say that I heard the same thing."

"I can't believe my little hometown has a serial killer. Wait 'til my brother hears this. He's in the army in Korea right now."

"I think they'll be a press conference later today to confirm or deny these rumors. You might want to hold off on telling him."

"If I do, someone else will tell him before me." He started fiddling with his phone.

"And the word is had, not has, a serial killer," I said. I figured he was already sending his brother a message.

"Whatever," he mumbled softly to himself.

Typical, I thought. Technology has sped up the transmission of gossip but not its accuracy.

A hot breeze smacked me in the face when I walked out of the coffee shop. During the half hour I spent inside, the bright sun had eliminated any touch of cool air the night had left behind. I ignored the morning heat and walked a mile before going to the sheriff's office.

People I had not seen before filled almost every square of the conference room. Anne saw me and pulled me into one of the side offices. Most of the original team sat or stood around a conference table that sat eight people.

"Come in, Jim, we're just tying up loose ends before the briefing. I have two questions for you," Special Agent Joe Rodriquez said.

"Sure," I said and moved to stand by Tony. I saw Rose signal me in a way I thought she was offering me her seat. I shook my head.

"Why did you approach Deputy Anaya and ask him to take you up to the sight where you found the first grave?"

"Bart Maverick, a local resident told me he saw someone digging what he thought was a grave up there a little before dawn. He was very adamant about what he saw. Since Deputy Anaya was off this case, and I had no involvement, I thought it might be interesting to find out if a body had been buried up there. It would be a simple enough task."

"Did you think it might be related?"

"No," I lied. "I actually didn't believe that Bart saw anything, but, like I said, it would be easy to check out. However, once I saw the grave and realized how close it was to the first two killings, I did begin to wonder."

"Did you know Logan Daniels followed you up there?"

"Not until I saw him."

"Did you suspect him?"

I felt like saying that was four questions, not two, but didn't. "Yes and no. I thought either Daniels or Karnes had to be the killer. It was a matter of elimination. However, I didn't suspect he was following us or that we would encounter him up there. That came as a surprise, a bad surprise."

"Who shot first?" Joe asked. He must have decided to double check what I had already said in my statement.

"Logan did. He came from behind Tony and me. Luckily, Bart saw him. We turned and Logan fired. I saw Tony go down, and I started shooting back."

"Did you warn him first?"

"No."

Joe nodded. "I wouldn't have either, but there will be people who will ask why not."

"I should add that he did shoot at me, too. Maybe a second before I started shooting at him."

"Good enough, thanks."

I saw Rose smile at me.

"Okay, team, any last questions or comments before we go out?"

Everyone stood up and left the room. Anne and I followed them out.

"We can stand in the back," she said.

The briefing was short and concise. The questions afterwards were not. Both Special Agent Joe Rodriquez and the sheriff handled the questions. I found it interesting that only a few in the audience represented the press. Most were state and county officials, and a few were representatives from federal agencies.

The investigation had moved quickly in the last twenty or so hours. I learned that in addition to the team finding Alex Karnes in the grave we discovered, they also found the rifle that Logan had used to try to kill Rhett and me. They had determined that the revolver he fired at Tony and me was the same gun used to kill Alex. They also found two older graves near the new one which held the remains of a woman and a teenage boy yet to be identified. They seemed to be optimistic in being able to identify the two bodies.

When the questioning stopped and the briefing terminated, people still wanted to linger. Rose and I didn't. We wandered outside and walked around the block. I knew right away something was bothering her.

"Today, we'll be wrapping up everything that we've done into something neat and tidy. There's still a lot of work to do, but the pressure is off. I get to fly that neat and tidy report with pictures back to DC tomorrow. Before you ask, yes, it will all go electronically, too. But the seniors in the FBI prefer someone walk them through everything in person, rather than read everything themselves."

"Makes sense, but why can't their staff there do that?"

"Because they can make me do it. You know, right from the horse's mouth. I need to go back there sooner or later anyway."

"A pretty horse at that."

"I don't want to go. Not that soon," she said.

I put my arm around her shoulders and squeezed, almost making her stumble. "I don't want you to go either."

"I better get back inside," she said when we finished the block. "At six tonight, the team has Spirits reserved for a celebration. It may get crazy, but I think we should go. Will you meet me there? I may not be able to break loose any earlier."

"I'll be there."

Chapter 49

Rose sent me a text at noon. She reminded me of the gathering at Spirits at six. She also said she wouldn't be able to break away until then. Her text helped me decide on my plans for the day. Someone else deserved to be brought up to speed on the investigation.

I drove to Nessy's diner with my Mustang's top down. Maybe it's just me, but driving in a convertible can be reinvigorating. The hot sun competed with the car's air conditioning, both losing out to the wind blowing all around me. Traffic remained light. I thought I got lost once but finally reached my destination. Two beat-up pickups sat next to each other in the small parking lot.

Inside, four men occupied a corner table. They reminded me of old ranch hands. I didn't see Nessy or Angel, so I grabbed a seat at the same table we used when I was there with Rhett. A few seconds later Nessy came out of the kitchen with a large tray full of food.

She smiled when she saw me but continued on to serve the food to the men. She talked to them for a few minutes, laughing at something one of them said.

"Jim, it's nice to see you again. I hear you've had an interesting few days. I'm glad you're doing okay," she said as she approached.

I stood up. "I'm fine. I wanted to bring you up to speed on everything, but it sounds like you're pretty well caught up."

"Not on any of the details. Carl came out last night and told me Logan had killed Ray and the others. He said he had no idea why. He did say you had to shoot him, because he tried to kill you, too."

"That's true."

"Please sit down and let me get you some lunch. I'll send Angel out with a menu. She'll want to see you, too."

I sat down. She must have taken that for a yes. She hurried back to the kitchen. Seconds later, Angel came out with a menu and a glass of ice water.

"Mr. West, I'm so happy you returned."

"Please, call me Jim." I hadn't expected my arrival would have the impact it did.

For the next hour, I ate my hamburger and discussed the investigation with both of them. They had to take a couple breaks to take care of the men in the corner and another three men who came in for lunch. Otherwise, they stayed at my table asking a lot of questions.

They both thanked me over and over again as I got up to leave. I had come out mostly for the car ride and as a diversion to get my mind straight. I thought bringing them up to speed on the investigation would be a nice thing to do. Both women had lost a good friend, and I doubted anyone else would be in a hurry to fill them in on the details. However, I hadn't anticipated how much they would appreciate it.

I felt good driving back. Better than I had at any time since I shot Logan. I had been in gunfights before, been stabbed, and beat up, but this was different. Having trouble sleeping after those past events, like what I'd gone through the last couple days, had to be expected. Sure, I dreamt about being shot at again. One would think that would be bad enough, but that wasn't what had me worrying about my mind.

In my dreams, I see Logan aim at me and pull the trigger. The action is always moving in slow motion, but my eyes are no longer focused on the gun. I'm staring at his face. A face that contorts like in that painting The Scream. Suddenly, his eyes turn a deep red and glow. That's what wakes me up. It's a dream I tell myself, simply a dream, but then I remember looking back at Bart. He is staring at me. Bart knows I saw what he saw, and he smiles.

The celebration at Spirits and Sandwiches rocked late into the night. Most everyone in law enforcement was there having a good time along with several EMS personnel. Joe bought a round, and then the sheriff bought a round. Someone from the mayor's staff bought a third round. After that, people were on their own, but that didn't slow the crowd.

Rose sat on a stool at the bar, and I stood next to her. After about an hour, those who only came to make an appearance started to leave. Rose and I found a free two-person table. We were both enjoying the celebration, but neither of us could shake the realization that tomorrow we'd be heading in different directions. We didn't talk about it. We had done that several times over the past year and a half.

"Look at that," Rose said and hit me on the arm to make sure I was paying attention.

I saw the younger of the two FBI agents sitting at the bar, laughing at something Konnie had said. They both leaned in so their heads would be close together,

"Are you responsible for that?"

"Yes. I love it. Konnie needed someone new, and poor Sid hadn't met anyone in town yet. It didn't take much persuasion with either of them," Rose said.

"Think there's a future there?"

"I do. I hope so, anyway. Did I introduce you to Sid?"

"I think so. He came out to where Rhett and I got ambushed. I saw him a few other times but didn't remember his name."

"He's a nice guy. Can you believe he has two years more FBI experience than I have? He can't be more than twenty-six or twenty-seven."

On our way out, Rose couldn't resist stopping by the bar to say good bye to Sid and Konnie.

"Yes, another successful match," she laughed when we were outside.

"Good for them," I said and meant it.

"Cheer up," she put her arm around my waist and squeezed.

That night I slept better. We talked for an hour about our future before falling asleep. Dreams of gunfights and demons were replaced with dreams of future vacations with Rose.

Chapter 50

The drive home seemed to take longer than the drive down to Alpine. I looked forward to getting home, whereas, I hadn't wanted to go help Janice. The wind picked up when I crossed into New Mexico, and a large tumbleweed rolled across the road ahead of me. A road runner sprinted behind it.

I had the radio on, but mostly ignored it. In my mind, I kept seeing Pat and Janice. I felt bad about their deaths, but my thoughts focused more on when they were alive. What had caused Pat to change so much? I knew it would forever remain a mystery,

I passed a sign that told me I still had thirty miles to Clovis when Deputy Anne Lanier called. We spent a few seconds in small talk.

"Listen, Jim, I called to tell you we got a big break on the case. We think we know the motive."

"That would be fantastic," I said.

"You know the two bodies we found near where he buried Alex Karnes. One was a woman and one a boy. They think he might have been a young teenager. They both were buried in their clothes which had deteriorated over the years. Well, in a thorough inspection of the boy's clothing they found a very thin wallet. They somehow missed it the first time."

"That can happen."

"The only things in the wallet were a five-dollar bill and a homemade identification card."

"Who was he?"

"That's the interesting part. The kid had covered up the last name and had handwritten over it on some white correction tape. It took the guys a little while to get to the hidden name, and it turned out to be Daniels."

"His son?"

"We don't know that for sure, but you haven't heard the best part. The card also has an address in Artesia, NM."

"That is a major break."

"The obvious theory is that Logan buried the two there years ago. No one here remembers him ever having a family."

"The team will have to do some research, but it shouldn't be that hard. I bet the kid covered up his last name because he was mad at his dad. That may indicate there were some family problems," I said.

"Yes. Everyone here is excited. Our best guess is that when Logan looked at Pat's map, he thought it led to where he had buried the two."

"Or very close to it. Too close for his comfort."

"It's always good to tie up loose ends. I can't wait to tell Rose, although she likely knows already. She should be in the air right now. Oh, one more thing, Logan had a wound on his leg. They think it was from a bullet grazing it," Anne said.

"So, I did hit him. That made him fall. He didn't dive out of sight. He fell."

"That's everyone's guess. Further evidence that he was the one who attacked you and Rhett. Not that we need it."

We talked for a few minutes more.

Twenty minutes later, I drove into my driveway. Home, sweet home, I thought. Chubbs, my loyal mutt, was happy to see me.

"Don't worry," I said as I sat down on my couch and petted him. "I'm not going to get involved in another situation like that."

I was serious. I didn't want anything more to do with death or demons. I didn't want to think or dream about them.

It may have been my imagination, but I thought Chubbs rolled his eyes at me. I don't think he believed a word I said.

Title: *Dead Men Can Kill*™

- Author: Bob Doerr
- Publisher: TotalRecall Publications, Inc.
- Paper Back: ISBN: 978-1-59095-759-2
- Book: ISBN: 978-1-59095-761-5
- Number of pages: 320
- Publication: December 8, 2009

When Jim West, a former Air Force Special Agent with the Office of Special Investigations, moves back to New Mexico, his goal is simple: start an easy going second career as a professional lecturer on investigative techniques to colleges and civic organizations. He never envisioned that his practical demonstration of forensic hypnosis on stage with a state university student would stir up memories of an 18-year old murder mystery. When the student is murdered three days later, West finds himself ensnared in a web of intrigue that pits him and the small town's authorities against a ruthless, psychotic killer.

An aggressive reporter for the town newspaper seeks out West for help with the story, but after one of her co-workers is murdered, she quickly aligns her efforts with West and the Sheriff. As West works closely with her, he begins to wonder if this could be the first real relationship for him since his devastating divorce a few years earlier.

The killer, though, has other plans for the reporter and the story takes fascinating twists and turns, leading to an inevitable, riveting confrontation.

Look out for a new hero on the mystery/thriller landscape! Jim West, retired military investigator, is resourceful, intuitive, pragmatic and always competent. All of West's abilities are tested when he matches wits with psychopathic serial killer William White, a man whose appreciation for murder is surpassed only by his delight in domination. Bob Doerr has crafted a must-read addition to the genre in Dead Men Can Kill, which evolves from absorbing story to absolute page-turner as West closes in on a killer who is supposedly dead. Highly recommended!

> --*Dallin Malmgren, author of...*
> *The Whole Nine Yards The Ninth Issue Is This for a Grade?*

A Jim West™ Mystery/Thriller Book 1

Title: *Cold Winter's Kill*™

- Author: Bob Doerr
- Publisher: TotalRecall Publications, Inc.
- Paper Back: ISBN: 978-1-59095-763-9
- Book: ISBN: 978-1-59095-764-6
- Number of pages: 288
- Publication: Dec 8, 2009

Cold Winter's Kill is a fast-paced thriller that takes place in the scenic mountains of Lincoln County, New Mexico and throws Jim West into a race against time to stop a psychopath who abducts and kills a young blonde every Christmas...

It was one of those phone calls former Air Force Special Agent Jim West never wanted to receive--an old friend calling to ask if he could drive down to Ruidoso, New Mexico to help locate his daughter who has disappeared while on a ski trip with friends. Jim found himself heading to Ruidoso even though he believed, much like the local authorities, that if she had gone missing in the mountains in December, her survival chances were slim. He didn't want to be there when they found her, but still he drove on.

Once in Ruidoso, Jim discovers a sinister coincidence that changes everything. It appears that someone is abducting and killing one young blond every year around Christmas. The race is on--can Jim locate his friend's daughter in time? But why is this happening and who's doing it?

Jim can't wait for the local authorities to raise the priority of their search, or for the pending blizzard to pass. In his haste he puts himself in the killer's sights. Will he, too, suffer from a cold winter's kill?

"**GREAT SUSPENSE!** In *Cold Winter's Kill* Bob Doerr grabs your attention from the beginning and holds it until the last sentence. Hard to put down!"

> *--Shelba Nicholson*
> former Women's Editor, *Texarkana Gazette*

A Jim West™ Mystery/Thriller Book 2

Title: *Loose Ends Kill*™

- Author: Bob Doerr
- Publisher: TotalRecall Publications, Inc.
- Paper Back: ISBN: 978-1-59095-718-9
- Book: ISBN: 978-1-59095-719-6
- Number of pages: 288
- Publication: Oct 27, 2010

LOOSE ENDS KILL is a fast-paced mystery/thriller that takes place in the historic city of San Antonio, Texas, and throws Jim West into the middle of a police investigation of the murder of an old friend's wife. The police already believe they have the killer in custody – West's friend.

West is drawn into this mystery by a call from the old friend who requests his assistance. West agrees to help his friend and digs deep to try to find another suspect. In the process he soon discovers that he is being followed and targeted for harassment, but by whom?

West quickly discovers that he didn't know his old friend's wife as well as he thought. To his surprise, he learns that she has had a number of affairs dating back for more than a decade. In fact, while investigating the murder, he realizes that his friend and he may be the only two people unaware of her philandering behavior.

Theorizing that one of her lovers could have had just as much motive as her husband, West starts turning over the rocks identifying one lover after another. In doing so, West unintentionally ignites an outbreak of more death and mayhem. The police and his friend's lawyers want West to go back home. The police even threaten to arrest him.

Soon, West believes the real killer wants him gone or dead. Deciding the only way to resolve the case before the outside pressures force him to leave, he sets a trap for the killer using himself as bait. However, he soon learns he may have only outsmarted himself.

A Jim West™ Mystery/Thriller Book 3

Title: *Another Colorado Kill*™

- Author: Bob Doerr
- Publisher: TotalRecall Publications, Inc.
- Paper Back: ISBN: 978-1-59095-785-1
- Book: ISBN: 978-1-59095-786-8
- Number of pages: 288
- Publication Date: September 06, 2011

It was supposed to be a short, fun golf outing, but when Jim West and his friend Edward "Perry" Mason stumble across a dead body in a restroom at a rest stop along I-25, things turn bad and then only get worse.

With the golf outing shot, West intends to stay in Colorado Springs only for a day or two. However, when two more murder victims turn up – one with West's name handwritten in her notebook - the heat on West skyrockets. The police instruct him to stick around, and soon he discovers that while the police may want to pin the crimes on him, the killer wants him out of the picture. Way out – like dead.

West's only ally is Lieutenant Michelle Prado, a tall red head with large green eyes that captivate West. Assigned to keep an eye on West, Lieutenant Prado decides the best way to do so is to keep him close. West and Prado do their own digging into the investigation. In the process, Jim wonders how close their relationship will evolve.

It seems to West that as the police focus less on him, the killer intensifies his focus on him. Barely surviving an initial confrontation, West realizes he must take the initiative. If he doesn't, or perhaps even if he does - he may end up as just another Colorado kill.

A Jim West™ Mystery/Thriller Book 4

Title: *No One Else To Kill*™
- Author: Bob Doerr
- Publisher: TotalRecall Publications, Inc.
- Paper Back: ISBN: 978-1-59095-423-2
- eBook: ISBN: 978-1-59095-424-9
- Number of pages in the finished book: 352
- Publication Date: December 4, 2012

2013
Eric Hoffer Award
WINNER
Excellence in
Independent
Publishing

No One Else to Kill, **Bob Doerr, TotalRecall Publications** - In this newest book in the popular Jim West series, Mr. West finds himself stood up and out of town. Looking forward to some R & R he keeps his reservation at the remote hunting lodge. Located in the Pecos Wilderness area in New Mexico it's a hunter's haven. Expecting to do nothing other than relax, he has no idea what the rest of the weekend holds for him. When a murder takes place, the hotel guest are detained and no one is beyond suspicion. The sheriff is called in, and while the investigation is underway, a second murder takes place. Both crimes are clearly related, but by whom and why? With time running out and unable to find a motive, the legal experts seek Jim's help.

2013
da Vinci Eye
FINALIST
Eric Hoffer Award
Excellence in
Independent Publishing

The cover for *No One Else To Kill* **is a 2013 finalist for the da Vinci Eye award.**

Bob's four previous novels in the series are titled *Dead Men Can Kill, Cold Winter's Kill, Loose Ends Kill,* and *Another Colorado Kill.* The latter two were selected as Eric Hoffer Award finalists for 2010 and 2011, respectively.

Bob Doerr's *No One Else To Kill* was awarded the Grand Prize in the "Books With Out Publishers" writing contest at www.ultimateherocontest.com

A Jim West™ Mystery/Thriller Book 5

Title: *Caffeine Can Kill*™
- Author: Bob Doerr
- Publisher: TotalRecall Publications, Inc.
- Paper Back: ISBN: 978-1-59095-562-8
- eBook: ISBN: 978-1-59095-563-5
- Number of pages in the finished book: 240
- Publication Date: 2017

This Jim West mystery/thriller, the sixth in the series, finds Jim traveling to the Texas Hill Country to attend the grand opening of a friend's winery and vineyard. Upon arriving in Fredericksburg, Jim witnesses a brutal kidnapping at a local coffee shop. The next morning while driving down an unpaved country road to the grand opening, he comes across an active crime scene barely a quarter mile from his friend's winery. A Fredericksburg policeman who talked to Jim the day before at the kidnapping scene recognizes Jim and asks him to identify the body of a dead young woman as the woman who was kidnapped. Jim does, and as a result of this unwelcome relationship with the police is asked the next morning to identify the body of another murdered person as the man who had kidnapped the young woman. A third murder throws Jim's vacation into complete disarray and draws Jim and a female friend into the sights of one of the killers.

A Jim West™ Mystery/Thriller Book 6

Title: *Greed Can Kill*™

- Author: Bob Doerr
- Publisher: TotalRecall Publications, Inc.
- Paper Back: ISBN: 978-1-59095-731-8
- eBook: ISBN: 978-1-59095-741-7
- Number of pages in the finished book: 280
- Publication Date: 2017

This adventure finds Jim traveling to Fabens, TX, in an effort to locate an old acquaintance who had written Jim a cryptic letter asking for his help in finding a briefcase. In Fabens, he discovers that someone has murdered his friend. Jim provides a copy of the letter to the local police explaining that he has no idea where the briefcase is or how to decipher the sets of numbers provided in the letter. Figuring there is nothing more he can do, Jim starts his trek back home. He plans to spend a night or two relaxing at the Lodge in Cloudcroft, NM, on his way only to find that he is being followed. An ominous, unidentified phone caller gives Jim an ultimatum - find the briefcase and turn it over to him within a week.

A violent confrontation in Cloudcroft verifies Jim's worst suspicion, a Mexican drug cartel wants the briefcase. The confrontation also brings the FBI into the picture. They also want Jim to continue his search. The search takes Jim to the New Mexican ghost town of Chloride where the final confrontation takes place and Jim finds out who the bad guys really are.

A Jim West™ Mystery/Thriller Book 7

Title: *Honeymoons Can Kill*

- Author: Bob Doerr
- Publisher: TotalRecall Publications, Inc.
- Paper Back: ISBN:
- eBook: ISBN:
- Number of pages in the finished book:
- Publication Date: 2022

Honeymoons Can Kill is a 68,000 word mystery thriller that is set on a cruise ship in the Gulf of Mexico. The eighth book in the Jim West series, this is the first book to bring back prior characters from previous books. Deputy Rose Luna (Greed Can Kill) joins Jim on a five day cruise out of Galveston, TX, and on the second day of the cruise, the couple encounters Sarah Stone (Dead Men Can Kill). Sarah Stone is now Sarah Lassiter having gotten married on the ship right before it left port. When Sarah's new husband is murdered on the second night of the cruise, the cruise changes from a relaxing vacation to a race to catch the killer before everyone disembarks in three more days. The book should be considered as rated PG-13.

A Jim West™ Mystery/Thriller Book 8

Title: *Double Bogeys Can Kill*™

- Author: Bob Doerr
- Publisher: TotalRecall Publications, Inc.
- Paper Back: ISBN:
- eBook: ISBN:
- Number of pages in the finished book:
- Publication Date: 2022

Double Bogeys Can Kill is the 9th Jim West mystery/thriller. In this book West finds himself in Myrtle Beach joining 15 retired air force pilots, to fill a void and allow the group to have four foursomes. The week, usually fun and something the pilots look forward to, quickly turns into tragedy as one of the golfers is murdered after the first day of golf. The pilots know West's background as a criminal investigator in the air force and lean on him to solve the murder. The Myrtle Beach police also learn of West's background and want him to be their inside man. West doesn't want the role, knowing it's a lose-lose proposition. He's right, and on the second night, the murderer seeing West as a threat tries to kill him. West survives but requires a trip to the hospital. The suspect pool shrinks down to his fellow golfers. Balancing his cooperation with the police with his golf is not easy as the whole group starts to turn on itself. Finally, West is confronted by the killer now crazy enough to kill himself and take West with him.

A Jim West™ Mystery/Thriller Book 9

Title: *Curiosity Can Kill*™

- Author: Bob Doerr
- Publisher: TotalRecall Publications, Inc.
- Paper Back: ISBN:
- eBook: ISBN:
- Number of pages in the finished book:
- Publication Date: 2024

West travels to Alpine, Texas, to help a friend's widow identify the body of her husband. He was killed in Big Bend National Park, more accurately described as the middle of nowhere. When a second person is murdered at the same spot, and the widow is then murdered, things really get strange. Jim is drawn into a hunt for the killer. Oh, and did somebody mention demons?

A Jim West™ Mystery/Thriller Book 10

PUBLIC SAFETY WRITERS ASSOCIATION
WRITING COMPETITION

Non-Published Fiction Book
First Place
Bob Doerr
for
Curiosity Can Kill

PUBLIC
SAFETY
July 13, 2024

WRITERS
ASSOCIATION

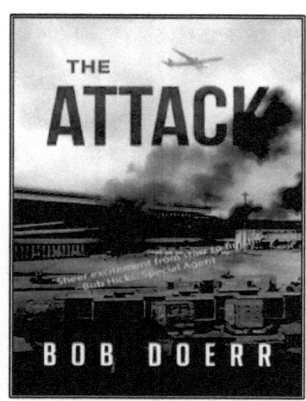

Title: *The Attack*™

- Author: Bob Doerr
- Publisher: TotalRecall Publications, Inc.
- Paper Back: ISBN: 978-1-59095-146-0
- Book: ISBN: 978-1-59095-147-7
- Number of pages in the finished book:
- Publication Date:

A terrorist team has just set off four explosive devices in an international airport close to New York City. The leader of the terrorists, Ahmad Khalin, survives the attack and plans to attack a second U.S. airport within the month. As Khalin makes his escape from the New York area he is involved in a shooting in Connecticut. Clint Smith, a U.S. government agent assigned to an ultra-secret agency, is at a restaurant across the street when the shooting occurs. He responds to the scene to see if he can help, but Khalin is gone. On a hunch, Teresa Deer, Smith's boss, sends Smith after Khalin. Smith's pursuit takes him to Bar Harbor, Maine; Wiesbaden, Germany; the Costa Brava, Spain; Northern Scotland; Lake of the Woods, Ontario, Canada; and finally into Saskatchewan, Canada, where the final confrontation takes place. Throughout the pursuit, a number of interesting characters add to the subplots and try to survive their involvement in the chase.

A Clint Smith Thriller™

Title: *The Group*™
- Author: Bob Doerr
- Publisher: TotalRecall Publications, Inc.
- Paper Back: ISBN: 978-1-59095-569-7
- eBook: ISBN: 978-1-59095-570-3
- Number of pages in the finished book: 288
- Publication Date: 2016

A fast-moving international thriller that pits a lone government operative, known as a hunter, against an unknown group of assassins who pose a worldwide threat.

Someone is killing off the world's rich and famous. The murders are sophisticated, requiring precision and skill. The international community is in an uproar but has no leads in its attempt to find the assassins. The victims were members of the Bilderberg Group, an international, loose knit group of the uber rich that meet annually. While the attacks have not had a direct impact on the U.S., Theresa Deer, Director of the Special Section, a small unit whose existence is known by only a handful in the U.S. government, sees this new age League of Assassins as a national threat. She sends her hunters out. Clint Smith finds their trail Switzerland where his discovery almost leads to his own death. The hunt leads him to Mallorca, Spain, where he witnesses a helicopter attack on a villa where a number of attendees from the Bilderberg conference were holding a follow-on meeting of their own. Smith picks up the trail a couple weeks later in Las Vegas, NV, and in his hunt finds out that he is no longer the hunter. He has become the prey.

A Clint Smith Thriller™

Title: *The Assassins*™
- Author: Bob Doerr
- Publisher: TotalRecall Publications, Inc.
- Paper Back: ISBN: 9781590951965
- eBook: ISBN: 9781590951972
- Number of pages in the finished book: 242
- Publication Date: 2018

A disputed election has divided the nation, and a handful of senior government officials have conspired to have the North Koreans assassinate the President of the United States. Believing the assassination attempt to be only days away, Theresa Deer, Director of the Special Section, a small unit whose existence is known by only a few in the U.S. government, is tasked to interdict the man intent on providing the North Koreans vital information about the president's itinerary for his visit to South Korea. While Deer succeeds in her mission, she is severely injured and finds herself being hunted by the North Korean assassins. Clint Smith is sent to Korea to help Deer get back to the U.S. and finds himself caught in a deadly game of cat and mouse with the North Koreans. With no one in the U.S. government to turn to for help, and the South Koreans now also hunting them, getting out of South Korea alive is looking unlikely.

A Clint Smith Thriller™

Title: *The Treasure* ™

- Author: Bob Doerr
- Publisher: TotalRecall Publications, Inc.
- Paper Back: ISBN: 9781648830846
- eBook: ISBN: 9781648830853
- Number of pages in the finished book: 242
- Publication Date: 2021

The Treasure is the fourth book in the Clint Smith thriller series. After a successful mission in South America, Clint heads to Las Vegas on vacation and to dig up a stagecoach strong box he had found in the desert earlier but had not opened. Upon inspection, he finds some old gold coins in mint condition and some well-preserved documents. He gives the contents of the strong box to a lawyer to find buyers. One of the documents, unfortunately, creates a maelstrom of violence and murder, and puts Clint squarely in the cross hairs of some Chinese assassins. Clint leaves Las Vegas to keep out of the spotlight, only to find himself going to Alaska in an attempt to rescue a female police officer who had been assigned to protect him in Las Vegas.

A Clint Smith Thriller™

Title: *The Enchanted Coin*™
- Author: Bob Doerr
- Publisher: TotalRecall Publications, Inc.
- Paper Back: ISBN: 978-1-59095-084-5
- Book: ISBN: 978-1-59095-085-2
- Audio Book Available:
- Number of pages in the finished book: 130
- Publication Date: September 17, 2013

We have all heard of tales of UFO's, ghosts, people who say they can talk to the spirits, ancient curses, and magical talismans. Most of us automatically dismiss them as false, figments of people's imagination, and understandably so. However, might not just a few of them be true? I don't know, but I heard this story from a young man the other day who swore the fascinating tale I have set forth in this book really did really occur, because it happened to him. You be the judge.

Title: *The Rescue of Vincent*™
- Author: Bob Doerr
- Publisher: TotalRecall Publications, Inc.
- Paperback, 6" x 9" ISBN: 978-1-59095-279-5
- eBook: ISBN: 978-1-59095-280-1
- Audio Book Available:
- Number of pages in the finished book: 160
- Publication Date: October 28, 2014

The Rescue of Vincent: Book 2 in The Enchanted Coin Series is a 31,000 word fantasy adventure targeted at Middle Grade readers. Imagine being a fourteen year old again and finding a coin that seems to give off a light of its own. The coin has your name on it, and instructs you to toss it into a fountain next to the Tree of Life. That's what happens in *The Rescue of Vincent*, and what starts my protagonist off on a magical adventure that many young boys and girls would love to have. This book is "G" rated.

Title: *The Magic of Vex*™

- Author: Bob Doerr
- Publisher: TotalRecall Publications, Inc.
- Paper Back: ISBN: 978-1-59095-309-9
- eBook: ISBN: 978-1-59095-280-1
- Audio ISBN: 978-1-59095-281-8
- Number of pages in the finished book: 140
- Publication Date: August 4, 2015

Samantha Gillespie's discovery of a magic coin results in her transportation to the strange world of Vex where magic is real and where she has to over-come a number of challenges if she ever hopes to return home.

What happened to Samantha was totally unexpected and quite frightening. It led her to an adventure that many might think impossible to believe, but it did. You be the judge.

This book is "G" rated.

Title: *Stranded in Space* ™

- Author: Bob Doerr
- Publisher: TotalRecall Publications, Inc.
- Paper Back: ISBN:
- eBook: ISBN:
- Number of pages in the finished book:
- Publication Date:

Stranded in Space: Book 4 in The Enchanted Coin Series is a 31,000 word fantasy adventure targeted at Middle Grade readers. Imagine being a fourteen year old again and finding a coin that seems to give off a light of its own. The coin has your name on it, claims to be magical, and instructs you to toss it into a fountain next to the Tree of Life. That's what happens in Stranded in Space, and what starts my protagonist off on a magical adventure that many young boys and girls would love to have. You be the judge.

This book is "G" rated.

Titles by Bob Doerr

Jim West mystery/thriller™ Series
Dead Men Can Kill
Cold Winters Kill
Another Colorado Kill
Loose Ends Kill
No One Else To Kill
Caffeine Can Kill
Greed Can Kill
Honeymoons Can Kill
Double Bogeys Can Kill
Curiosity Can Kill™

A Clint Smith Thriller™ Series
The Attack
The Group
The Assassins
The Treasure

Mouse Gate™ Series
The Enchanted Coin
The Rescue of Vincent
The Magic of Vex
Stranded in Space

Author Bob Doerr Uses his special knowledge
to provide authentic details in his novels
about how law enforcement agencies do their work.

For a complete list of books by Bob Doerr,
a preview of upcoming titles and more
visit his website.
www.bobdoerr.com